the IMPOSTOR

the IMPOSTOR

Georges Bernanos

translated by J.C. WHITEHOUSE

University of Nebraska Press, Lincoln & London

Original title: *L'Imposture*

*Cet ouvrage publié dans le
cadre du programme d'aide à la
publication bénéficie du soutien du
Ministère des Affaires Etrangères et du
Service Culturel de l'Ambassade de
France représenté aux Etats-Unis.*
This work, published as part of
the program of aid for publication,
received support from the French
Ministry of Foreign Affairs and
the Cultural Service of the French
Embassy in the United States.

© Librairie Plon, 1927, 1991
Translation © 1999 by the
University of Nebraska Press
All rights reserved
Manufactured in the
United States of America
⊗
Library of Congress
Cataloging-in-Publication Data
Bernanos, Georges, 1888–1948.
[Imposture. English]
The imposter / Georges Bernanos ;
Translated by J. C. Whitehouse.
p.   cm.
ISBN 0-8032-1290-9 (cl: alk.
paper).—
ISBN 0-8032-6153-5 (pa: alk. paper)
I. Whitehouse, J. C.   II. Title.
PQ2603.E58751513   1999
843'.912—dc21   98-35947
                                    CIP

Acknowledgments

I wish to express my gratitude to the British Centre for Literary Translation at the University of East Anglia in Norwich, England, for the residential bursary that allowed me to revise and improve the early draft of this translation during May 1997, and to the University of Nebraska Press for its prompt and encouraging response when I offered it the manuscript. JCW

Father Cénabre's fine voice was slow and grave. "Some attachment to the good things of this world is legitimate, my son, and protecting them from others seems to me to be a duty as well as a right, provided we're not unjust. Nevertheless, we need to act prudently, discreetly, and with discernment . . . Living as a Christian in the secular world calls for proportion and measure. For balance, in fact, in all things. We can hardly resist such attacks at the purely natural level, but we *can* control them if we are very patient and diligent . . . We should defend only what we need to defend, without prejudice to anyone. Then we shall keep our peace of mind, or regain it if we've lost it."

"Thank you, Father," Monsieur Pernichon replied, his voice betraying his obviously sincere feeling. "I must confess that the battle of ideas sometimes produces more heat than light. But the example of your own life and thought is a great comfort for me." (His mouth was still twitching, making his bearded chin tremble as he spoke.)

"I accept," he went on, "that someone else could have been entrusted with the annual report. Some of my colleagues are better qualified. For instance, I would willingly have stood aside in favor of the senior Catholic journalist, but from the very beginning he gave up all claims to what was his by right . . . We could hardly have foreseen that a seasoned fighter holding back like that was going to thrust Larnaudin into the limelight . . ."

"I've no objection to Monsieur Larnaudin," replied the fine, slow, grave voice. "In fact, I've rather a high opinion of him. I've always benefited to some extent from his criticisms, even the unfair ones. You see, my friend, the useful thing about doctrinaire people is that because they're so different from us they stimulate certain of our faculties that custom and the experience of life weaken. They provide us with useful points of reference."

He gave a harsh laugh.

"I admire you!" Pernichon cried out fervently. "In all this sound and fury, you still observe other people calmly. You're priestly on the altar and everywhere else. And yet not even someone as well disposed as you are can turn a blind eye to the harm Larnaudin's polemics, bias, and obstinacy have done to our very worthy cause. Yesterday evening I heard your eminent friend Monsignor Cimier urging us to give pledges and more pledges, for that was the way forward! Well, we *have* given them, all except one. I mean, that we should name, yes, *name*, and formally disown one or two fanatics with no mandate at all and a following of only a tiny handful of gullible fools. Is that too much to ask for?" (Sweat had finally broken out on the little man's forehead, which seemed to give him enormous relief.)

Pernichon wrote the religious column in a radical paper subsidized by a conservative financier for socialist ends. What soul he had flourished in the threefold equivocation, feeding like a patient and industrious insect on the humiliation the position involved. He was virtually a stranger in the offices of *The New Dawn*, and his brooding and prematurely decrepit form, further disfigured by a limp, was best known in the very distinctive group of writers without books, journalists without newspapers, and prelates without a diocese that exists on the fringes of church, politics, society, and academia. Its members are so anxious to sell their services that supply is often greater than demand, and the bottom is always cruelly threatening to fall out of the market. Once the slump is well underway and the saturation point is reached, their short-lived and hence valueless commodities are dumped in outer offices and left to rot away.

He had studied at the junior seminary of Notre Dame des Champs, playing out until the very last moment what he half knew was the comedy of a bogus vocation to the priesthood. Then, once he was over the hurdle of the baccalaureate, he had disappeared from sight for a long time until the decisive moment when he was commissioned to write signed weekly contributions — first uplifting news items and subsequently *Letters from Rome*, written in the house of a small caterer in the rue Jacob — to a parish publication. Who else could have apparently managed to turn that kind of obscurity to his own advantage? But he was able to save up for his future fame by putting aside one small coin after another like his ancestors from the Auvergne, who had ploughed their sweat into an unproductive land in summer, coming to Paris in winter to sell the chestnuts the pigs refused, slowly piling up their savings until their ridiculous dream collapsed about them, leaving them released rather than requited. Eventually, they were hurriedly cleaned up, for the first time, by the old woman who washed and laid out their bodies before the public health officer's visit.

His *Letters from Rome* were not, however, entirely without merit. They were as good as other less well-known ones written in the same spirit by conceited and disappointed men as a vehicle for the bitterness they exuded drop by drop. The wording might, of course, vary from one writer to another, but not the deeper hidden meaning, the enduring malice, the unmistakable longing for the worst and, disguised as a desire for social harmony, a pathological hatred of any remaining sense of honor in the Church.

Pernichon looked respectfully at the priest's magisterial face for a moment and then smiled, clearly showing the mass of premature wrinkles on his own. He spoke again.

"I've given up the idea of making you angry with anyone . . . but yesterday the Nuncio was saying . . ."

"Can we please not mention him?" Father Cénabre asked. "His Holiness's determination to upset no one will eventually look like an insult to our republican ministers . . . democracy likes a show, and we send appallingly low, scheming little prelates. And he doesn't even understand Greek! At Senator Hubert's . . ."

He rubbed his hands over his cheeks. For a moment, he was lost in thought, and then said quietly:

"What's the point? Neither do you."

"You're forgetting," cried Pernichon, forcing out a laugh, "you're forgetting that I took the prize for translation from Greek in 1903, in the Paris seminary. It's a pity . . . I should have preferred to do something more literary . . . but the sad events we've lived through . . ."

"Tagore says that the secret of peace is not to expect good fortune . . . St Thérèse said it earlier . . . these meetings, my friend, have something strange and bitter about them . . ."

His hand, tapping irritatedly on the scarlet cloth of the Louis Seize desk, called them edgily back to their business. The clock struck eleven.

"I'm afraid I'm tiring you," said Pernichon. "I know that you rarely keep late hours. But these all-too-infrequent occasions when I can rest in the solitude you live in, a stone's throw from all the noise and bustle of Paris, do me a world of good! I always come away filled with certainty and faith. The way you look at events and people is so calm, and even your mischievous remarks are so indulgent and refined! I'm proud, I repeat, proud, my eminent master, to see you not only as a protector in the worldly sense of the term, but also as the spiritual director I hardly deserve."

Father Cénabre looked at the clock, sank further into his chair and, raising his right hand for silence, spoke with striking authority:

"My friend, I appreciate your patience and your submission to a priest who spares you neither rebukes nor occasionally rather severe criticism. But I'm very reluctant to hear your more or less weekly confession. You know that I find it hard to carry out my ministry, and that my modest efforts as a historian take up the bulk of my time. And a pious young man shouldn't be seeking absolution from such a controversial figure. Of course, you'll be welcome to my advice if you find it useful, but I'd like you to go to another priest for the sacrament. You have a wide choice, if you prefer not to go to some excessively simple curate . . . so today is the last time."

They walked to one end of the enormous room. Canon Cénabre sat on a very ordinary simple straw-bottomed chair near a similar prie-dieu on which his penitent knelt. To enlarge his study, the priest had had the dividing wall knocked down, opening up a storage room with whitewashed walls and a red-tiled floor. It was as if Poverty, which he hated so much, had suddenly breached the wall and burst into the famous library, a miracle of disciplined luxury for the few connoisseurs capable of appreciating its exquisite detail. For Cénabre, the contrast seemed precious. He had scantily furnished the bare little corner with a wretched table, chairs whose straw was yellowed with age, and simple shelves on which, however, those with taste could admire a very fine and extremely rare collection of naively bound missals, the treasures of rural piety through the ages. On the bare wall hung a cross which, as a final touch of sophistication, was the only one in the house.

Pernichon's murmuring recitation of the confiteor was already rising and falling in the surrounding silence, for he affected an impeccably stressed Latin. With his head bent forward and a painful smile on his tightly closed thin lips, Father Cénabre seemed to be listening closely to the familiar sound, although as yet all he was aware of was the smell that accompanied it. A dull, flat odor, not so much foul as sickly, did indeed hover around the puny and joylessly envious man. But his conscience was even more sweetly fetid than his smell.

It was not that the piety of the young editor of *Modern Life* was mere hypocrisy. Indeed, it could perhaps be said to be sincere, as it had its roots in his innermost being, in his obscure fear of evil and the hidden desire to attain it deviously and with the least possible risk. What little he had in the way of social or political doctrine was governed by the same longing to yield to the enemy and hand over his soul. What the fools around him called his independence or boldness was merely the outward, though misunderstood, sign of his morose yearning for total surrender and the final elimination of self. Anyone opposed to the cause he claimed to serve already had his heart, and any objection from his opponents found a secret welcome in his mind. Any injustice against his own kind immediately aroused in him not revolt, or even cowardly connivance, but, in the hidden depths of his womanish soul, a hatred of the victims and an ignoble love of the victor.

His inner life was similarly muddied, ambiguous, airless, and unhealthy. Although he took liberties with the Church's teaching, he made a show of scrupulously respecting her moral precepts. He certainly kept certain major rules of his game, but he also feared Hell with such a covert envy of those who braved its torments that he merely thought that he despised them. Anxious to avoid any fuss in this world or the next, he managed his conscience with a certain distaste, rather like a retailer surveying a shop with no customers, and gave the impression of a frighteningly static and decaying adolescence that had outlived itself and survived into adult life. Once, when it had looked as if he might be in danger of dying, he had braved the ordeal of a general confession. The experience of stirring up the sour residue of his empty life had taught him the frightening lesson that the sum total of all his faults did not provide the matter for any real remorse.

Cénabre heard all the usual admissions in their usual order. Indeed, Pernichon liked to make a quick, methodical confession, begun in a ridiculously authoritative way and conducted and completed like a clinical lecture. Simple priests were left at a loss, hardly daring to absolve such a well-informed penitent. Never before, however, had the author of *The Florentine Mystics* deigned to interrupt the flow before the final sigh, which sometimes even turned into a discreet and irreproachably guileless cough. Once again, the little man was heard in silence. When he had finished, however, and was surprised at the continuing silence, he looked up and caught the priest's motionless and sinister eyes looking straight into his.

Curiosity does not have such somber fire, scorn such sadness, or hatred such bitterness. Deathly pale, Pernichon felt that he was held in a vice, suddenly slit open and probed to the depths of his being. He could not hold or beat down his confessor's incomprehensible gaze and for a second tried desperately to see in it the almost imperceptible deflection, the oblique flame, of madness. It simply fell straight down onto his shoulders. He could literally feel its shape and weight, as if it spurned the chance of merely passing through his wretched conscience and was moulding it, kneading it with disgust, playing a light on it. Even feeling ourselves to be the mere objects of an intrusive keener perception is intolerably humiliating, but our shame reaches its peak when the lucid gaze of others fully exposes our own degradation to us. And Cénabre's gaze, free of all idle curiosity, suggested a roughly comparable but even more offensive type of attention, a means of assessment involved in all the higher and more spiritual types of shame: the kind we pay to things so totally and substantially base that they do not merit a specific judgement.

One might wonder what the priest was comparing Pernichon with in his own mind, since all we consider in that particular way is what we have dishonored in ourselves.

"My friend," he suddenly asked, "*how do you see yourself?*" As he did so, his scrutiny became less intense.

"How do I see myself?" Pernichon breathed. "I don't really see . . ."

"Listen to me," Cénabre went on gently. "The question may seem strikingly simple. We all judge ourselves, but, whatever our intentions, very insincerely. Our picture of ourselves has been endlessly touched up. It's a compromise. *Observation* is a mental act taking place at two or three different levels, whereas *seeing* involves only one. What I'm asking you to do is to look at yourself simply and directly, to catch sight of yourself with your fellow human beings as you live out your life among them."

"I see what you mean . . . " said Pernichon, freed from his initial anguish. "I must admit . . . that I'm full of contradictions."

Cénabre thought silently for a long while, and even a more perceptive man than Pernichon might have assumed that he was praying.

"I also admit," Pernichon immediately continued, "— and I'm sorry to have to raise this objection — that the kind of introspection you're suggesting . . . isn't one that . . . well, it's rather unusual. I always thought that in such matters we shouldn't be too methodical or attentive. I might have been afraid of . . ."

"Don't be afraid of anything," the priest answered icily. "But don't answer if you prefer not to."

"No, I'll do as you ask," the little man continued wretchedly, full of a burning zeal. "Of course, I can't tell you anything you didn't know already. Whatever efforts I make, in spite of my small number of real faults, sensuality is a constant trial. You know that, too. But perhaps it's good to be made to repeat it and feel the shame of it again."

At first Cénabre said nothing. The wick of the simple oil lamp within reach on the table (he could not bear any other kind of lighting) spluttered and gave off a thin line of black smoke inside the glass. As the priest leaned over and stretched his arm out, Pernichon saw his long fingers trembling. Almost immediately, the bright new flame lit up the bony, leonine head, the extremely pale, almost livid, forehead and cheeks. The sudden and totally unexpected appearance of the tense features produced a sense of vague remorse and a feeling that he had been intolerably indiscreet.

"So," Cénabre finally said, "sensuality is a trial for you, is it? Perhaps that's how the mind sees it. You think you have strong passions. And yet, I think, you accuse yourself only of what are, at least apparently, minor faults."

"I didn't expect such criticism from you," Pernichon murmured, immediately regretting the rash phrase, for the same icy voice, so icy now that the almost imperceptible northeastern accent was neutralized and undetectable, did not trouble to reply directly.

"You've nothing to fear from sensuality. You don't deceive me, and perhaps not yourself. Oh, all that's scarcely of any interest. It's hardly worth bothering with. In spite of what people always think, any experienced priest attaches no more than symptomatic importance to sexual life. Anyone who turns it into the sole object of his investigation is certain to make a serious mistake. Indeed, it's only of interest, only provides useful information and illuminates the high ground, when it gives us a blurred and semicomprehensible image, a material sign, of the contradictions in the innermost life of a real human being. Even though it has to have its own independent existence and history, its own specific character."

"Perhaps one needs to accumulate a lot of failings to deserve the reputation of being a lofty soul?" Pernichon asked timidly, more irritated by the tone of these rather obscure observations than by their meaning. "I'm listening to what you say in a spirit of submission, but however severely I judge myself, I'm allowed to be aware of the efforts I've made and the temptations I've overcome! Perhaps I've not been able to advance very far along the way to perfection, but at least I've not given ground. The wound is still open, of course, but I haven't been swallowed up by sin, thank God."

He was breathing heavily, with his hands to his face, and once again his forehead was covered with sweat.

"For both our sakes, this final meeting will be taken to its ultimate conclusion," the voice went on. "I'm to blame for having waited so long. You see how right this first probe has been and the revealing outburst it has caused. I've seen the abscess bursting, my son."

"Father," said Pernichon, choking with astonishment and anger, "I can't understand why you're being so harsh with me!"

"I've listened to you many times, in this same place, with one question on my lips: *Do you think, then, that you're alive?*"

"I can't believe," Pernichon repeated, "that true apostolic zeal is expressed with that kind of hatred."

It was as if, as he heard the words, only "hatred" affected Cénabre, who almost lost his usual self-control. He flushed, struck the table sharply with the flat of his hand as his face turned a deeper red, and continued in a quieter voice.

"Please forgive the momentary outburst of bad temper. I'm

not, and could never be, an apostle. A critical mind is my most important characteristic, or at least it absorbs all my other faculties. In the end, concentrated attention devours pity."

He took Pernichon's hand.

"My friend, I'm astonished by the partiality of those rather foolish, limited, and indiscreetly zealous priests who foster the illusion of so many good people that they're struggling with all the demons of lust. The military terms they use merely make such commonplaces all the more ridiculous. It's all a matter of fights, attacks launched or repulsed, defeats or victories . . . Ah, my son, what do you expect me to say about that illusory struggle, where wretched people try to judge themselves in terms of the *saints*, including the most discerning of them, whom I think I can claim to be familiar with? Much more . . ."

He pressed Pernichon's hands more warmly.

"That's not only an error of judgment," he went on. "There's a very high level of perverse duplicity in it. To take your own case alone, if I may, I think, and take it as being obvious, that far from resisting external temptations you try very hard and consistently to keep alive a level of concupiscence that grows less toxic with each passing day. The well has dried up, but you stir up the mud in it to be able to smell it, at least. So as not to overtax your strength, you like to live out the lie that you're subject to endless sexual temptation, when in fact your sexuality is barely strong enough to provide you with real occasions of sin. Why are you talking about a struggle inside you? It's all too easy to see your suspect thoughts, your lukewarm desires and actions that come to nothing. Anyone bringing such fantasies to life would be doing you a cruel injury. What your desires want to consume is that shadow, not something living. I'm talking to you now more from the point of view of knowledge than that of ministry. A rake throws himself into his pleasures like a madman, but at least he looks like someone who doesn't hang back all the time . . . whereas *you* . . . my son, your interior life has a minus sign."

Pernichon gasped sharply, like a bather entering cold water.

"Your idea of yourself," the voice continued with a kind of dreadful tenderness, "isn't wrong. It's like those mathematical equations where all you have to do is invert the signs. Your mediocrity tends naturally towards nothingness, the state of indifference between good and evil. Painfully keeping one or two vices alive is all that gives you the illusion of living."

Pernichon stood up at these words, waiting mutely before his torturer.

"The experience of life, and more so my modest historical researches," Cénabre resumed, "have shown me how few lives are positive . . ."

"I respect your character and yourself enough to let you finish. But what you are saying belongs to the category of remarks that one ignores," the journalist burst out with some dignity.

"In that case, my final ones to you will be all the less hurtful," the priest answered. "Your presence has been the occasion, not the cause, of all that has gone on. All you have done wrong is to have been here with me, at this time on this day."

He breathed in noisily, and when had finished, the blood seemed to have drained away from his cheeks and forehead again, leaving them livid and pale.

"There comes a time, my son," he went on, "when life lies heavy on us. We should like to put the burden down, have a good look at it, and make a choice, keeping what we absolutely can't do without and throwing the rest away. Remember what I've said to you in confidence, aloud, this evening. I'll try to make that choice. I have to. I'm ready."

He stopped abruptly and looked down. Then extremely violently, he screamed "Get out! Get out!"

No doubt anyone but Pernichon would have done as he was told, but there was something potentially tragic in his clumsiness. And fate always saw grimly to it that he was in the wrong place at the wrong time and kept him there to the bitter end, a perfect way of using the ridiculous or the odious.

"I'm sorry to have been the unintentional cause . . ." he started to say.

"Cause of what?" Cénabre begged him. "I've told you, you caused nothing. Why should I humiliate you for no reason? But just listen to this observation: the world is full of people like you, and they stifle the best by sheer weight of numbers. Why did you join in our battle of ideas? You'll leave it without regrets, but with little profit."

Despite its vulgarity, Pernichon's face now looked truly human and almost noble.

"Nevertheless, I didn't choose the winning side," he said.

"That's because the winning side is the masters' side, and you're painfully aware that you aren't one. But you live in their shadow, and you find it reassuring when they flatter your vanity."

For a moment he was silent, and then added quietly:

"And you needed something to bargain with."

"No, Canon," Pernichon cried. "My enemies have never seen me as a man who could be bought, I tell you!"

"My son," said Cénabre, "don't be angry if I use my special knowledge of your inner resources and moral abilities. You're a born middleman. Why should the Catholic party — or, to use their own language, Catholic circles — tend to create an abundance of such people? Because, in an increasingly interdependent political society almost exclusively made up of rigidly disciplined groups with no room for individualism, they're the ideal haven for old-fashioned opportunists. In theory, it looks easy to move from radicalism to socialism. In practice, it certainly isn't, because it means changing one set of voters for another. But believing in God and accepting the light yoke of the Church is a very convenient position! One is *in* a party without being *of* it. From that point of view, there's nothing less rigid than dogma, for some people even think it generally proposes indifference in political matters. With all the distinctions and shades of difference, there's a very wide range of choices for the dilettante. In a world of more and more concessions and enticements, an ambitious young man who hates a fuss and works methodically can go as far as he likes without losing the valuable privilege of being an ally rather than a party man, and an ally from outside at that, who has to be watched and can't be taken for granted. He's rather like those unfortunate ladies who, in holy wedlock, for which they certainly weren't made, still have a rather unappealing whiff of their past."

"You really are being very cruel," said Pernichon shakily. "Even if what you are saying is for my ears alone . . ."

"It's all yours," said Cénabre. "Do what you like with it."

Suddenly an irresistible inner change transformed his features once again. The smile froze on his lips, his gaze hardened, and his hands were visibly trembling again. Even his anger seemed to have been swallowed up by some more violent and mysterious emotion.

His lids drooped slowly. The ensuing silence was difficult to break.

From the very beginning of the sudden and unforeseeable attack, Pernichon had had no means of resistance. Although he was used to a certain kind of linguistic fencing and oblique allusion, direct violence paralyzed him and quite literally froze his will. He did not know what to make of such cruel, calculated harshness, switching from abuse to painful bitterness and then incomprehensible solicitude. His initial stupor eventually gave way completely to fear and then to a worse confusion. For what was perhaps the first time, the journalist caught a clear glimpse of his inner self, pale and dazed, before it disappeared again, like a dream in the light of morning . . . It was not so much Cénabre's words, with their vague suggestion of anger and scorn, as the complete change in the subtle priest and the way in which he communicated a compelling inner vision shown by an attitude and voice that dragged Pernichon's inner core into the open like a muscle suddenly jumping out of its covering in a surgeon's hands. Being seen as a skillful and ambitious man who weighed his chances, a doubtful friend and a watchful enemy, would not have offended him. The attacks he had just suffered, however, had hit a deeper, more secret and more sensitive spot, the point of balance, as it were, of his humble existence: the idea, which was now an habitual and integral part of his thinking, of an inner struggle, the need to be able to classify himself, a certain stability. His self-concept had been brutally uprooted, and the suddenly persuasive hypothesis of a life with no spiritual reality breaking into his normally very carefully managed conscience had been enough to shock him into seeing how totally chaotic that conscience really was. There are very many other people who watch more or less strictly over their actions and yet, like sailors observing the stars without looking at their compasses, are unaware of where their will or their perverted instincts are taking them. The horror lies not in the strangers whose paths cross ours but in the features our devastated soul will suddenly meet and not recognize as its own.

"Canon Cénabre . . ." Pernichon began, with a last desperate attempt to be polite and respectful to his dangerous companion. He did not manage to finish, however. What humiliation had not been able to do was achieved by fear, which is much more pressing than shame. Moving away a few paces, he looked clumsily for his overcoat, which had been thrown over a chair behind him, struggling to push his arms into the sleeves, sobbing painfully yet tearlessly, crouching, tense, as if his whole skinny body and not merely his face were twitching. Then, in despair, he disappeared into the dark hall. The hinges squeaked as he went out even though he had closed it carefully.

Father Cénabre, who had watched him go, stood rooted to the spot for a considerable time, apparently as amazed as his visitor had been, moving so little that even the shadow on the wall did not tremble. An observer would have been struck by his clear gaze, which was not that of someone in a dream, but more like that of a bold and determined disputant concentrating on defeating a half-beaten rival and trying to work out what he is thinking. From the corner of the room it might have looked as if he was simply contemplating the door Pernichon had left by, but in fact he was looking somewhere quite different. Neither Pernichon nor anyone like him could have kept alight such a fire in his sombre eyes, which were focused on another subject in another place. And more than one skeptic would have been embarrassed to admit that he seemed to be addressing the bare cross on the wall. In any case, there would have been no time to settle the question, for, suddenly moving forward as quickly, promptly, and precisely as if he were parrying a thrust, Cénabre dashed the lamp to the tiles, smashing it.

Moonlight immediately flooded the room. The action had been so violent that the wick had probably gone out before touching the floor. For a moment the oil could be heard gradually gurgling out of the crystal-ware holder. The sound then faded and with it, it seemed, the memory of the extraordinary outburst of the priest renowned on both sides of the religious divide for his elegant skepticism.

One of Father Cénabre's idiosyncrasies was to accept domestic help only from an old cleaning woman who was said to have been his nurse. She was always up early, had finished her work by noon, and did not show her face again. Around the short, solid shape barely visible in the calm of the night, the solitude and silence were unbroken. The figure then moved slowly and carefully away and a door slammed. In the empty room, the moonlight lay motionless. Father Cénabre was back in his bedroom.

The author of *The Florentine Mystics* had long been able to disconcert the critics. Skilled at capturing attention by stealth, his sole aim was to charm. He would withdraw before reaching a conclusion, leaving friend and foe alike baffled. One faction had got hold of him, just as it took up with any doubtful element, not from a taste for scandal but from a desperate need to deceive itself, to put on a mask, to hide its poverty. In powerful Roman spiritual milieux, the intellectual demimonde is very like its sexual counterpart, with the same vanity, envy, welcome for complex hatreds, and passion for denigrating the better elements that show it up for what it really is, the same naive lies and pretenses and gullible belief that it has deceived the other side. Of course, the prostitution found in townhouses looks down on that of the streets, but in urgent cases the professional service is automatically provided, and seen from a certain point of view, it always involves connivance and compliance. It is never clear whether one will meet doubly submissive whores or good mothers on the mezzanine floors of the rue des Martyrs. So the faction includes decent young men, austere old ones, very talented writers, and priests of mostly irreproachable morals, and there is no obvious reason for confusing them with mean adolescents, patriarchs eaten up by envy as if it were a kind of leprosy, or black-robed adventurers with faces like shifty croupiers who have been expelled from every diocese. What they all have in common is a penchant for prevarication and sloppy thinking.

Father Cénabre had often made good use of their show of enthusiasm without, however, returning the favor. All that their small minds understood and approved about him was that he was unable to come to a conclusion, that his ideas lacked cohesion, and that his almost sensual curiosity and restless criticism worked at cross-purposes and to no avail. His *History of Arianism* had disappointed them precisely because of its positive, definite qualities, but they had delighted in the chatty and allusive tone of *The Florentine Mystics*. He was an illustrious writer who knew his readers and would have despised them if he had been capable of such a feeling. As it was, he merely loathed them. His epigrammatic judgments had long been their guide, and they honored him for being suspect. Their ambiguous sympathy and protective admiration were an irritant to his self-esteem, and he made them pay dearly for his purely nominal gratitude. He was hard put to praise them, but never tired of ridiculing them, and, surprisingly, his obvious but unrecognized mockery had inspired the best of his writing, his choicest and most flowing pages. All he gave in return was the most savage irony. Perhaps in their vanity they set a high value on the hard-won praise wrung out of a man they saw as strong and solitary (although in fact he was merely solitary) by an alliance of the weak.

The bedroom windows gave onto a street in Paris at its most provincial. Up there, at this time of night, the distant swell of sound from the Place de Rennes seemed lost and pathetic in the solitude and silence. Through the darkness, gasping and groaning in their pleasure, cities call to us profoundly. The noise and glare of every street we cross follows us into the darkness, frightful, plaintive, becoming gradually more and more muted until we reach the edge of a new tumult which adds its own heartrending voice. Yet "voice" is not the right word, for only forests, hills, fire, and water have voices and speak their own language. We no longer really understand it, though even the coarsest of us cannot quite forget an old and hallowed harmony, a strange and wonderful affinity between things and our minds. The voice we no longer understand is still that of a tranquil friend or brother, bringing peace. The lowest of men, those devoted to carnal hedonism and the cult of the self whom our modern world has honored as gods, have foolishly believed that they have recreated that voice when all they have done is strip nature of the antiquated forest gods, dryads, and nymphs and replace them with their own barnyard sensuality. Their fast-aging leader filled streets and woods with his tireless lechery. In his wake, a crowd of disciples rushed into the sacred solitude, basely dreaming of taking it over for their gluttony, melancholy, and post-coital sadness. The contagion gradually spread to the very ends of the earth, and even remote desert islands heard their secrets, witnessed their couplings, and echoed with their grotesque sobbing in the face of old age and death. There is no meadow, dewy and dappled in the innocent light of dawn, without their traces, like greasy wrappings on lawns in public parks on a Monday morning.

And yet, although it is a characteristic of human beings to impose themselves and their depravity on the natural world, they cannot grasp its inner rhythm or its profound meditation. They drown the voice but question it in vain. It continues its sublime song as a vibrating string chooses its harmonics from among a thousand possibilities and responds to them and to them alone.

With towns, those landscapes of girders, iron, and stone, things are different. How can we expect them to call us to joy, since they were built in pain and sweat? Or to freedom, since they are the fortresses in which a defeated Adam, faced with the obduracy of things and the elements, took refuge? Or to life, since these temporary dwellings are the guardians of nothing but our bones?

Father Cénabre had moved imperceptibly nearer the window,

as if the uncertain light from the street reflected through the panes offered a refuge in the dark room. He was standing motionless in the embrasure, apparently lost in thought but in fact concentrating on the dull and muffled noise from outside. His recent violent reaction had certainly not been merely an angry gesture, for no one was less capable of such pointless aberrations. He had suddenly found the light unbearable as it fell on the cross and the wall, a visible sign, as it were, of an interior enlightenment he would have liked to extinguish and push desperately out into the darkness. One of the features of major spiritual upheavals is that they take place in the physical world, so that a severe disappointment, for example, is forever linked to a specific place and time, not only by material association but in a kind of compenetration, as if a certain deep harmony in our inner life had been distorted by the battering ram of passion. The priest's sudden rebellion had indeed been no more than a delayed defensive reaction, and the cell with its sandstone floor, the walls, the books, and the bare cross were hostile witnesses, silent so far but likely to raise the question he was unwilling to answer. That was why he had left them in darkness.

It had been a disastrous mistake. What he had done raised a further and equally urgent problem. It was the end of one stage of a journey and the beginning of another unknown but more important and terrible one. Madness can lie dormant and undetected until a cry or some other manifestation convinces the victim of his insanity. For weeks, Cénabre had refused to acknowledge consciously certain types of thoughts whose violence he still scarcely suspected. He had now unthinkingly revealed his inner self and called everything into question. The subtle analyst who always subjected everyone to his irony, even the tragic saint of Assisi, had a horror of self-examination. He instinctively sensed how dangerous his critical approach, so greatly admired by foolish onlookers, was for himself, for we do not stake our own destiny on a random hypothesis, which was all he could use in his analysis and was indeed the only driving force behind it. The thought that he had had for some time, however, was growing stronger every day and taking over and foiling his carefully laid plans. He had pushed it aside, but to his amazement it was back, part of the fabric of everyday life, always there. In his sudden outburst against Pernichon, he had recognized it once more.

The scholarship of the author of *The Florentine Mystics* was as serious as his heavy and hard features were manly. The wide reading and sheer industry it presupposed might be misleading, since he had been happy and bold in his choice of subjects, but he seemed unable to approach them quite head on and tackled them obliquely. The same was true of the way in which he governed his own life: the specialist in moral analysis could not bear to look squarely at himself. Over a long period the obscure scruple that had been irresistibly pushed to the surface of his mind that evening had, with a struggle, been kept back to the lower level of pure feeling. It had to be acknowledged, of course, as a sense of restlessness and malaise, a reduced or morbidly deviant activity. It *was* all that but also something quite different. Since he had been careful not to put his finger on the exact location of the pain, however, the suffering was still vague, diffuse, easier to bear. Once we start to question and define it in our own minds, it is almost impossible to make any proper assessment of the feeling that starts as mere melancholy and then develops into remorse, a distortion of divine charity and just as avid, since, unless it has everything, it has nothing.

Unfortunately, and however much it may upset crude materialists, it is neither good nor safe to feel oneself, in one's fleshly integument, quite sheltered from the workings of the soul. Avoiding any scrutiny of intentions and insisting on seeing moral events as nothing more than their effects on the vasodilatory system leads to very severe disenchantment. We can contradict but not totally deny ourselves. Examining our conscience is a useful exercise, even for amoralists. It defines and names our remorse, thus holding it as it were in a sealed container in our soul for the mind to reflect on. If we repress that remorse, we run the risk of giving it flesh and substance. We may prefer a vague suffering to being forced to blush for ourselves, but we have brought sin into our very flesh, and because it has a twofold nature it will not die. It will grow marvelously fat on our blood, feeding on it like a persistent and unremitting cancer, letting us come and go and live as we wish, apparently healthy and at worst uneasy. As we move secretly further and further away from ourselves and others, our body and our soul split fundamentally asunder in a kind of semilethargy that is suddenly shattered by massive and overwhelming anguish, the hideous bodily form of remorse. We shall wake to the despair that no resistance can redeem, the very moment of the death of the soul, when a wretch puts a bullet into a brain that can no longer do anything but suffer.

Some of the readers Cénabre had irritated rather than won over by his charm and desire to please had perceptively sought in his recent work the strange, painful tone seeming to indicate wounded pride and self-doubt. The customary slightly pedantic irony grated now, seeming perhaps to be outside the author's control. Once it had had its function within the text, but now it sometimes appeared to overflow from it, explode, and be pushed back with difficulty. The author's art — or rather his felicitous way of proceeding — could be described as writing about sanctity as if there were no such thing as charity. Poor Renan, with all his limitations and his everlasting and rather unimaginative blasphemy, merely transposed two orders, inserting a miraculous being into a world without miracles, and was prevented by his own vanity from seeing the enormously comical nature of the simple undertaking. For anyone who can read, his *Life of Jesus* is a farce, with all the appropriate ingredients except naturalness and flow. But Cénabre had never denied miracles and even had a taste for the miraculous. He never approached major spiritual figures without a sense of veneration, and his very curiosity was so forceful that it had the appearance of love. All it was given to him to imagine was a spiritual order without charity at its head. It was probably impossible to read his work without a sense of unease, but the only person capable of drawing his secret from him would be one of the saints he had mutilated. His analyses were tasteful and inoffensive and — a sign of naivety and pathos — he even prudently omitted those heroes whose major historical status seemed established for all time, preferring to rescue virtually unknown, minor, and hopefully more tractable saints from their reassuring obscurity. Yet he had never managed to control them. However simple, gentle, ingratiating, and persuasive his literary art, they would not yield to him. The preface to his last book alone ran to fifty pages, full of reticence, reservations, and allusions, as if the poor fearful author was putting off the inevitable confrontation for as long as possible. The fact of the matter was that as soon as an uncooperative witness was called, the equilibrium was broken. Even the limited importance given to facts was too great, for an action, a word, even if stifled by the laborious text, was enough to break the spell, and the major role allotted to commentary simply highlighted the painful impotence more harshly. The unequal struggle was both tragic and laughable. At times his oversophisticated ideas would melt into thin air, exposing the implacable reality they had hidden. At others, they would lurk in the background, allowing the conquering hero to emerge. A fruitless search would follow his unsuccessful attempt to grasp his subject. The number of pages increased, the book grew inordinately long, like a fitfully interrupted nightmare. Then suddenly the author, who had seemingly been rocked to sleep by his own monotonous purring, woke up, lost his composure, and threw himself into the argument again in a kind of rage, arousing only disquiet and amazement in the reader. What caused the sudden anger was the fact that like a stench betraying the presence of a corpse, an appalling irony — perceptible to no one else but stinging Cénabre's self-esteem — rose through his lies from the truth he had twisted and abused. Anxious to escape from himself but deeply drawn to the imaginary characters he had almost unconsciously substituted for real ones and tried to see as real, his tragedy was that at the end of the tortuous road he had taken he never met anyone but himself. What he had denied to his saints was denied to him in his turn, and every attempt to hide the fact made his own deprivation clearer. It was as if in order to give his ghosts a little reality he had stripped away some of his own substance, some of the lies that would have offered him a disguise, as they had done for so many others until their dying day. He saw himself in all his nakedness.

He went closer to the window, leaning his stubborn brow against the panes. The street was empty and resonant, and he turned away wearily.

And so it came slowly and carefully, gradually finding its own level. Never had he spent so much time so agreeably in everyday actions as he did at that solemn moment, drawing the curtains, lighting his bedside lamp, meticulously laying out his clothes for the night. He was enjoying this waiting period, seeing it as if through an onlooker's eyes with a grave and silent joy. His footfall on the carpet, the sound of a glass on the marble chimneypiece and the sound of his breath, coming a little faster after the exertion, caught his attention closely and delightfully. For the last time he was observing himself in his usual setting, surrounded by familiar sights, grasping the scrap of life like the crew of a drifting boat staring at the motionless disappearing shore, and his thoughts were already dragging their anchor.

He knelt down and prayed as usual. So far, he had never failed to carry out to the letter certain duties of his clerical state. Prayer was one, as he found it easy to submit to external discipline and physical constraints. They provided him with an indispensable support and safety from a profound disorder that was likely to take him far beyond the ambiguity his nature rejoiced in. On that evening too he uttered the words slowly, reciting the whole of his usual prayers properly before slipping between the covers and closing his eyes.

Immediately the thought of finishing once and for all with the anxious doubt that had been suffocating him for weeks came to him, and he tried to give it form in his mind. It was stronger now, and he unconsciously struggled to fit it into one of his usual psychological categories. It seemed to him that his perfectly ordered life meant that a mental crisis was at very least unlikely. He had, he told himself, simply reached a dead end, and his work had scarcely begun. It was, he thought, impossible to do without a system of ideas forever. There was such a system to be drawn from his writings. But, like a sharp physical pain, he felt the need to collect himself.

This, he thought, explained his increasingly profound feeling of tedium over recent months, the irregular pattern of work, keen sense of wasted effort, sudden lack of ideas, and vague but ever-increasing bitterness towards his subject matter, the simple men whose simplicity had betrayed him.

In the darkness, he could hear his heart thumping in his chest and was struck by how irregularly it was beating. He realized that he did not want to grow old before he had proved his worth and made his mark. He now felt nothing but indifference for that alien breed, the readers whose unthinking adulation had given him his elevated status and who were now waiting for him to lose it again in a new and unexpected way. Only the most embryonic, fleeting, unstable forms of error satisfied them, and once it had taken shape they would abandon it. They were passionately interested in everything suspect but either apathetic or pitiless towards renegades.

In his reverie he had reached the stage where certain words sometimes seem to have a life of their own, thrusting themselves forward in his mind and violently interrupting the flow of thought as if they had burst out from the depths of his being. "Renegade" was one of them, and the shock of hearing it was so great that he unwittingly repeated it aloud.

He tried, and even managed, to smile. In his mind, the old-fashioned word still had no clear meaning. He did not know why it had occurred to him. In all probability, few books had been more minutely examined or more severely criticized than his . . . but he was safe. Even the strictest censors now found fault only with the general trends in his writings, in which their hostility had never been able to detect anything deserving condemnation. Who was there to trouble him? However close the scrutiny, he was blameless. Not only did he faithfully meet his major obligations, he also scrupulously carried out his lesser duties, taking care to make no changes or disturb the pattern and order of his days. There was also an element of proud scorn for sloppily abandoning a discipline, in short, of a sense of dignity. Although he seldom said mass, it was with the agreement of his superiors and because he was genuinely short of time. He always read his breviary, however. Father Domange heard his confession every month, and that look at the past gave him serenity for a time. The elation and eager hope of youth had gone, but once the general trend had been settled his life had flowed on as if carried along by its own weight . . . he closed his eyes tightly, like a stubborn child, wanting to see the monotonous journey through time . . . but where was it taking him?

Quite independently, his thoughts, like an animal that had broken free, were already running along the road that was finally open before them. Not only was he no longer in control of them, they were outside him, something extraneous, a falling stone . . . yes, his writings did have a meaning he had never known. They were still being studied in an attempt to find a heterodox statement. He too had played that childish game. At that very moment, the familiar jumbled arguments were thrusting themselves chaotically forward, as if for a final effort. But he was deeply afraid and only too aware that the chaos was merely an eddy on the surface of deep water. Already his sudden, single, precious, dangerous thought had run ahead, out of all reach, and was dropping swiftly through the darkness like the weight on a sounding line. It would not stop until it reached its destination, if there was one. A man clinging to the edge of a cliff by his weakening fingertips could not have listened more fearfully to the sound of stones hurtling pointlessly down into the void below him. The sheer drop opening up before him finally tore a single word from Cénabre. "God!" he cried.

Scarcely had his feeble voice died away when a massive, leaden silence suddenly struck him like a blow. The attack and the mental collapse were so abrupt that he jumped out of bed in an attempt to escape . . . around him the bedroom was still alive in the pale light, with everything in its normal place, and in the mirror he could see his staring face . . . but things seemed to have lost their individual meaning, not to answer to their usual names, to be dumb. His look now seemed to express not so much terror as total astonishment . . .

"I no longer believe," he cried bleakly.

We are troubled by temptation and cunningly tormented by doubt, but Cénabre was the victim of neither. Between such trials and the brute fact expressed in his cry lay the precise difference between absence and nothingness. The place was not empty: there *was* no place at all, nothing.

Quite literally he felt neither regret nor remorse but simply the astonishment of a man who, thinking that he has been advancing in a certain direction, discovers that he has been making no headway and that his progress has been an illusion. Had he so wished (but he did not), his reason would still have insisted that at that moment he was no different from the man he had always been. The whole of his past had flowed out like water through the mysterious breach, and all that his undiminished consciousness could now see was actions more futile than dreams and a life ordered, regulated, and shaped in terms of a world with no existence outside his own imagination. What others took to be his life, his real personality, had come into being in circumstances just as ephemeral and insubstantial. Repeating the same actions over the years had barely created the ghost of himself or given it any reality. That, at least, was how he pictured it. For belief, slowly broken down by a delight in deliberate doubt and the sacrilege of loveless curiosity, had vanished completely, like a hitherto pointless physiological function once an organ has been destroyed.

And yet the looking glass still showed the unbearable reflection of features transformed by fear and a wretched, defeated body. Under his light nightclothes he was shuddering, sweat was trickling down his loins and legs, and in his open shirt-front he could see his scapular trembling on his hairy chest as his heart raced. His furtive inward-looking gaze, his jaw, slack in his anguish, and his bitter mouth all looked strangely vulgar, but the dreadful sight nevertheless held him, drawing him into a secret and almost unavowable complicity. The humiliation of his flesh was sweet, if the word can be used to describe such confused pleasure, for in the chaos that had engulfed him, he despised himself so savagely that he still had at least the illusion of some remaining lucidity. He desired so keenly to see the depth of his shame, however, that he stared into the reflection of his own eyes, trying to see the expression on his face.

Once he had done so, he gave up the struggle and abandoned himself. In his contorted features, his gaze still seemed clear, attentive, and even, he would have sworn, mocking. "You're lying, lying, lying!" He said no more, but his soul, raised up and as it were drawn out of itself (just as an orchestra, hanging on to the repeated first note of the theme, suddenly plunges into it with the full force of the brass) took up the accusation even more vehemently: "He's right. You're lying. You're acting out a sacrilegious little comedy. It's not true that you've lost God. And in any case you'd have felt the loss no more than you've felt the need of him. Today, you're what you were yesterday. If you're shivering, it's because you're cold. It's just that you'd like to believe that a man like you only gives in to trials that are made for him, worthy of him. God can't die in you without a bit of a show, a bit of thunder and lightning."

The sharp realization that his distress was bogus and inane was the last straw, breaking the final link between the past and the present and leaving him in limbo. Faith had disappeared as if it had never existed, and it seemed to him at that moment that he had never lived. He would have given anything to have felt some resistance, a rift, even if the pain were searing, anything but this silent decomposition of the being he had thought real but which had vanished and left nothing in its place. Now, however, it seemed that he would be locked into the supernatural silence forever.

He went wretchedly back to his bed with his head bowed. The abject submissiveness he felt showed how far he had fallen and how impossible it was to return. He was less like a liar caught out in his lie than a trained animal performing poorly. He was yielding now, but doing so might well bring no consolation. Yet there did seem to be an outlet for the stagnant, fetid waters of his soul. Feelings that were new yet familiar to his deepest self and undeniable, even though he still had no name for them, welled up from a swampy soil. To his astonishment, the strongest of them was curiously like hate.

He got up almost at once and lit his lamp again. He was no longer trembling. His sweat-soaked shirt was sticking to his back and thighs, but he was no longer aware of their icy touch. His heart was beating regularly and strongly again, and he was already resolving to get the whole matter over and done with and take a hard, clear look at the problem, whatever it cost. That was all he was aware of, for he thought that he was calm again because he had reached the critical point at which anxiety claims, demands, postulates the presence of a friend, anyone, a witness. Now, he could no longer be alone.

It was strange that the image that immediately forced itself onto him was that of a man so unlike him and so unlikely to understand him — Father Chevance, once the parish priest of Costerel-sur-Meuse and now on the ancillary staff of Notre Dame des Victoires. It was the first name to occur to him, either because the number of friends one can wake up at two in the morning is small, or perhaps for a different, deeper, more urgent reason. Cénabre could not have said and pushed the question from his mind forever. He was already living in his dream from which he could expect no quarter.

Apparently quite composed, he picked up the telephone. Father Chevance had a small room on the top floor of the Saint Etienne building in the rue Vide-Gousset. He looked up the number in the directory. The night porter, woken from his nap and bewildered by such a late call, had to have his instructions repeated three times.

"Please ask Father Chevance to come urgently. It's serious."

"Is someone ill?"

"Dying," Cénabre answered calmly.

The author of the *Life of Gerson* had known Chevance at the junior seminary in Nancy. Fifteen years older than Cénabre, he had at the time been the deputy supervisor of the youngest boys. The relationship between the two men had been unremarkable but was never to lapse completely. In 19———, Chevance, by then the parish priest of Costerel, had had to leave the Verdun diocese after a minor scandal cleverly exploited by the radical press. Quite naively, he had taken it into his head to exorcise a mad girl, the terror of two villages. In his defense, however, it must be said that he had carried out the ceremony most discreetly at the request of the poor girl's only remaining relative, an uncle who had been the verger at Notre Dame de Grâce, in Lérouville. Unfortunately for Chevance, the only result of three lengthy stays in the departmental lunatic asylum had been a worsening of her condition, and its chief medical officer had declared that she would very soon die. Her unexpected recovery after the exorcism had seemed foolishly provocative to sensible people and capable of seriously damaging "religious harmony" in the diocese, the end for which Chevance was in fact sacrificed.

Despite the consolation and encouragement of the bishop, who "condemned only the imprudence and recognized the good intentions" of the repentant priest and offered him another parish, the unfortunate man thought that his reputation was irretrievably damaged and his honor as a priest in danger. It never occurred to him that he had been the victim of an injustice, and the indulgence of his superiors, their "goodness," as he called it, broke him. From that time he saw himself as unworthy of the priesthood, or at least of any kind of authority. In his child-like mind there were certain contradictions others would have found intolerable but which persisted because he accepted them unquestioningly. Thus, although he did not doubt that he had done his duty and behaved charitably towards the mad girl, it was equally clear to him that his superiors had had every right to be annoyed. The fuss caused by such a simple action was a virtually irrefutable proof of his unforgivable clumsiness, even if he could not quite see how. All the intervening years had not weakened the scruples his holy simplicity imposed, and he would still relate his humble tragedy in the same tone of voice, full of a remorse that would shine in Heaven.

As a result of Cénabre's intervention, the diocese of Paris had taken him in and found him a modest post at Notre Dame des Victoires, for which he was enormously grateful. In this obscure role, the former parish priest of Costerel-sur-Meuse ceased to exist in the eyes of men and simply disappeared. His extraordinary shyness, which for a time had been pushed into the background by the responsibilities of his modest position, increased from day to day, becoming a touching and ridiculous infirmity that the world found amusing. No doubt it was his cross, but every cross is a refuge. It was an odd little foible that hid his boldness in spiritual matters and extraordinary sense of the grace of God from most people. The timidity was not exclusively physical, as is sometimes the case, but also involved a real fear of the judgment, or even the notice, of other people. However hard he tried to live unnoticed and wipe out all traces of his past life, the chance encounters living in Paris entailed threw him into disarray. In this connection many of his colleagues from his former diocese, where he was remembered as a harmless enough fellow, were unwittingly an occasion of torture, for he more or less imagined that it was solely because of Cénabre's protection that he was tolerated as one of the most insignificant members of the educated and sophisticated Parisian clergy, of whom he never spoke without a certain comical reserve.

In the long run, that reserve was to look suspect. Some saw it as a sign of intellectual poverty, others as a covert reproof. What happened was that as the years passed his spiritual influence grew and became harder to ignore. Ultimately, even his excessive prudence created a legend around him that was fed by his innocent ruses. Thus, although he was working outside the regular parish hierarchy and was accustomed to performing the lowliest tasks and being a permanent jack-of-all-trades, it had occasionally fallen to him to stand in for one or two of his brilliant colleagues at confession. Gradually, although still on a supply basis, he had come to spend the greater part of his time in the confessional. At first his great worry had been that he might seem to be poaching on others' preserves, since it might not be possible to avoid the risk of attracting pious penitents of some consequence away from their legitimate confessors. Never had a fashionable preacher, drunk with social successes, shown the zeal and perseverance in charming his beautiful female sinners as Chevance did in trying to find and keep the most neglected, despised, and unenviable sheep of the flock. Cooks out early with their baskets on their arms, shopgirls at midday, crunching the walnuts they had had for dessert with a couple of small coins in their hands for Saint Antony of Padua's box, horse-faced sanctimonious ladies, humble and disastrous old men, schoolboys avoiding the chaplain — he accepted them all joyfully and found the fact that he could hear the confessions of anyone, however mediocre, quite reassuring. Unfortunately, if these second-hand penitents were not noticed for any other reason, it did not take long for the sharp-eyed curates to recognize, amongst Father Chevance's regulars, one or two of those maniacs who are the amusement and terror of every parish, riddled with imaginary faults and hankering after something spicy and sacrilegious, seeking out a strict confessor as their unacknowledged sisters might seek out a lover who would beat them. Once the maddest had been excluded, Chevance, among his weak and fallen penitents, was illuminated by a strange and almost unforgivable supernatural light. The scandal he had come so far to escape and for which he had probably been born tracked him down even to his attic. A wit went so far as to call him "the charwomen's confessor," a name that immediately caught on and was all the rage in right-thinking Catholic salons. Aynard de Clergerie, the historian, once briefly thought of taking an interest in the strange old man and had him sent to his house on some complicated pretext by one of his friends, a vicar-general whom the unfortunate priest would certainly have dared refuse nothing. In the end, however, Chevance's shyness and rather servile politeness proved an obstacle to the kind gentleman's benevolence. Had it not been for the good offices (which were judged to be indiscreet) of Mademoiselle Chantal de Clergerie, the daughter of the eminent author of *The Church in the Twelfth Century*, his fall would have been quite complete.

Cénabre went to the door, felt for the knob, and opened it, taking his visitor's arm and leading him into his room without a word, which the "charwomen's confessor" found disconcerting. He did not have the courage to speak first and feared that his silence meant that he had failed in some elementary duty. He was even more taken aback by such a mysterious interview so late at night and scarcely dared look at the man to whom he owed so much. As the Canon had simply thrown a fur-lined overcoat around his shoulders without putting on his soutane, the startled priest was confronted by a view of his bare feet in slippers, strong legs in black trousers, and, beneath the open coat, his massive chest. The strange attire also disturbed him.

"Sit down," said Cénabre, not unkindly. "Sit down, and first forgive me for disturbing you . . . forgive me for this ludicrous fancy."

Father Chevance, who was standing by the bed, sat down on it. The base squeaked horribly, and he stood up again at once.

"Canon — my dear and illustrious friend — I will ask you . . . I would need to ask you first about your health . . . and also about the sick person . . . for whom . . ."

"Nobody's sick," Cénabre answered curtly, "and nobody's dying. I'm even sorry for the lie, the exact meaning of which I'm afraid will escape you. However, I've no right to claim that I lied lightly and without thinking. I had to speak to you, at once, without delay, that was all."

"I'm at your disposal," Chevance murmured, with ever-increasing anxiety. "I may have done something wrong involuntarily. The indulgence people have shown me isn't without risks. I should like to break, if I could do so tactfully, with many of those whose friendship is nevertheless a great honor to me. It's ridiculous for a poor priest to let himself be seen at the house of the excellent Comte de Clergerie or that of His Excellency the Nuncio, for example. But enough of that," he added, since his interlocutor's face had been growing more somber as he spoke. "I'm ready to hear you . . ."

"My friend," said Cénabre, "I thought of you today because your simplicity has always been a great help to me at certain times in my life. The world, and I'm talking about the one I see most of, is full of bare-faced liars."

Chevance threw up his hands, desperate and protesting, but regained control of himself almost at once and looked down without replying. Cénabre's indirect response to both actions was a cold stare.

"I need you to agree to be my witness tonight," he said abruptly.

Chevance's voice was shaking with astonishment.

"I can't grasp . . . I don't understand . . . how you can need me . . . or even have some use for me . . . and who could take seriously . . . for a man like you . . . such poor support . . . at least I can talk openly to a colleague, tell him what I really think and feel . . . this conversation . . . today . . . tonight . . . I don't want to offend you by calling it a little odd . . . even astonishing . . . this conversation, whatever its result may be, coming after . . . others just as odd . . . circumstances . . . which might seem to be to some extent . . . a snare of, oh, of the devil!" he cried with astonishing naivety.

He reflected for a moment, with Cénabre's harsh gaze still on him.

"I shall shortly have to talk to you, I expect, about the trust someone admirable and exceptional honors me with." His voice was no longer trembling. "Mademoiselle Chantal de Clergerie was born to edify and teach me. I watch her with a kind of fear, truly with terror, moving towards God, to the highest peaks of contemplation. Quite simply, the Holy Spirit has come down on her, and she has already left us . . . ah, I know who I'm talking to! I haven't much time for reading, and I read little, but I know that you have experience, a great deal of experience, of holy people, chosen souls . . . It's true, thank God, that Mademoiselle Chantal is still unknown, but it's hard not to be afraid for her . . ."

"Can we forget Mademoiselle Chantal for the moment?" was all Cénabre said in reply.

He seemed to hesitate again and then looked pityingly at Chevance, who was still taken aback. It would have been hard not to feel superior to the old man with his childish confusion, his forced, servile smile and trembling hands.

"My friend," said the author of *The Florentine Mystics*, unconsciously reverting to more elegant language, "I'm going through the most sudden and acute crisis imaginable. I may be calm again now, but I certainly wasn't a short while ago. When all the spiritual powers of one's soul are in turmoil and upheaval, there's no question of being in control. One cries out in distress, and I didn't attempt to stifle it. I'm not ashamed of it. I want to tell you, and you alone, about the deep distress that explains and excuses certain resolutions and actions that malicious people have said slanderous things about. I've already been accused of being cold and insensitive. You can see, I'm afraid, that neither reputation nor perhaps talent (however insignificant my own is) is any protection against such extremely humiliating attacks. I sincerely hope that for the present I shall not be called upon to ask you to support me. But if I talked openly about such things to those who admire me and think that they love me, they wouldn't understand what I was saying. Your simple and sincere heart will be a better judge. Don't hold back, my friend. In the midst of all the trials that await me, I set great store by the consolation of knowing that secretly and silently a priest as spiritual as you is helping me by being compassionate. And I may say that if providence were to decree that things should turn out that way, you would keep me in your memory."

As his words fell into the silence, he saw their true and ignoble meaning and felt intensely annoyed with the simple man they were addressed to. Since he had to offer a believable reason for what could easily have seemed an inexplicable action, he had simply come out with the truth willy-nilly. What he perhaps would not have dared to admit to himself was clearly expressed in his embarrassed phrases. Despite the terrified role he had been semiconsciously playing, everything was gradually falling into place, as if his still-lucid mind had drawn up its plan right from the outset. His cry of distress had been feigned. He had always accepted, at first instinctively and later by conscious choice, the absolute need for a secure position and convincing excuses. Consequently, his falsehood had been shaped from within by his deep hypocrisy and had been its first victim, and could only be separated from it by an effort of the reason.

"Do you mean," Chevance asked despairingly, "that you're thinking of relying on me in such a serious situation? It seems to me . . . if you don't mind . . . I'm sorry . . . that this is just a nightmare . . . or if you're just testing me, why? I have the greatest respect . . . and admiration . . . for your gifts and your reputation as a writer . . . your services to the Church . . . it would be so easy for you to catch me out, and to laugh at me — quite properly — when I'd shown you what a fool I was." His voice was begging now. "But people would know what I'd done and there would be more talk about me again, and who knows, perhaps they would eventually tire of my follies, of the scandal I caused. I've paid so dearly, Canon, for a tactless mistake I made when I was young . . . I don't want to raise all that again. All I'm asking is that you won't drag me into the limelight simply for fun. Don't add to my troubles. If I lose the honorable and . . . very advantageous . . . situation that I have very kindly been given in another diocese, where there are so many worthy people . . . what will become of me? My dear, good friend, I can see, and I admit, that over the last few months I've been imprudent. I've let myself be pushed forward and done one foolish thing after another . . . Don't make me pay too dearly for them!"

There was a strange look on Cénabre's face as he watched the old man pleading with him, and he suddenly shrugged his shoulders impatiently.

"You seem to think me capable of being strangely smallminded," he said. "I apologize for distressing you. But surely you can see that it's too late for me to turn back now? In any case, I still intend to stick to my original choice. Yes, however bizarre you may find it, I need you in one of the most serious and indeed tragic situations in my life, a terrible and decisive ordeal, a time of inner turmoil — "

He stopped abruptly, as if the better to see the former parish priest of Costerel-sur-Meuse, who, to his astonishment, was pushing the prie-dieu discreetly toward him like someone no longer willing to shirk his responsibilities and saying very calmly, despite the beads of sweat on his brow:

"In that case, Canon, I'm ready to hear you."

He made the sign of the cross.

The anger in Father Cénabre's voice was barely contained.

"I wasn't asking you to hear my confession, my friend. *Don't be in such a hurry!*"

He stressed the final words deliberately, grinning so savagely that Chevance blushed to the roots of his white hair. Suddenly his humble gaze shone with supernatural assurance.

"I can do nothing else for you," he said, his voice still shaking. "In myself, I'm nothing. Let God take my place. I'll certainly not be foolish enough to rely on my own insights, indeed I won't."

He pulled out a large cotton handkerchief and feverishly wiped his forehead and cheeks.

Cénabre's powerful hand was pressing the old priest's shoulder, and Chevance seemed to falter beneath its grip.

"If you're worried about your peace of mind, Father, or about compromising yourself, leave now."

"Canon," the priest cried with tears in his eyes, "I don't deserve that!"

The insult produced a keen sense of a slight to his self-respect, something he had not felt for many years, and for a second he realized how strongly and irresistibly it was welling up in him. He had been innocently expecting Cénabre to confide in him about some serious fault too difficult to acknowledge to anyone else. There was none that would have repelled him, no filth that would have made him flinch. Already his hand was rising in blessing, and the divine pity that filled him was quivering in his palm, inseparable from the spilling out of his own life. His look was so humbly beseeching that Cénabre responded to it in spite of himself.

"I've lost my faith," he said, adding immediately and much more calmly, "tonight has been a struggle with terrible darkness. I can no longer put off a decision that intellectual honesty, if nothing else, demands . . . the question I've avoided for so long needs an honest yes or no."

While he was speaking, he had been walking up and down with his head bowed. As he reached the end of what he was saying, he stopped opposite Chevance, whose naive features showed enormous relief. Either from disappointment at some failure or embarrassment at having opened up his heart for nothing, Cénabre turned pale.

"Why didn't you speak sooner?" the older priest asked quietly.

"No one is safe from that kind of trial. Even I . . . but a mind like yours probably feels it more keenly. In circumstances like that, struggling is pointless. You can't do much for yourself. Try to let yourself be calm, my dear friend and mentor. Let God come to you of his own accord. I'm going away to pray for you."

He picked up his hat from the bed and turned towards the door, about to go and do as he had said.

"So that's all!" cried Cénabre with a forced laugh. "You think that's all there is to it? You find me shattered and beside my-self — the fact that I approached you is enough to show just how badly I was affected! — but that's all you feel. Or perhaps you think I'm capable of being so tortured by childish imaginings? You must know, my friend, that belief isn't snatched from a man like me without a terrible struggle. Circumstances rather than any wish of mine have made you the only witness of this tragic adventure. Go on! Off you go."

Once again, Chevance's eyes filled with tears.

"That's not it at all," he muttered in despair. "I would have asked for light for both of us. But I couldn't have abandoned you, my patron, my faithful friend! In God's name! You would soon have seen me again!"

"Are you sure?" Cénabre cried furiously. "*I have seriously been thinking of killing myself tonight!*"

Neither Cénabre nor anyone else could have said why the idea came to him or where it came from. Nor could he have said whether it was a lie. Once it had been put into words and accepted as something more than a pointless provocation, the attitude of the old priest and his silent terror, which was so different from his usual agitation, immediately gave it a sinister reality. Cénabre had probably not truly contemplated suicide: he had never had the thought and had spat out the threat as if it were a curse. Once again, however, he felt with an absurd fury that his rash words were as binding as a declaration. It was like being in a dream, a kind of frantic nightmare in which the dreamer struggles in vain only to see the free space around him shrinking and as every escape is gradually blocked. It might have been unwise to summon Chevance, but he had wanted a friendly and readily useful witness, and all he had stupidly managed to do was give himself away. He could not tell against whom or what invisible obstacle the hatred that filled him was directed.

Chevance was now looking straight at him, sadly. Without complaint or reproach, but with the greatest dignity, he simply said, "I can no longer listen to you outside the sacrament of penance."

Once again he made a move to leave, but Cénabre forestalled him.

"Do you think I am capable . . ." he began to thunder.

"We are all capable of anything," the old priest replied humbly. Immediately, however, his expression hardened, and his words hit home.

"I'd rather believe you to be the victim of such a thought than think you capable of attributing it to yourself falsely."

He hesitated for a second and then said, sadly and movingly:

"I can't allow you to use me to offend God."

Cénabre smiled bitterly.

"I offer no further defense. You're free to go. No one's stopping you."

He watched Chevance steal rather than walk towards the door with his hat under his arm, looking so pale, weary, servile, and submissive that he was furious with himself for letting the ridiculous little priest escape with his secret. In his heart of hearts, however, he was even more keenly aware of the unbreakable silence and the incomprehensible solitude he had been imprisoned in for some hours. Prayers, threats, lies, cries of fury or despair, nothing, it seemed, could break the magic circle. He was like a man crying on a seashore.

Fury won, however. The same mysterious hatred still seeking its object, which had already roused his anger against the whey-faced journalist, now shook him as he faced a new enemy. There was no attempt to restrain himself. He simply stretched out his arm and the frail old priest spun round, his open hands seeking something to clutch for support. His nailed boots slipped on the polished floor and he fell on his knees with his hat beside him, a pathetic figure.

Shame rather than pity drew something like a moan from Cénabre. He stood mute before his grotesque victim, scarcely seeing him, his whole attention fixed on the internal event, the irresistible outburst, the unknown and supernatural force, trying to understand the sudden violent passion in his breast.

He neither saw Chevance stand up, nor felt the old man's hand take his own, nor heard the very soft voice, still shaking with a childlike fear. Yet suddenly it was terribly audible. His whole body drew back imperceptibly, rather like a hunted beast. Then some expression returned to his features.

"I should have liked you to bless me," Chevance said sadly. "I should have liked to ask you for that favor before I leave you forever."

His voice was so tender and full of God-given pity that even the proudest and most supercilious heart would have been moved by it. He was no longer avoiding Cénabre's somber eyes, but meeting their gaze. The compassion in his ardent soul came down on the celebrated priest like an eagle swooping on its prey.

"In the terrible trial you're going through at present, any other action of our ministry would of course be impossible for you," said the charwomen's confessor. "But which of us, even in the clutches of Satan, could not validly give a blessing, in the name of the Father, the Son, and the Holy Ghost? Ah, my friend, that's a certainty! Without sacrilege you could call down on a friend scarcely less wretched than yourself the grace you're deprived of for the moment. Listen to me. At least make that sign, even if you do it indifferently or with all the wrong intentions. At this moment, when every heartbeat could mean blasphemy and defiance, what does it matter whether you believe or not? If you can't ask for pity for yourself, oh, at least, at least make the sign that gives it to the sinner! All I ask you to do is to wish for my happiness!"

Tenaciously and impressively, the priest was trying the only possibility left to him, making the final appeal Cénabre might heed. He could see, hold in his gaze, virtually touch the frantic, mortally wounded soul. All he hoped for was a single sign, even if it was barely voluntary or lucid, something like the scarcely detectable movement of the eyes indicating acceptance on the frozen face of a dying man or woman, the breach through which God's awesome pity, which he sensed strongly all around the still-living sinner, could bring all its weight to bear. In a flash, he knew not how, he had his revelation and was to forget it just as quickly. He was completely caught up in what he had to do and did not weigh his actions. Well beyond the limits of his own reason, a world away from his puny body, which even then looked as humiliated and fearful as ever, his charity alone discerned, judged, and acted. We cannot see as the angels see. The strongly built man with the smooth, pale forehead and lowered eyes he was fighting for in the darkness was still there before him, but in Heaven they were embracing.

Gradually, Cénabre became aware of his surroundings again, although he had to make an enormous effort to break out of his inner contemplation. What was taking shape inside him was unlike anything else, could not be grasped by any intellectual process, and remained distinct from his own life, which had nevertheless been shaken to its very roots. It was, as it were, the jubilant *self-realization* of another being. He could see neither the meaning nor the point of the prodigious turmoil within him, but the voluptuous passivity of all his higher faculties at its epicenter thrilled every nerve in his body. At that level of self-abandonment and total disintegration not even the most compelling argument, nor any threat or insult, could have drawn so much as a sigh from him. Its grip was so tight because he had been seized so unexpectedly, and his resistance had been broken at a blow.

He was still looking stupidly at Chevance, whose voice, alternately commanding and begging, had from time to time impinged on his hearing without moving him, even though he remembered his words, stored them in his memory, and retrieved them mechanically. As the new and appalling happiness poured through him, the suffering and the final appeal were meaningless, or at least he had to climb back gradually from the deep, dark places of his joy in order to grasp what they meant. The time it took showed him just how far he had fallen. For however pitilessly he harries us, the angel of darkness, the master of our will, feels the flesh he has deceived shudder beneath him at the final moment as it scents death. All this flashed through Cénabre's mind.

At last he could see, could focus on the old priest trembling no longer with fear but with pity. Although he did not recognize them as such, he found the missing strength to flee and the desire to do so in the gaze of his last friend. For months he had not felt even the absence of divine grace, which he could now dimly perceive again like the face of a drowned man beneath the waters or a plaintive cry in the fog. The insight, or rather the charity, of the man of God had inspired him to beg from his wretched colleague the only thing he was still capable of: not even a silent imploration or even an attempt at sympathy, but perhaps only a movement of compassion for his fall.

None of this showed on Cénabre's tense features. They still bore the marks of his recent frenzy, for the vertigo had struck suddenly and without warning. There had been no outward sign of the equivocal joy he had initially and definitively experienced. Perhaps the human face cannot express such an emotion. Nor was there any sign of his final hesitation, his last false step on the inevitable road. Yet the mercy of God was now assailing him, throwing itself upon him, embracing him so violently that his very body seemed to be responding to it. There was no new gentleness in his gaze, but the kind of fleeting, dazed gleam seen in the eyes of someone who has been stunned. As Chevance had asked, he raised his arm in blessing. Everything was over in an instant. His rational mind was functioning more rapidly, his anguish lifted in a moment, and the nightmare opened up like a cloud, revealing the sterile part of his soul that had long ago been consumed by irony. The eminent historian's much-vaunted critical sense took over. Something he could no longer name veered away from him. The tragic scene, the key to which he had immediately forgotten, now seemed no more than an unbearable parody of a real drama, and he thought he could see just how ridiculously pretentious it had been. He caught sight of his ashen face in the looking glass, and his shaking hands and all the remaining signs of the anguish his reason had just escaped filled him with shame. He would have liked to remove every trace of them at once, like an actor tricked into accepting a poor part furiously throwing off his tawdry costume.

If his return to normality had been less sudden and total, he might have vented his anger and disappointment on Chevance once again, but he was in too much of a hurry to finish with the whole episode and, after the incomprehensible fit of madness, to take up again the thread of his daily life — in short, to be himself once more. Although he did not know it, he was exhausted. With a deep sigh, he simply said to Chevance:

"I'm not going to try to understand anything about this crisis. It seems that I came to my senses, my friend, when I saw that you were about to succumb to my contagious madness."

Chevance's despairing cry was still echoing in the closed room, but Cénabre's icy words killed it immediately. The old priest seemed to understand, bowed his head, and for the moment was no more than a sad little man.

"How little people know us priests," the slow, grave voice continued. "How separated from the world we are. Many people see my own modest self as a writer trained in intellectual disciplines, attentive, cautious both by nature and profession, familiar perhaps to the point of disillusionment with the most delicate questions of conscience . . . and yet the first time I'm faced with the temptation to doubt — which I've studied so often in my books — I lose all self-control and babble and act like a madman.

Obviously one hardly needs to scratch a mature and experienced priest to find a seminarian's rather wild faith, fears, and scruples. You know that, my friend, as we all do. That's why you've already forgiven me."

"Oh, God . . . no doubt . . . it's true . . . Canon," Chevance stuttered oddly in reply. "I haven't . . . I can't really . . . how could you think that I still remember those . . . well, those . . ."

He was never to finish what he was saying. The calm superiority of the interlocutor staring at him so severely cast a spell on him, and he was clearly at his mercy.

"It would have been wiser to take your advice from the start," Cénabre went on overbearingly, but without raising his voice. "Yes, in a situation like that, there's no point struggling. Avoiding temptation is better than meeting it head-on, and if I went beyond my strength, I've certainly been punished enough. There's no simpler or more effective remedy than peacefully doing our duty in a spirit of trust and acceptance. Nevertheless, I still have something to do. It's right and proper that to some extent I should make amends not for my offense, as your charity has done that, but for the scandal I've given. My venerable friend, I want you to hear my confession . . ."

"No!" The retort, which Chevance would have liked to withdraw, shot out. "I think now," he stammered, "I have reason to suppose . . . far from giving a definitive judgment . . ."

Then, as if his courage really had failed him, the rest of his words were lost in a confused mumble. His wretched head drooped even further. He seemed to be doing his utmost to face up to some painful effort he had to make. His body, so strangely humbled, seemed weighed down by unthinking fear. Suddenly, in the midst of his ridiculous distress, the same cry was wrung from him again:

"No! I can't lend myself to this sacrilegious pretence!" Immediately, his eyes seemed to be pleading for some help that could never come, but as they met Cénabre's solicitous and almost tender stare, he started back so spontaneously and timidly that the Canon's features reddened.

"Are you afraid of me?" he asked quietly.

Now that he was calm again, it was quite clear how unwise he had been in almost enjoying bewildering the, to him, extremely transparent priest. The author of the *Life of Gerson* was not a man to suffer gladly the trickery purely physical strength might easily resort to, and at that moment the most violent outburst of anger would have frightened him less than the signs of the panic in which his sophisticated knowledge and experience recognized the total and overwhelming rebellion of an invincible heart. It was possible to bear scorn and recognize what hatred can do, to sidestep heated indignation and deal with it from behind, but poor implacable little Chevance was going to escape his grip forever.

One more word and it was finished. There would always be this obscure judge to whom he had entrusted his confidences for an hour and who was now lost in the crowd again, a thousand times more dangerous and elusive because he was anonymous. For the moment, no doubt, the charwomen's confessor's budding reputation would give him rather limited authority over a few minds, but it was not what he might do that Cénabre feared. His will, which was now struggling to wipe out even the memory of the crisis that had almost broken him or at least destroyed his rest, his works, and his reputation, had come up against a fateful obstacle. The secret of his new life was going to leave his house and travel around the world. The certainty was too much for his already bruised pride. He felt that the trick would either work at once or fail completely. Without anger, but deliberately boldly, he asked:

"What are you going to tell people about me?"

"Good heavens, Canon," the priest cried, "there's nothing *for* me to tell them."

"Oh yes there is," Cénabre replied after a moment's silence. "Whether you've really understood the situation or not I hardly know, any more than I know when what you foresee will actually happen. What I want to know is whether you believed me when you found me just now, completely distraught and disorganized. Were you sorry for me? Was that the sort of ordeal someone low and insincere might go through? Didn't I put up a struggle? Didn't I suffer?"

The strange look in Chevance's eyes stopped him.

"And, since I don't expect an answer to those questions," he went on, "don't you think that it will take a little time for your ordinary decency to cope with the weaknesses and contradictions peculiar to someone whose intellectual life you know so little about? And what should I have to do to satisfy you completely?"

The old priest replied immediately in a low and even more respectful and deferential voice, but his words were pitiless:

"Canon, there is only one thing *for* you to do. Leave everything. Give it all back."

Still smiling, Cénabre made a gesture that perhaps indicated incomprehension followed by amazement. The wonder was that Chevance noted the smile, took possession of it, and returned it with joy, like a docile pupil responding to an indulgent master. Waving his long, thin hands, he went on with what he had been saying.

"This is what I'm trying to say, Canon. We're so wretched . . . that sometimes our whole life . . . drifting . . . without our knowing it . . . to some degree . . . from God to the Devil. I'm expressing myself badly. What we should imagine is more a spring lost in arid and polluted land. What I see as the most precious thing the Lord gives us is our physical and spiritual sufferings. But over time, the use we put them to may have corrupted them. Yes indeed: man has soiled even the very substance of the divine heart, that is, suffering. The blood that flows from the Cross might kill us."

He took a deep breath and went on.

"You've waited too long, Canon. Really and truly, you've deprived yourself of too much. There's nothing else to be done with the anguish you spoke about. It's come too late and in spite of you. You won't use it. Rather, it will destroy you, cast you into hatred. Don't blame God, Canon. He offered you the anguish, so to speak, as one persuades a child to drink his medicine, a sip at a time. You were unwilling even to take a sip, and now you have to drain it at one go. Drink it down quickly! All you'll find at the bottom of the glass is a final draught that will be more bitter and burning . . . my God, how clumsy and unconvincing I am! What I'm trying to say is that your ordeal is sterile and unproductive. It belongs completely to the aspect of your life you have to reject. Keep *nothing* of it. It's rotten through and through. I can see, *see your work itself.*"

"Do you know it?" Cénabre asked coldly, but without malice.

"No, no doubt I don't," Chevance retorted. He then thought about what he had admitted, realizing how unconvincing it must sound. There was real despair in his eyes, despair about the dazzling certainty his words had just revealed but no longer expressed or would ever express again.

For an instant he was on the brink of excusing his apparent lie by appealing to the superhuman insight that justified it. He had not the strength. For a second time a word from Cénabre had been enough to catch him, drag him down from the heights, and make him a poor wretch again.

"I'm supposing," he said in shame, "simply supposing. But I

would have liked to . . . I *know*," he went on, "that you *have* to wipe out the past . . ."

His voice choked, tears came into his eyes, and, as he could not finish what he was saying, he begged Cénabre several times to go away, an injunction whose real meaning God alone knew.

There was no reply for a long time.

"All that could hardly be said," the Canon finally replied, "about a man who had neglected all his duties. Fortunately, there's nothing like that in my case. All mine have been carried out punctiliously, if not enthusiastically. I've respected them even if they haven't been a labor of love. Of course, I can't hope to justify myself completely. But tell me whether on reflection you don't find it childish to claim to leave your past behind, as one might a night's lodging? It's not that we have the past at our disposal, that *we* hold onto *it*. It's the other way round."

Chevance said nothing.

"Nevertheless, I shall bear in mind some of the hurtful things you've said to me. It's true that my work fills up my whole life and that a priest who is as humble and zealous as you are might be scandalized when he sees how greatly I am *apparently* attached to worldly vanities and *really* too passionately interested in the things of the mind — in short, that I am not enough of a priest. Since I had no major or even any serious omission to reproach myself for, I took it too much for granted that one can do without keeping a watchful eye on the soul, the strong and subtle self-examination that our old masters called, rather beautifully, our orison. Criticism is a poor substitute. What you might call my long-term professional familiarity with the lofty and consummate spirituality of the men I had been writing about led me astray, for I unconsciously saw myself in them. Unfortunately, charity can bring us together and make us one, but the intellectual world is solitary, clear, and icy . . . oh, our intelligence can penetrate anything, like light going through the thickness of a crystal, but it can neither touch nor embrace. Its contemplation is sterile."

His voice quivered slightly with impatience and then lost its confidence as he uttered the last few words.

"Anyway, why am I talking like this? It must sound stupid to you. It is, because it's futile. From now on, no more reasoning for me. I want my life to be simple, regular, ordinary. I want nobody to experience or be distressed or scandalized by the temptation you've seen me on the point of surrendering to like a coward. Nobody will know what I'm suffering, and I shall try to forget it myself. If I deny the past, I shall only do so in secret, for what I did wasn't reprehensible, even though my motives or intentions may have been . . . why should I run the risk of troubling my fellow men? I am taking my life up again at the point where I left it, tranquilly — if I can! — and firmly, like a ploughman straightening out a furrow . . . no, I didn't lose my faith! That's not what happened. I was mad. It was simply that I came close to forgetting that abstinence and virtue aren't the same thing, that there still has to be an impulse of the soul, a passionate seeking, a painful and pleading cry to the Father and an invincible hope. Why all the talk about overthrowing everything? What does it matter whether I'm in one place or another? Our attitude isn't important, and you'd also agree with me that in my present position there are appearances to keep up . . . as you very well know from your own pastoral experience, it's on the inside that we need to start again, to reform. It's not easy, my friend, but I don't think it's beyond me. I was, you might say, inert and insensible, but not dead, as this crisis has shown. My intellectual search led me astray for a while, but I never stopped loving God . . ."

At these words the priest, who had been listening humbly to Cénabre's words, staggered as if struck. Extreme anxiety shone in his eyes, and his old body, still clumsy in his terror or anger, was thrust completely forward, as if to shield a sacred presence behind him.

"Don't! Don't say that!" he shouted, violently and savagely. "No! *You don't love Him!*"

Cénabre recoiled at the outburst, his arm raised as if to ward off a blow.

"Monsieur . . . my dear friend . . . Canon," Chevance cried out piteously, "have pity on me, the poor wretch God has given you to today and who can do nothing for you! I can see you falling like a lead weight. Oh, God, I shall have to answer for this, for *you*. Do you really want me to be lost? I've no strength, no eloquence. I'm a stupid priest. People aren't hard enough with me. No one is such a coward as I am. Why was I chosen tonight? You need explanations and a true picture of yourself, and all I can do is feel your wretchedness without being able to express what I see. I can do nothing to help you, God knows! How does He expect me to make myself known to you? He knows that I would have preferred anything, even sacrificing my own life, to what I have to confess to you and the humiliation of having to make such an incredible admission. Look at me. I must keep every scrap of the shame and offer it in its entirety . . . the only proof of my mission I can give you is my word, my wretched oath. I swear, I swear to you that the Holy Spirit is inspiring me in this. I swear that you are as open to me as a child's look is to its mother. I can *see* you, *see* your soul perishing. And that has been revealed to an old fool incapable of doing anything useful with it. My God, all I can do is bear witness to it again and again in rage and despair, knowing full well that I can do nothing!"

Even the hardest of men would have found what was before Cénabre's eyes at that moment intolerable. The holy madness of his puny adversary was of course now totally beyond his comprehension, and the least help from outside would have given him the strength or self-possession to smile at it. Yet something within him was moved by the sound of a familiar voice, the last to speak in such a way, and he had a strange and bitter feeling that he would never again know such supernatural pity, for he would never again want it. In his very heart of hearts perhaps he even hated it.

"Blasphemy and revolt would be a thousand times better for you," the former curé continued with his hands folded across his chest. "Oh, Canon, there is some love of God in blasphemy, but yours is the coldest hell."

He uncrossed his hands, let his arms fall, and stood for a moment facing his redoubtable adversary. Neither the look of astonishment on Cénabre's face nor the bitter set of his turned-down mouth seemed feigned. His deep and solemn silence demolished or perhaps merely neutralized Chevance's words more than any angry or mocking cry. For a moment longer the old priest tried to bear the silence. Then, with a kind of moan, he was gone.

. . . . .

"Ah, the well-meaning old fool has woken me up completely," Cénabre said aloud. "I won't go back to bed tonight."

Chevance's flight had left him filled with a quiet joy barely tinged with ironic bitterness. Far from disturbing him, the memory of his frail adversary's ultimate failure would probably be a help in any similar ordeal in the future. It was as if he had tried out his own madness on the old priest, as a laboratory animal is injected with germs of tuberculosis or plague.

Smilingly, he wondered aloud whether he had been mad enough to provide a worthy interlocutor for "the maniac," and whether he could have done anything but turn "the poor fellow's" head by honoring him with his confidence and seeking his

advice. Chevance obviously could not have expected such a prodigious adventure from a Canon and must have thought it more
likely that he had brought it about himself, and had therefore
been sent away in desperation rather than disappointment.

These and other similar words were in fact uttered aloud for,
to his great astonishment, he was *thinking* aloud, a common
weakness amongst solitary people but something which Cénabre, for whom silence was natural, had always previously found
deeply distasteful. Now, however, he was instinctively seeking
out the murmur, listening avidly to his own voice, and finding
enormous consolation in it. For a time, as he paced heavily
across the room, he went on talking to himself in the same way,
occasionally laughing strangely.

Nevertheless, he washed and dressed very calmly, determined
to spend what was left of the night in his library. He could hardly
wait to be back there with his beloved books, in front of the
white sheet of paper that was shining in his thoughts like a light-
house. He could see the page he had written the previous evening and was burning to finish it. Indeed he was already doing
so, for his memory, seemingly pushed beyond its normal capac-
ity, was running line by line through the article for the *Weekly
Review* he had started a week ago. It was a very subtle and perti-
nent refutation of a recently published (and rather mediocre)
book by Father Paul Berthier on Blessed Thérèse of the Child
Jesus, whose heavenly smile, a temptation for the facile and the
foolish, will always be the most bloodstained and best-defended
rose in the gardens of paradise. Still speaking in a low voice with
occasional bursts of the same incomprehensible laughter, he re-
cited the most felicitous pages to himself. He had always been
very fond of upsetting some of those edifying priests whose pallid zeal flows ceaselessly through unreadable books. But was it
the writers he really liked to disturb or the holiness he could

never reach? It seemed to him that he had never hitherto felt so avidly impatient, perfectly in possession of his material, or clearer minded.

Anyone seeing him in the rosy light of the distant lamp with the pale moonlight in the windows, his sturdy shoulders rolling imperceptibly beneath the stretched cloth of his soutane, the powerful jaw muscles and fearless neck, would have envied him his tranquil power. It was, however, already dying, destroyed from within.

"What on earth have I got to laugh about?" he suddenly asked himself, finding the tone of his laughter astonishing although he still did not quite know why.

At that point, he went diagonally over to the door, blowing out the lamp as he passed it. The livid predawn light held back at first, crept along the high curtains, and then, lying on the floor at the foot of the cold, wan windows like some sly beast, refused to go any further. Cénabre caught sight of something on the floor he did not recognize at first. He picked it up and held it up to his eyes by his fingertips with considerable surprise and slight disgust. It was Chevance's neck band.

It was nothing in itself, and indeed he saw the square of fabric for no more than an instant. A problem that seemed to call everything back into question had just arisen . . . Problem is perhaps too strong a word. It would probably be truer to say that an awesome and immovable objection had been raised, hesitantly at first but then increasingly urgently, in Cénabre's still-troubled mind. Although he did not know it, he was at the point where our inner balance is a miracle of lucky coincidences and fortuitous harmonies, and the slightest obstacle creates a huge wave, like a reef in swirling waters. He had no choice and could no longer either subdue or evade a hostile thought.

It was quite clear that the band had fallen off as the old priest had lost his footing when he pushed him. He could see his body stretched out, his rough black woollen stockings showing under his soutane, his legs twitching like a child's.

"Why did I hit him?"

Now that the inexplicable fit of anger had passed, there was of course no way of explaining his sudden violence and extraordinary loss of self-possession. However much he might want to regain his usual impassivity or need to persuade himself that he had done so, the strange and obdurate little fact would not go away. As long as any doubt remained, there was no way of reducing the night's events to manageable everyday proportions. Cénabre's composure and rather arrogant and imperturbable irony were so well known as to be already almost legendary, and it was therefore not easy to explain the way he had brutally destroyed the pathetic little journalist and even harder to account for subsequent events.

"Why did I hit him?" he repeated, still murmuring. "I must have been beside myself."

That single obstacle was enough to block his mental processes. All he wanted to find out was what had led him to attack, with such fierce hatred in his heart, an enemy now gone, wiped out, annihilated . . . hatred of whom, of what?

Once again he was startled to hear himself laughing. It was not so much laugher as a strangely triggered, unrecognizable, convulsive, involuntary snigger, which for some time had been forming a mysterious background to his reflections, so closely linked to his most intimate and unavowed, or unavowable, thoughts as to be unnoticeable. What had suddenly caught his attention was a certain basic clash, not between the laughter and his inner thoughts, but between it and his attitude, his outward appearance, each of his grave and measured actions, indeed all his external characteristics. His astonishment disappeared as rapidly as its cause, leaving behind no more than an obscure anxiety, a secret watchfulness. As he walked to and fro across the room with a show of indifference, he waited and listened, between each word and the next, for the sound of the alien laughter again.

As he did so, he put the crumpled, stained band, stinking of the snuff Chevance took in great quantities, down on the table, went back to the windows, and opened the curtains wide. It was no help, however, for the lonely street and the noise of the wind reminded him of the old priest, and he imagined him crossing the city on his way back to his desolate hotel room, which he had seen one evening. Yet what was uppermost in his mind was not the memory of Chevance but his complete, irrevocable, and pitiless solitude. Only now did he seem to grasp just how alone, isolated, cut off from his fellow men — by his strange nature rather than by space or time — the old priest was. What could such a wraith matter, as either friend or foe? In the throng, he was like a foreigner unable to make himself understood, and even if by some remote chance he tried to do so, every attempt would make the original misunderstanding worse and the priest still more confused, as happens when there is an absolute and irreconcilable difference.

"Poor old man," he said sadly.

And immediately, he heard his own laughter for the third time. It was brief and stifled, but his watchful mind had immediately plucked it out of the air. Once again, but this time more clearly, he realized just how much it jarred with his bearing and facial expression, even though the latter filled with tenderness and pity as he uttered the words. The clash was clear and compelling in a different way. He could not yet grasp its cause, but it had taken no more than a second for him to pinpoint the exact location of the pain at the heart of his self-esteem. The priest whom Monsignor Dutoit, in a famous lecture, had called "the most subtle and perceptive man of our time" heard his own crude laughter.

The coldness and forced smile of the author of *Tauler* were well known. Everyone was aware that in fact he rarely smiled. The mobility, vivacity, and occasional sudden fixity of his expression (which disappeared almost equally rapidly when he closed his eyes) made up for everything. Few people had heard him laugh, although the lucid and charming P. J. Toulet had written that one evening, at a dinner at Madame de Salverte's house, the priest's unexpected joy had almost made him cry out in anguish. It is possible that Cénabre was quite aware of the strange anomaly or dangerous weakness. Whether he was or not, however, what he had just overheard was much more bizarre. The snigger, which he did not recognize and could not control, had clearly come from himself. He had listened to it with disgust, his attention suddenly caught, as one becomes aware of a repulsive creature at one's feet in a sudden and momentary flash of light. He did not recognize it and could not attribute it to a purely physical cause or separate it from some secret, private part of his mind for which there was perhaps no other outlet. The thick whinnying in his throat, however astonishing, had no real existence of its own and was triggered by . . . a noise? Not a noise alone, an echo . . . but an echo of what?

He could not have said, and yet his anxiety was so powerful that he could now think of nothing but the new conjecture. He even tried, childishly, to reproduce the sound he had only heard fortuitously, trying his best to find his little game of hide and seek grotesque. What came out of his mouth, at first timidly and then angrily, was nothing like the earlier laughter and had quite a different ring. He stopped.

Although he was still afraid of going mad, he would at that moment have given anything to doubt himself and the evidence of his senses, to believe, for instance, in some kind of auditory hallucination of the kind critical commentators on the saints attach such importance to. No one, however, would be able to understand the fear torturing him, if such an equivocal explanation were ever deemed possible. He already knew that the humiliating laughter was simply an external manifestation of the full and certain reality of the flesh-and-blood life from which he had always wanted to remain aloof. It was impossible to deny the clear evidence of his senses, and he could only delay its inevitable effect.

Certain specific types of renunciation are not susceptible to analysis, since sanctity is constantly drawing from within itself what the artist borrows from the world of forms. It becomes increasingly interior and is finally lost in the depths of being. We no longer see the relationships between acts and motives. Once that contact has been lost it can never be recovered, and as the observed facts become more and more subject to their own logic, they seem in fact to separate, to dissolve, as it were, in the absurd. To tie up the broken thread again we would need to achieve the impossible and raise ourselves in a single bound to the lofty aim glimpsed by the heroic individual from the very beginning of his movement towards the heights, an aim that his fierce and patient desire has possessed in advance, that is, the deep unity of his life.

Cénabre's life also had its key: an almost absolute hypocrisy. It was not, as is the case with others, merely a constant search for a moral alibi or anything that could be confused with ambitious self-interest, but something more: a liking, a passion, a frantic desire for lying that led to a real and truly monstrous dichotomy in his being. The origin of the fearful duality lay in the very distant past, no doubt in his earliest childhood, when the peasant boy, riddled with pride, instinctively and almost innocently played out the gloomy comedy of a "vocation to the priesthood" in his family home. And he certainly did so in a sad and dreary way. Some hypocrites, even if they are diligent and punctilious, occasionally have their weak moments when they make up their role with a kind of imaginativeness and exaggeration in their pretence that, for a time, frees them from themselves. Few men have the terrible single-mindedness necessary to create their lie from the inside, but for years it had been given to Cénabre, now stumbling for the first time, to resist and overcome every revolt of the soul. In the past, in the junior seminary in Nancy, the singular Father de Saint-Genest, who died as a missionary in Hué, accused himself of being unable to overcome the revulsion he felt for his pupil, who was nevertheless extremely hard working. When he was asked why, he would simply reply "I think he is incapable of love. HE DOES NOT EVEN LOVE HIMSELF." Yet the youngster was studious, obedient, a glutton for work, irreproachable. Once the first step had been taken, however, his heart had closed and would never open up again. In seminaries, it is not too unusual to come across precocious and determined boys pushed toward the priesthood by the illusions or sometimes the blind vanity of those near to them, who no longer have the courage to leave and eventually resign themselves to its obligations as they would to those of any other career. At least they are mediocre priests, easy to recognize, with the ambiguity of their sad lives atoned for by worries, suspicions, and all the pathos of a failed vocation. Cénabre, however, did not lie by halves and never had.

And if the lie he was living had not been absolute, without reservations, and totally accepted, he would not have had the courage to hold out, for he was a man of strong feelings. If he had not withdrawn into the very center of the fortress, no doubt he would have been driven from the outer walls. He was too proud to settle for mere appearances, too subtle not to see how frail they were, and had committed his whole self. No one seeing the strange child conscientiously, assiduously, even fervently following the exercises of the double annual retreat with all the concentration of a devoted craftsman working for his own satisfaction could possibly have accused him of duplicity. When Father de Saint-Genest had watched, frowning gravely, intent on the daily meditation, for example, and asked him rather brusquely to give him an outline of the reflection that he had found so absorbing, he had always replied at once with obvious sincerity. His attention had never wandered for a minute from the topic suggested, and he had honestly taken it as far as he could. His quick intelligence, marvelously attuned to interior observation, had assimilated both the language and the spirit of the inner life, and in that field he had already shown an exquisite sensitivity. Similarly, his confessions would have deceived the wisest of men (only the stunningly elliptical judgement of a curé d'Ars could have seen through them) for they were equally sincere, with nothing omitted save the perverse and diabolical negation that was gradually turning him to stone. Nor did he hide even his most personal trials, such as doubts concerning his faith or his unsurmountable horror of the Passion of Our Lord, the thought of which was so painful to his nerves that he involuntarily turned his eyes away from crucifixes. What is even more incredible is that his confessor, Father Brou, after giving him fairly harsh penances that were always carried out in full, ordered him never to go to sleep without having dwelt on each of the major episodes of the Sacrifice of Calvary. He did as he was told, and it cost him such an effort that the sweat would sometimes stream from his forehead, and some nights, through the thin wooden partition, his neighbor would hear him moaning softly.

Thus he performed each of his duties punctiliously, working at his own downfall with enormous willpower. Perhaps he really was already possessed. Perhaps one of those seminal faults that germinate so slowly but so tenaciously and can corrupt a whole race was to be found in his childhood. No one will ever know. There may be a different and more acceptable hypothesis. Any actor can become so immersed in the part he is playing that for a time he leads an existence strangely modelled on that of the imaginary character, even taking the scrupulous search for verisimilitude into everyday life.

Cénabre's powerful nature, about which so many people had been mistaken because they had been thrown off the trail by an apparent readiness to take the easy way out, hated to see a task left unfinished and was unstinting in all it undertook. The young orphan who had been abandoned by everybody (one of his grandfathers had been involved in robbery with violence in Metz and had died in a penal colony, his father had been an alcoholic, and his young widowed mother had washed and mended linen for the local housewives in her tiny cottage in Sarselat and had died in the Bar-le-Duc workhouse) was not one of those people for whom options are possible. He wanted to get on and was keen to make a name for himself but was doomed to grow up where he was, where a single ill-advised act could cost him everything. Not only was he forced to enter the priesthood, he also needed to stand out amongst his better-placed and privileged rivals. A premature and unfortunately unflagging shrewdness already told him that his superior intelligence alone would have been enough to put him in a difficult position and that his best course was not so much to try to stand out as to make up for his origins and past by irreproachable behavior and manners. The fear of being caught out in his new and still flimsily constructed lie gradually led him, after several timid experiments and attempts to break free, to keep to it extremely strictly and closely, even when he was completely alone, and in his heart of hearts. It could have deceived Cénabre himself had he not fairly promptly lost the desire or the courage to see himself as he really was.

Such dissimulation might seem surprising in a youth who had scarcely left childhood behind. One might think, without being overdramatic, that it was not until later that the unfortunate youth entered into the full and perfidious possession of his lie. The delights were short-lived, for when such a lie is total, it involves the whole of life and governs every thought, and there can be no rest on the arid road that has to be followed. All the work undone at the end of one day has to be begun again the next, until the twofold being reaches its point of perfection, its full-blown horror, realizes that there is no place for it on earth, and dissolves into the supernatural hatred that has brought it into being.

What justifies this way of seeing things is that however much we might want to find a natural cause for such tragic aberrations, it is hard to know how to account for their subtlety, their quality of pointlessness and superfluity, that clearly indicates the presence of lucid pleasure and delectation. It is difficult to imagine, for example, the youngster in the seminary in Nancy subjecting himself, really and not merely ostensibly, to the highest practices of the spiritual life without gaining any benefit from them. No doubt he refused his interior consent and only committed the superficial part of the soul we call intelligence or attention, yet it is not easy to see why he was not tempted to go further and give God something more — just one act of love, or at least of goodwill — when the soil had been plowed and needed only a single grain of seed. His nature was to be sure astonishingly arid, and we can begin to understand why his pride was afraid of surrendering its place of last resort when it had already given up everything else. Or it may be that he never experienced the need, which so many others have found irresistible, to inspire and offer friendship, to love and be loved, though he understood that if he took that path his lie would be too heavy to bear. But more than anything else the most effective weapon against grace was his extremely tenacious intelligence, which was driven by a kind of curiosity and fuelled by a certain cruelty and soon revelled in its mysterious and skilfully hidden conquests. In the young brain the persistent and as yet invisible work of a lifetime, the brilliant and sterile books, models of clever, perfidious, remorseless analysis, so complicated in their inspiration that they would always dupe some of their readers, was already taking shape. Their roots plunged deeper into the life of their author than anyone suspected, reaching a level at which they occasionally revealed something of himself he had already forgotten, the pain of humiliations that had outlived the memory of what had caused them, deceptions that had lost their point but left their mark on him. He had once explained to Monsieur de Colombières that he had always been attracted by sanctity and curious about its most remarkable and hidden forms. In fact, his harsh nature found it difficult to conceive of the exceptional spiritual state whose causes his intelligence sought to explain.

He remained motionless for a moment and then hurriedly left the room and went into his library, closing the door carefully behind him. As he took his first step, his foot hit the lamp on the floor, and he had to grope around irritatedly in the dark for another one, which had not been used for a long time. It weighed so little that he realized at once that there was no oil in it. Finally he reached the chimneypiece and found one of his eight-branched solid-silver candelabras, a present from the Princess of Salm, and lit the candles feverishly. As he put it down on the fabric on top of his desk he saw that his hand was trembling.

In front of him, waiting for him, was the sheet of white paper he had longed for. He pushed it away, stood up and absent-mindedly flicked through the pages covered with his small, bold, carefully punctuated and exquisitely neat handwriting without actually reading them. Occasionally his eye was caught by a particularly felicitous phrase or a familiar paragraph, and then he would immediately look away. He would have liked something, *anything*, to break the silence and was almost unconsciously waiting for some reasonable excuse, or the dawn itself, to do so.

Never had the night been so dense and silent around him, lying in ambush just outside the circle of light, lurking watchfully in all the dark corners and folds of the curtains, the undisputed mistress of the world outside, of the deserted street, of the city, at the hour when even debauchery is falling asleep.

The street, however, was not quite deserted, as suddenly there was the sound of footsteps on the paving stones, coming closer with a kind of mechanical regularity and then stopping all at once. The ensuing silence and emptiness seemed so much more intense that Cénabre felt it strike to his very heart, and he reacted defensively for a moment . . . he snatched up the white page furiously and hurled it violently into the wastebasket.

His confusion and shame were as indescribable as his more acute but less deeply felt disappointment. The calm he had regained was perhaps no more than an illusion, simply another snare. The night might perhaps live in his memory forever, since he could not undo what had been done. Perhaps he had yielded not because of some unforeseen external obstacle but because he had not had the strength to stand up to events. He snarled, rapidly scattering what remained of the manuscript. Looking up he saw, in the darkest recess at the far end of the room, the Cross standing out against the whitewashed wall.

Immediately, he heard his own laughter.

This time, there was no attempt to escape from it or stifle it: he listened to it courageously and wanted it to be as it was, no less shrieking or vile. With his whole being he accepted it and made it his own . . . his reward was an immense and unexpected lightness and ease, overwhelmingly reminiscent of the relief when an abscess bursts. He felt, first with astonishment, then with certainty, finally with exhilaration, that the now intolerable activity inside him had found a way out and was discharging itself. A child in the dark coming upon what he believes to be a ghost and then touching a familiar and harmless object with his little hands would feel something, but only something, of that joy, for he would simply stop being afraid and would not despise or try to take his revenge on what had frightened him. Cénabre, however, opened himself up completely to those bitter and hitherto largely unknown delights.

He looked down, saw Berthier's harmless book on the table, and laughed again, this time uproariously. If there had been a witness, someone to whom his fear had been transmitted, the unbearable scene would no doubt have come to an end more quickly. Since it was taking place in secret, however, it moved slowly from the real to the nightmarish and finally to a kind of supernatural infamy. That terrible internal joy bursts out so often in the debates the human soul conducts, but we do not hear it. No doubt evil can break out of its solemn empire and give itself up to us as it really is only in rare and unusual circumstances.

Anyone seeing him as he was then, still impressively vigorous and healthy, large and calm with massive shoulders, strong and bold in his bearing, and yet shaken by mad laughter, would hardly have been able to believe his eyes. Something that hell normally keeps jealously for itself was now being unreservedly, incredibly, brutally, insolently given away. Was it the cynicism of a soul already lost, or perhaps the sluice gates being raised in a final merciful attempt to let out the hideous secrets of the soul, the poisoned thoughts stifled for twenty, thirty years, the forced unwilling, material but still liberating avowal, the miraculous outflow channeled by the actions and voice of a hypocrisy reaching the highest level of concentration, the ultimate degree of evil now incompatible with life, as the belly sometimes rids itself of a poison with which it has suddenly been saturated.

And yet in the midst of the mounting frenzy the ever-watchful witness remained lucid. However strong and pressing the enemy's grip may be, he has not been given the power to replace completely our life with his own. In his overflowing joy, as in the very perfection of his ineffable despair, doubt remains, like a worm. The feeling of the fragility and precarious nature of a pleasure unable to live in us or to blend with us is imposed by force and maintained by violence, for no experience in this world can give us a convincing idea of Hell.

What had once been Father Cénabre had now, of course, only a vague and confused notion of why he was so furiously agitated. If he had seen and heard himself clearly, he would have been so horrified that he would immediately have done what in fact he was not tempted to do until later. It may be that the divine pity was merciful enough to blind him for a time, or never to let him see the wretched depths to which he had sunk. The fact that many people perceived a final stubborn and almost childish and silly illusion in the sinister priest would seem to suggest it. The writer so passionately interested in all the trials, and particularly the strangest ones, that saints undergo, was an unwitting dupe of his own critical obsessions, for the idea that he might be possessed never occurred to him.

What he gradually felt was an immense fatigue. The night was almost at an end. His heavy eyes looked increasingly less often outside the circle of light at his feet. With every moment that passed, sleep was gaining a firmer and firmer hold. Although he was still incapable of grasping the degree of violence that had lifted him so high only to drop him like a stone, he was obscurely aware that his strength had decreased incredibly and his life was being spent and scattered. Once he was on the downward slope, his will had collapsed and his very being had simply faltered. Yet again, he realized with terror that his balance had been destroyed, that the routine transitions that give the interior life its measure and rhythm no longer existed for him, and that all he had known of joy or pain during that dreadful night had been the overwhelming and twofold fury whose strands had come together in the same shared anguish.

The cause of the brutal relinquishment was almost comically simple, but it became more complex virtually at once. A few moments earlier, he had proclaimed his freedom aloud, and was now repeating the declaration softly and uncomprehendingly. Suddenly an ironic and almost inaudible voice, as always at the back of his mind muttered "Free from what?" Then it quickly grew inordinately loud, drowning everything. "Free from what? Free from what?"

He burst out laughing and soon found the ringing sound intolerable, quite aware that the hostile cackle was tearing him apart. The words he had involuntarily uttered were of no great import, but they had touched a vital spot. The past he had rejected and discarded forever and thought he had escaped from had left him an equally hollow and empty future with a new and equally wearisome lie to assume . . . free from what?

Try as he might to escape, he felt trapped again every time. In any case, if he had gone on struggling he would have been beside himself. He preferred to look the new catastrophe straight in the face. Sadly, even in the state of near madness he could understand what had brought it about and analyze it with some lucidity. What would he have done with freedom if he had regained it? It had come too late, even if he had ever been worthy of it. After his harsh, deprived childhood, the severe discipline he had voluntarily accepted was still the only solid and positive part of his life. Without it and the constraints it and his lived lie imposed, what meaning would his life have? What purpose could it serve? What use could each day be put to? No other discipline could ever have completely satisfied him, and in any case he was too old to embark on an alternative falsehood. He had no vice to indulge and indeed considered most of them to be foolish and stupid dissipations for which he had a poor man's scorn . . . so, what was to be done? Could he not simply consider a crisis with no result to be totally unimportant and unreal and go back to the task he had put aside the evening before? It would be *his* secret; no one would have found out anything about it except a priest too scrupulous to speak out and who would only be disbelieved if he did.

. . . No, he thought, he could not go on.

He did not try to find a reason why, but everything new repelled him, even though the break between past and present seemed clear and decisive. It would be pointless to claim that he had never been aware of the old laborious lie in his life, but simply by forcing itself glaringly obvious and naked into his fully conscious mind it had deprived him of a tiny but essential and indispensable suggestion of unrest and ambiguity, rather like those materials that are highly toxic once their chemical equilibrium is upset in the presence of another specific substance. He certainly could not forget the ordeal he had just endured, and the memory of it meant that any peace was necessarily unstable and precarious. He might still be able to deceive others, but could no longer deceive himself. Certain involuntary emotions, such as the dull anger he had felt so often, bitter distrust, the passionate, painful, insatiable curiosity the heroes of his books aroused in him were no longer mysterious. He had thought that he loved them, as a historian might treasure the contemporaries of Louis XII or Charlemagne as childhood friends or familiar figures in his own circle. He no longer had any real doubt that he hated them. It now seemed ridiculous to be interested in the tedious pursuit of an imaginary good or the terrible emptiness of their destinies. Perhaps, he thought, he had unsuspectingly been driven on by the hope of wresting a secret from them, but he now knew that they had none, that there was nothing. A strikingly arrogant thought.

His success, reputation, and authority were no longer of any interest to him. For a man in the limelight, standing still means slipping backwards, and he was convinced that there would be no more moving forward and no more confidence for him and that the force behind his work was exhausted. Even his boldness, which the foolish found scandalous, was boldness only in relation to the relative order of his own life and to a certain harmony that had now been destroyed and seemed frivolous. He sought nothing, wanted nothing.

He felt the same vertigo sweeping him up in its hellish swirl, the same emptiness in his breast, the same burning forehead and icy shoulders. Nothing could have expressed the blind violence and disorder in his mind better than a wild cry, but the silence was majestic and undisturbed, deepening and more motionless around his despair with each passing second. In every fiber of his being (for, at such times, the whole body has a concept of pain and death) he felt that he had passed the point of no return and that his fall would accelerate of its own accord. He had no hope and could no longer even imagine going back or coming to a stop in his vertical descent. And yet he was still too much alive to endure it and simply let himself plummet. He felt himself touching his round, stubborn head, his muscular arms and chest almost naively and pathetically. It is impossible to grasp the fatal idea when it swoops on our soul like an eagle. It was in him. Before he could even name it, it was in his heart. If he could not halt the inevitable fall, he thought, then at least let him speed it up and be done with. Such were his thoughts when he saw his own pistol in his right hand.

There was no question of drawing the barrel toward his temple. He threw himself on it in that dreadful moment when Hell is no more than a feeling of hatred, a single flame on the soul in peril, piercing everything, consuming even the angels and stopping only at the foot of the Cross. His action was horribly precise, sharp, and irresistibly powerful. Nothing but a miracle could have stopped him, and there *was* a kind of miracle, for the trigger jammed. Cénabre had clenched his hand so convulsively that his finger had been injured and was bleeding onto the steel edge. He thought the safety was on, and was astonished to find that it was not.

He carefully took the pistol in his left hand and gently squeezed the trigger. There was some resistance for a moment, then the metal sear slipped out of its notch. The barrel was trained on nothing in particular, but pointing toward the wall. The bullet clipped the brick and ricocheted into the door, which merely shuddered slightly. Blue metallic-smelling smoke rose slowly towards the ceiling and disappeared.

Just as carefully, he put the gun back in his right hand and pushed the cold little mouth behind his ear. He was so completely sure of himself and what he was doing that he allowed himself a minute's respite, not a minute to think about his actions. Strangely, his impending self-destruction seemed obviously and even monstrously stupid, and that was its ultimate bitter joy. All that had happened during the night, each act and thought, was a series of bizarre and illogical events. Of his own free will, he was about to add another equally or even more incomprehensible and crazy episode to the painful nightmare, as if he were exacting some mad revenge. His mind was illuminated by a moment of hatred. His past did not flash before his eyes, and he had no time to weigh out his future. The illumination lasted no more than a moment . . . he had very little time to wait. At that moment, however, he happened to catch sight of the clock. His neck was stiff, and the pressure of the little steel mouth had become extremely painful. His shoulders ached as if he had been in the same position for a long time. Staring stupidly at the black hands, he could hardly believe his eyes. When he had seized the weapon for the second time, he had happened to notice that it was five minutes past three, and now it was ten minutes to four. His hesitation, which had seemed so short, had lasted for forty-five minutes.

He might have felt disbelief, but he did not. When he thought of his long dream while his finger was on the trigger he started with terror, not so much of death as of the risk he had run of suddenly slipping out of a dream and into death. A cramp in his finger, pressing the trigger without realizing it, and it would all have been over for good. A suicide, but one carried out blindly, which would have meant that he had been a victim of the whole incomprehensible period of delirium. He realized with fury that one terrible night could have robbed him of first his life and then his death.

Once again he clasped the butt of the revolver, trying to calm down and concentrate. If anyone had told him, at that point, that the decision was probably not irrevocable, he would have quite sincerely laughed out loud. He was certain that he would not see the dawn. Yet his mind, already unwilling to accept his fate, was secretly resisting, edging slyly towards images of horror. He heard the dull, muffled shot. The point of the bullet was drilling through the frontal bone, bursting the wall of his skull. His eye was blown out of its socket, a white globe lying on the table in a pool of scarlet mucus . . . the clock struck four.

The cry he heard was not that of a dying man, but a real roar of impotent rage. He slackened his grip on the gun. What was even worse was the fact that his brain was already working more freely; the strength he had fought hard to concentrate had dispersed, trickling away in pointless musing . . . he was starting to observe, to become a spectator again.

He hurled the weapon away so violently that it turned on itself and bounced twice before hitting the wall. Almost immediately, he ran and picked it up and put it back on his desk, within reach, looking at it in turn angrily, dismally, and strangely confusedly and humbly . . . in fact, he was thinking of nothing in particular, trying out one idea after another. Then his features froze, his cheeks turned pale, and he suddenly drew up his large body with such a sharp reflex movement that it seemed to jump. The glittering brown revolver shone in his hand once again and moved quickly up toward his forehead. Each of his actions was that of a man gathering momentum and moving off, for the final onslaught of temptation, after the victim has been lulled into a momentary sense of false security, is always the shortest and most violent. Never before had the awesome priest been closer to death. And yet, even then, something in his heart broke. The frantic and apparently irresistible impulse slackened and collapsed, and his shadow flickered on the wall. It was not his flesh that was affected but, so to speak, the most delicate and vital point in his will. Without for a moment losing consciousness, he fell face forward on the carpet with his arms outstretched in the form of a cross and rolled around sobbing and abandoned, his whole being disintegrating hideously.

His jaws were clenched and his face thrust into the thick woollen pile of the carpet. A convulsive movement threw him momentarily onto his back, then he rolled over again, bellowing, to escape the unbearable light.

It was as if the opposing forces fighting over their prey had now cast aside all pretense and were wrestling like two combatants at each other's throat over a corpse. He was in that extreme anguish where every link is loosened and the shamefully distressed body takes part in the collapse of the soul, no longer expressing pain through any abstract sign but sweating it at every pore. It was an abominable but magnificent spectacle, enough to repel pity. There is no mask that temptation cannot wear, and the idea that Satan is purely a logician is an illusion held by not a few naive people. Many a shifty old man sees him as an opponent in an academic argument, but if he does the observer is still at the stage of games and trifles. Sometimes, though not often, the black desire to harm wins out over quicker and less bitter delights. When that happens, evil shows itself for what it truly is, not a way of life, but an attack on life itself. Thus the frantic hatred Cénabre had previously exercised so shrewdly was finally flowing quite outside the safe and ordered regions of the conscious mind. His tortured and abandoned body was a frighteningly accurate image of an abused and profaned soul, for the horror reached its height when his robust physique seemed to offer no further resistance and endured suffering, devouring it as we devour shame. For an instant, his humiliation was indeed complete.

Stretched out full length, with his head in the hollow of his folded arm, the priest was no longer moving. The wave of pain had passed over him without annihilating him. He was completely abused. Regaining consciousness in the posture of a tortured animal was no longer even humiliating, or if it was, the humiliation was of the kind that follows sexual pleasure, a baleful self-detachment. He vaguely felt that he was no longer an observer but the passive subject of some cruel double experiment or the stake in a relentless struggle. The outburst of hatred had initially been so searing that it had wiped everything else out of his mind, but it had been totally isolated, a spurt of pure, essential, impersonal loathing, and he still did not now what it had been directed against. He was pinned to the floor by an overwhelming sense of self-contempt coming from a different and more mysterious source within him that had been momentarily eclipsed by the searing spasm, although he confusedly felt that once it had broken out it would have expanded and swept everything away, shattering even the framework of his soul. The two forces had certainly seemed to become one for a moment, but it was clear that they were working in opposite directions. The hatred, however harsh it might be, had stiffened his will and made him look to his defenses, whereas the humiliation had undermined his resistance, wearing it down slowly, stubbornly, and with terrifying cunning. If one of the two had first deferred and then prevented his suicide, it was the hatred.

Father Cénabre knew that. He could see that in return for the life it had saved at the final moment it was grabbing, attacking, breaking down from within his self-esteem a good more precious than life itself. It was not a matter of laughter or insults, for either would be more likely to strengthen and encourage him, but of a strange and bittersweet sadness unlike anything save a kind of tender, heartrending, distant moan with a power and fullness that the ear could recognize from afar merely from its tone. It echoed in his own heart and would have melted the hardest heart. His very flesh responded with a kind of langor like love or its ghost. Meaningless tears filled Cénabre's eyes like water passing through stone, and with extreme anguish he felt them wet on his face. He wanted nothing to do with them, for they were merely the tangible and inscrutable sign of a horrifying presence, tears shed to no purpose. Simply accepting the situation, abandoning the pointless struggle and making a gesture of defeat to the victor, was the only way of opening up their real source, and he was more afraid of such a deliverance than of any torture. In his distress and shame, he hated and despised himself but was utterly and totally incapable of *pitying* himself.

This self-contempt was his only fixed point in the total collapse of his world. Pride, which works mysteriously and extremely subtly and powerfully once it is threatened, seemed to be yielding a part of itself when it was merely offering the tortured soul a false and sacrilegious image of the divine humility, for a powerful nature forced out of a state of grace seeks a new stability far beyond the self-satisfaction that is the only serenity the fool knows. The apparently mindless rage that turns it against itself is perhaps no more than the first bout of vertigo in the terrible intoxication that reaches its perfection in the absolute silence of Hell.

Once more, all Father Cénabre remembered of the three dangerous attacks of anguish he had just suffered was what he had done, which now seemed hard to explain. Both the revolver on the desktop and the tears he still had not managed to stop bore witness to his madness, but what *was* it? He wondered whether the sudden overthrow of a carefully ordered and very private life and the weakening and indeed collapse and momentary disappearance of his well-known critical sense could have any other cause than some still-unknown physical illness. To judge by the severity of the symptoms, the illness was serious. He examined his athletic body, his still-youthful appearance and his lofty and somber expression in the mirror, shrugged his shoulders in disdain and, for a moment, wanted so totally and strongly to die that he seemed to feel his reason shaken once again. The nightmare was perhaps still with him.

He struck his chest with both clenched fists.

"I am calm. I am calm again," he repeated coldly and angrily, with something of a rhetorical note grandiloquent enough to summon death or dementia into the self-contained room. He was trying with all his might to thrust what he was already calling his mystical crisis completely away from himself and into the void of the past and his dream. Such a sudden collapse, he thought, with nothing inside preparing the way for it and no preliminary reflection, could scarcely have any connection with the obsessive scruples of which his study of the human soul had provided so many instances. If he had lost his faith, it seemed to him he had done so almost imperceptibly, and, apart from the ridiculous fear he felt, he could see no difference between the man he had been yesterday and the one he was today. And the fear had in fact disappeared. What proved it was that now he would not call poor, silly old Chevance back for anything in the world, and could not imagine why on earth he had done so in the first place . . . and yet . . .

He left the room, went back to his bedroom, and sat down on the bed. Faced with suffering, we are all children, and as long as we are not totally prostrate and have still preserved the center of our resistance, the point, as it were, where body and soul meet, a chink in the armor, adults and children alike see no remedy for their afflictions but naive and futile flight. That humble thought also occurred to Father Cénabre. The International Society for Psychological Studies, of which Frau Eberlein was still the president (she later went mad one winter's night in her hideous Schlestadt home, which was full of maddened, wild-eyed animals) had managed to persuade the illustrious historian to promise to take part in its Frankfurt congress, or at least to be present for the formal closing session to give a lecture on mysticism in the Lutheran Church. It had been arranged for the twentieth of January, nine days later, but the congress itself had already been underway for a fortnight. He decided to set off for Germany that very day. The idea that someone so well known for punctiliously meeting his professional commitments, faithfully keeping appointments and scrupulously dealing with his correspondence, could disappear so suddenly and unexpectedly soothed him to some degree. Was it, he wondered, a tentative *trial* disappearance, a preparation for something more serious later? . . . he closed his eyes.

. . . . .

He found himself out in the street, his breath almost taken away by the cold morning air. The damp mist exhaled by the still-gloomy city was slowly clearing, sinking to the ground like stagnant water only to be pushed away by the new air, no doubt into the depths of cellars built of iron and cement that had never known the warmth of any rich full-bodied wine. He was walking quickly with his traveling bag in his hand, hampered by a hideous tweed traveling suit that had grown too tight for him since his last holiday and which he had pulled out of his trunk a short while before with no thought for stains or creases. The expression on his face was far from amusing.

He knew absolutely nothing about the streets of Paris. The fact that they were so deserted at that time of the morning puzzled him. He was incapable of paying attention to the simplest landmarks or even reading street names on their blue enamel plaques and was fairly vaguely following signs such as a corner shop, a second-hand bookseller's stall, or a familiar house that only he recognized. He was totally lost in his thoughts, suddenly making out some remembered place he had accidently reached. The iron covers on shop windows, the thousands of shutters, and the empty pavements all seemed to belong to a strange town. Eventually he reached the rue Sébastopol.

It was not until he had gone as far as the rue de Rambuteau that he realized that he had not informed his daily cleaning woman or even his concierge, or left any instructions, and saw just how unwise it had been to leave so early. He wondered what people would imagine.

He decided to post a letter to young Desvignes, who sometimes did unpaid secretarial work for him, before his train left. But what time did it leave? He had come so far without knowing or even trying to find out . . . that kind of absentmindedness may seem a small matter to the odd incurable sufferer, but Cénabre now saw exactly and clear sightedly what it meant and had no illusions. It was totally out of character, and he did not recognize himself. He was meticulous and traveled only rarely, and in the past he had drawn up a timetable for every journey with an attention to detail that his few close friends found amusing. He would not have been upset by the mere fact of breaking with such habits or obsessions, even though they played an essential part in his life, but he was now forced to admit that the break had been unintentional. His forgetfulness had been blatantly obvious and undeniable and a humble, if irrefutable, indication of some deep inner disturbance. The scales had been stripped so brutally from his eyes that the unfortunate priest, worn out by a pointless struggle, bowed his head and was tempted to turn on his heels and go home defeated. There passed through his mind a brief picture of the room he had just left, once friendly and familiar but now forever stamped with terrible memories . . . he suddenly held his breath and swallowed. Abruptly, he realized that he had left his desk just as it was, with the revolver on the table, the broken lamp, all the signs of the mysterious struggle, and the soutane thrown into a corner, a scene that would no doubt look even more mysterious in the cold light of day. That final proof of his incompetence overwhelmed him, and he was already edging forward along the boulevard, returning to his fate.

As he was walking along, calmed a little by the physical effort, the shame of having given in to fear was once again stronger than the fear itself. When he reached the rue de Rivoli he was pale with rage and determined to keep to his original plan come what may, even if it meant risking a scandal. He would flee to Germany and if possible even farther, since he had to escape, putting off explanations and excuses until later. The departure marked his defeat, but a defeat accepted rather than merely endured is never a total disaster. He was giving ground but still hoping for revenge. And standing up again to the strange enemy who had already struck him down without first decisively examining his conscience would really be asking for defeat, or at least further more humiliating ramblings. He grunted to himself that he needed a change of air, and the simplicity and ordinariness of his advice to himself were sweet and refreshing.

Dawn had broken by the time he reached the parvis St Laurent, and the clock on the Gare de l'Est, rosy in the early light, showed five in the morning. On his left, a sleepy waiter, pale beneath his grime, was opening up his establishment with a great rattle of hardware. He gave the early passerby a look that could have meant anything. Cénabre went into the café almost humbly and took a seat.

He had felt so alone that he had gone in almost instinctively, like a soldier on a deserted battlefield crawling nearer to a stranger to die. With a deep sigh he sat down on the narrow bench along the wall, watching his single companion coming and going with something like bewilderment, his mind emptied of all thought and filled by an inscrutable tenderness. The waiter, already awed by his mysterious customer, who he sensed might be a peaceful drunk recovering from a night of enviable delights, wordlessly pushed a bowl of scalding hot coffee and a large glass of brandy across the table. Then, with a professional discretion indicating a budding friendship, he shuffled around in his slippers and began frantically rubbing the tables with a greasy cloth again.

For the second time, a kind of pity welled up in Cénabre's heart, and in his eyes he felt once more the same inexplicable and universally redeeming tears, already offered and deferred, the supreme invention. Many are those who have thought themselves finished with the soul forever and who have awoken in the arms of their angel, having received the gift of tears at the gates of Hell, like a new childhood. His head sank into his hands and he let himself go. All he could do to defend himself was to distract his attention and leave it in the void, letting himself weep without cause as one lies down to sleep or to die. In a later written account, he described himself as weeping from physical and mental weariness, but he knew that he was lying. In fact, as the solemn tears ran between his fingers onto the squalid marble-topped table, all his weariness drained away with them, and he felt a powerful force stirring within him against which his broken will could barely struggle. Who then had brought him to that place, so far from his little world from which he had drawn his substance, where his pride had flourished and he would have fed his remorse, only to cast him alone, so laughably disguised, completely at his own mercy? If any regret had thrust its way to the surface of the darkness inside him, if a memory of a youth soon destroyed by calculation and fraud but nevertheless for a time innocent and full of faith had merely passed into his field of consciousness, it would have been enough to break the silence he was desperately maintaining against a victorious God. As far as it is possible to make a judgment in such cases, it was clearly here that his destiny was fulfilled. No one is cast into Hell unless he has first thrust aside and drawn away from the terrible but gentle hand of God without having felt its grip. No one is abandoned unless he has committed the essential sacrilege of denying not the *justice* but the *love* of God. For the terrible Cross of wood may stand at the first dividing of the ways in our life to admonish us gravely and severely, but the last image we see before we take ourselves away for ever is that other Cross of flesh, the two outstretched arms of the grievously suffering Friend, when the highest angel turns away in terror from the Face of a rejected God.

The moralist has nothing to say about such permeating evil. His thesis, so crapulously impoverished that many a freeborn spirit has sunk into absolute indifference rather than accept such a crude vision of the spiritual world, is that the perfect inner life is the result of a kind of balance of the instincts. Accidentals are seen as essentials, and from this fundamental error there arises a theoretical construct that in what it wrongly puts forward as obvious and its wayward logic can be compared to mechanical explanations of the phenomena of life. It could of course be said that the sinister priest — now weighed down by thirty years of lies so perfectly incorporated into his life that they had become, as it were, his own substance, his deep and inescapable nature — had gradually and almost imperceptibly traveled an immense distance to throw himself into the hands of Him who, even in Cénabre's proudest heyday, had perhaps wanted to grasp and absorb completely into His own magnificent light — but had never blessed — the monstrous knowledge that love, glimpsed for an instant in the divine abyss, had suddenly dissolved into darkness. Nevertheless, however cunning the enemy may be, even his most ingenious tricks can harm the soul only in a roundabout way, as a town may be taken by poisoning its wells. He clouds our judgment, soils our imagination, rouses our flesh and blood, uses the contradictions in our nature with infinite skill, leads our joys astray, makes our sadness more bitter, and distorts our actions and intentions, but even when he has overthrown everything, he has still destroyed nothing. He needs *our* final consent and can only obtain it if God has not had His say. For however long he thinks he has delayed divine grace, it will burst forth, and he awaits its necessary and inevitable outpouring with immense dread, for his patient work can be swept away in an instant. He does not know where the lightning will strike.

When Cénabre looked up, he saw the humble witness of the scene watching him with a strange, stupid pity, as moving as certain of the momentary gleams in the eyes of animals. He fled the place.

Poor Pernichon answered Guérou's scornful silence as best he could, with a brave smile.

"Canon Cénabre's work does nothing but good," Bishop Espelette declared. "Fools speak ill of it, and that's the only proof I need."

His frail voice stumbled so clumsily on the final syllable that he seemed to find it necessary to finish his sentence with a sharp, coquettish little laugh, wringing his delicate hands as if begging his listeners to pay no attention to him.

Guérou turned in his armchair, painfully twisting his soft, enormous head with its unforgettable eyes around on his shoulders and staring at the prelate with the greatest curiosity. For a short time his face itself, misshapen under its fat, kept something of the same look, but the muscles soon tired, and a kind of tense smile played on his still-handsome lips before disappearing into the folds of his cheeks and the waves of flesh that fell to his chest, tightly buttoned into its garnet colored waistcoat.

"I've no idea who's accusing him of what," he said gravely. "In the past, theology has often been a consolation for politics, but I wonder whether there's still anyone left who can bring all these controversies to an end. They're so movingly complex that our liveliest chatter seems crude in comparison." He made a sign to a small, bald-headed man. "I have heard it said that those close to Monsieur Combes, and the minister himself . . ."

"You have been wrongly informed," the stranger replied flatly. "The eminent statesman I had the honor of working with for ten years never took part in such discussions in my presence and had too great a respect for other people's consciences to willingly run a deliberate risk of upsetting them simply to satisfy his own curiosity. And indeed, his even-handedness with regard to metaphysical matters has always seemed to me to be absolute."

"What a lot of rubbish has been talked or written about such things," exclaimed Lavoine de Duras from the dark corner where he was sitting, making the observation with a whole range of smiles. "Those persecuting us were basically decent enough. It has to be said that Roman diplomacy has been good at gaffes . . ." he squeaked in an attempt to tone down the rather bold expression. "I hope Your Grace will forgive me but, at a decisive moment, did the Church not have her Chambord in the person of Pius X?"

A discreet murmur strengthened the allusion to the heroic period in the life of the ineffectual simpleton speaking at the moment, who had once been a subprefect thanks to the good offices of his cousin Doudoville and had ever since played the part of the democratic and voltairean nobleman, even though in the depths of his childish heart he was almost equally afraid of Hell and revolution.

Over the tea table, the Bishop of Paumiers glared murderously at the man who had spoken so naively to him. Then, stroking his cheek with his fingertips like a prostitute putting on her rouge, he hissed. "Is a gaff not an instrument used by the Fisherman?"

Once again, there was a half-hidden gleam in Guérou's eyes, and the same smile slipped fleetingly over his face.

Combes's former colleague stepped forward, holding out two ossified fingers. "Please accept my applause . . ." he began.

Guérou was already coming to the eminent churchman's help, however. "Do what I do, Jumilhac. Learn how to appreciate your share of a subtle witticism. There's no need to shout it from the rooftops."

"Please, please," was the reply, "I had no intention of stressing . . . I simply meant that it is the honor of the Church of Rome, and perhaps her salvation too, to keep within herself . . ."

"His Grace will be glad to accept the obviously impartial evidence of a former member of the Paris Consistory," Pernichon generously cried.

The Bishop of Paumiers bowed graciously.

"I should like to add," the former principal private secretary continued curtly, glaring at the author of *Letters from Rome*, "that for years I have had nothing to do with doctrinal concerns."

"Let me bring the matter to a conclusion," the bishop pleaded, bathing his audience in an irresistible smile. "We are among friends here. We say what's in our hearts." He laid his index finger on one of the buttons of his soutane. "However, don't give my little quip a meaning I didn't intend it to have. I was simply being mischievous, but not at all malicious. It was rather like a son's joke about his father. No doubt our priests, in our diocese, feel able to make harsher ones about us," he finished, with a paternal smile.

At the other end of the famous salon, however, Lavoine de Duras's hackles were rising. Purple with fury, he was shouting at a tall, unfortunate-looking young man:

"No, we will not . . . we don't admit . . . it cannot be tolerated!"

"What are you talking about?" Guérou asked.

"M. Jérôme has just told me about an unspeakable conversation he heard in Florence at Prince Ruggieri's house. It's being said that there's an attempt afoot to sabotage Canon Cénabre's candidature for the Institute by using a new condemnation of his work wrung out of the Congregation of the Index by surprise tactics!"

"I don't approve of the move," Jérôme protested, deathly pale.

"You don't approve of it," the fool cried, beside himself with rage, "but nevertheless you see it as inevitable. Unless I'm very mistaken, that's very close indeed to approving of it."

"I'm assuming the worst and acting accordingly, Monsieur le Vicomte," retorted Jérôme, clearly infuriated. "In any case, Canon Cénabre is quite capable of defending himself. However, if such an abuse can't be avoided, there must be some form of compensation, and I'm assured that we shall be able to obtain it easily, because the Congregation is made up of men of the greatest probity."

"I'm aware of the step you're alluding to," the Bishop of Paumiers said softly, "but aren't you afraid that an indiscreet word. . . ?" From his pocket, he drew out a mother-of-pearl case and swallowed two pastilles one after the other.

"His Grace is right," put in Madame Jérôme, who had said nothing so far. "These arguments, as everyone here knows, lead nowhere."

For the tenth time she took a slim volume out of her handbag and seemed absorbed in contemplating its pink cover. Since the previous evening, she had been considering giving it to the bishop, and was now looking for the right moment to do so. It was a collection of her latest poems, published through the generosity of a lover. Entitled *To My Master*, it was dedicated to her husband.

"I see that our gracious colleague is holding a brand new book," Guérou observed with his usual perfidy. "From here, poor invalid that I am, I can smell fresh ink, and also, unless my nose is playing tricks, a country scent. My bet is that we have some new poems."

"You win, *maître*," the poor woman replied, her fury showing on her face as she realized that she had once again been caught out in her besetting sin. The only thing her enormous vanity feared, however, was a void, and for the moment it staved off her desperate desire.

She stepped forward.

"Could I ask Your Grace to accept these poor efforts? Probably the only thing about them that will stay in your mind will be their intention. I've nothing to offer the public except the humble joys of my family life, and the one thing of value in these simple poems is their sincerity."

"I was waiting impatiently for them to be published," the prelate answered amiably, resting the book on his lap. "I had been told it would be soon."

"I've written a few lines on that very subject in *Christian Annals*," poor Pernichon sighed. "It's a comfort for all of us, when religion is often the excuse for all sorts of confused writings, where the emotion is dubious and sometimes impure . . ."

The impetuous vicomte, however, was again throwing down the gauntlet.

"I've no special competence in the matter, and I admit it. But I would like to say that we are being swallowed by a wave of exaggerated mysticism so unbalanced that, as well as being likely to discourage right-thinking people, is arousing antireligious fanaticism. What my eminent friend Father Cénabre cannot be openly accused of is of having written wise and passionately interesting books about sanctity, easily accessible to any educated man but also capable of satisfying philosophers and historians."

"Perhaps there is sometimes more in them of the historian than the philosopher, or at least, strictly speaking, the theologian," the bishop conceded, "but we also have to take into account the importance of the positions taken up by rationalist critics and the need to keep up, whatever the cost. The fact of the matter is that here, as in every other field, the Church must not let herself be left behind by anyone."

He gently laid his tiny fist on the pedestal table, no doubt mistakenly believing that in so doing he was showing his implacable resolve to live and die a member of the avant-garde of his time.

No one but himself, however, was taken in by his boldness. Intellectually, he was a great coward. Although he could not grasp the fact, since his whole feeble being lacked any fixed point and was not susceptible to any kind of honest assessment, he was nevertheless vaguely aware of what was lacking in him, feeling it in the emptiest and warmest part of his undeveloped and gentle soul: his vanity. He had perhaps been thought a rather surprising but certainly not a scandalous choice for the diocese, as he was known to be active, educated, almost embarrassingly gracious, anxious to please, and of irreproachable morals. None of his predecessors had taken up the crozier with a greater desire to do good and to give of himself wholeheartedly. Like all the strong passions of men, ambition keeps us in a strange state of indifference toward others, which in the worst of us is like a kind of ingenuousness akin to the sinister image, in our adult corruption, of the illusions of childhood. Like the child throwing his arms round his mother's neck and thinking that he is giving her the world with the kiss from his sweet little mouth, the ambitious man does not learn until later, after harsh experience, how to hate those he has robbed, for at first, when he is too happy to be in command not to hope to be obeyed with delight, he loves them. "From now on, I belong to you," the bishop had written to his flock in his first pastoral letter, and, while he was writing the words, his private secretary, who was already fired by a holy zeal and anxious to admire his master, saw the tears streaming down his cheeks and thought that he himself was about to be overcome.

No one, alas, is less worthy of love than he who lives solely to be loved. Such people, however skillfully they may be all things to all men, are simply mirrors in which the weak man soon learns to hate his weakness and the strong man to doubt his strength, and they are equally despised by all. So great was the unfortunate bishop's disappointment that he could feel it through the threefold thickness of his guileless pride. He was offering himself: what more could anyone ask? His goodwill went no further, and on the rock of that misunderstanding he came to grief.

We think only the mad are unfortunate, and yet the solitude of the foolish is worse. A certain spiritual mediocrity, which is always venial, can turn a priest's life into an absurd and tragic adventure. The bishop of Paumier's ideas, or what in his self-importance he saw as such, were those of the least-inspired academic. He was incapable of deliberate betrayal and had a child-like faith unbroken by all the whims of his superficial intelligence. He had had the senseless dream of being a priest only for his time and was one for all eternity. "I am of my time," he would say, like a man giving an account of himself, without ever realizing that whenever he did so he was denying the eternal sign with which he was marked.

How could he be aware of it? His conscience was silent. He was like a dancer, never touching down or coming into contact with earth in all its solidity and certainty, moving in an insubstantial element thinner than the air, making unforeseeable twists and turns no observer looking up at him could make sense of. "I get round obstacles," he still said, but in the void where he traced his illusory and quickly effaced path, he sought only himself and was himself the object pursued and the prey desired. For although he was a priest by situation and perhaps by vocation, a part of him nevertheless conspired constantly against the order he was committed to maintaining. That was the tragedy of his pitiful fate.

So he believed in Progress and made of it an image to his own measure. Very proud of being an agrégé, he had acquired many new notions without freeing his intelligence from the tyranny of visceral reactions. He thought in terms of the loves, hates, envies, and rancors of his adolescence, and such and such a phrase of his that might be quoted for its boldness or novelty was in fact no more than an abstract expression of a particular humiliation experienced in his youth but still acutely felt. This baseness was pathetically ridiculous to those in power, whose friendship he craved even though he was unaware that their only emotion for him was a heartfelt scorn, for by and large the successful hate their flatterers. To no avail at all he made innumerable pledges, wrote resounding letters, seeming always to be somewhere between a protestant minister and a rabbi, humbly competing with such official functionaries for their places. Never had his pride taken such bitter blows, but he was at the age when the errors and vices of our younger days take on flesh and blood and are eventually loved for their own sake in direct proportion to the disappointments and tears they have caused us.

"Father Cénabre has strengthened our faith," Jérôme resumed, seemingly shaken out of his usual reserve by his wife's first words about her book of verse, at least to judge by a fleeting and barely visible reddening of his coarse-grained skin.

Through half-closed eyes he glanced toward Pernichon, for although he never praised anyone without a pang, he was more painfully envious of his own wife than anyone else and was not about to forgive the wretched young Auvergnat for his indiscreet admiration of an intolerable rival.

Once he had everyone's attention, he bent his small wedge-shaped head to one side over his right shoulder in a gesture familiar to all. Then, in his best diplomatic voice, reedy, cracked, and always surprising, he spoke as if delivering a dire and ominous augury.

"We think too much of the critic and historian and neglect the priest too much. There's nothing ostentatious about it, but his zeal is known to one or two people who could speak on his behalf if, as is very probably the case, they weren't held back by honorable scruples. I am no doubt not one of that favored band, but I know enough about the matter to be able to smile at certain instances of malicious gossip or even a silence that is not always impartial. It won't surprise anyone here if I say that for one or two privileged people the Canon is an incomparable advisor and, it should be said, confessor."

He gently stroked his thin and unimpressive whiskers and seemed to be savoring the ensuing silence like a connoisseur. Everyone turned to look at Pernichon.

"I *am* one of that privileged few," the young man said. "Or at least I *was*, a short while ago, but now all I am for the Canon is a respectful admirer of his intelligence and talents."

"But *why?*" shrieked Madame Jérôme, apparently without thinking.

The faint murmuring on all sides made her blush in turn, and she continued in a choked voice that gradually strengthened as it went on:

"No doubt I seem very bold, but isn't it true, Your Grace, that someone like Father Cénabre is to some extent outside ordinary laws and that it is permitted to be a little partisan in his favor? Monsieur Pernichon may well have come to his decision quite naturally, and we needn't suppose that . . . ! Oh, make me be quiet!" she cried, laughing toothily. "I can't get out of this all on my own! I'm just terribly inquisitive, and that's all there is to it!"

She gave her melancholy little adversary an odd look, in which mere scorn jostled for place with a kind of maternal sympathy, for she had not yet entirely given up the hope of adding this tiny prey to her spoils and sincerely pitied his lack of courage.

To everyone's surprise, however, Pernichon answered extraordinarily swiftly.

"I haven't seen Father Cénabre since he came back from Germany."

He took his time, adding almost reluctantly and in terror at his own boldness, in an anxious, quavering voice he was trying desperately to control:

"And I shall never see him again."

His astonishing reply was received in icy silence, followed by a strange kind of grating noise, and a final sharp note as the vicomte snorted his displeasure.

"I'm sorry to have been the involuntary cause of . . ." Madame Jérôme began.

"Please don't be distressed, dear lady," the Bishop murmured, seeming to hold an imaginary hand between the palms of both his own. "Our young friend has given us the wrong impression. He's too wise and prudent to commit the whole future so rashly. Thank God, he's still at the happy age when the word 'never' has, and could have, no meaning."

"Let's say, at least, that it was far from being a wise or prudent word," said Guérou, paternally. "But here, we are all one family, although in a happy state of mutual independence. And — heaven forbid — if we were not entirely free, we should first and foremost have to respect the freedom of the youngest, and hence the most alive, of our members."

No one could draw the hidden painful truth or potential

tragedy from an everyday incident, a word, or even a look as could that strange man. The slightest quiver or the smallest waves of suffering were perceived by a kind of infallible discernment, and his extraordinary sensitivity captured them at once, like a delicate receiver. Any yielding or imperceptibly flawed will, any anxious or failing psyche, was immediately detected, as if spotted by a hovering bird of prey, and his curiosity would swoop down on it, a curiosity so piercing and eager that its hapless and unwilling victim would be infected by it, like those women whose sensuality is aroused as soon as they come unwittingly into the proximity of a fixed and secret desire.

Pernichon's confusion increased as he heard Guérou's indulgent words, and the silent and agitated circle seemed to tighten round him.

"I took the decision regretfully, and I should have liked . . . it would have been better to say nothing . . . if I hadn't had reasons for believing that my change . . . my change in attitude . . . with regard to someone I still respect and venerate . . . might have been wrongly . . . unfavorably interpreted . . . some malicious talk . . . perhaps . . ."

"Such scruples are the downfall of youth," said a very gentle voice from the other end of the salon. "Life is indulgent and takes care of everything. All we need to know is how to use it carefully and wisely, just as we don't use dangerous explosives to dig out a mine in one go, but to remove one by one all the obstacles that we can't get rid of with picks or shovels. I'm taking the liberty of telling you this, with the simplicity of a man of my age who has nothing but sympathy for a gifted, legitimately ambitious young colleague anxious to do good. For some time, my dear Pernichon, I have deplored one or two imprudent if venial actions on your part that have been at odds with what we know of you — your moderation, your correctness, your maturity, so unusual in a young man. To speak openly, as I think we should, your article in *New Dawn*, for instance, caused too much of a stir to be praised."

When he had had his say, Catani slowly and carefully lowered his ashen head onto the cushions. The ferocious old man, of whose work probably no one at all could quote a line, as for the last half-century he had written only under impenetrable pseudonyms and appeared in obscure and ephemeral journals, rather like a thief moving from one lot of furnished accommodation to another to throw the police off his track, nevertheless had the reputation among clever innocents even more cowardly than himself of being (to use their astonishing language) a very high-class religious informative journalist whose decrees were irrevocable.

The no doubt unexpected blow caused Pernichon, who had been trying for a moment to calm down again, like a duelist deprived of all sense of relative distances after the first clash and timidly seeking to judge them from the point of his sword, now no more use than a foil, to slip up again.

"I don't understand," he said. "Actually, I thought I was being helpful to Monsieur Dufour by undoing the bad impression created by a piece of probably ill-judged praise in the *Sunday Welfare Services*, whose program he judges to be dangerous."

"If I may say so," said the former member of the Consistory with an air both politic and dignified, "I'm afraid you're quite unintentionally making a mistake here."

Pernichon went red with anger.

"With my own ears . . . I heard that."

"It's a matter of a date," remarked Jérôme, his eyes gleaming in a motionless face. "My dear Pernichon, you're wrong to ignore dates. Before you do anything, consult the calendar."

"I had to take the swiftest possible action to undo the damage," Catani declared, without deigning to look at his victim, "by having a last-minute note printed in the . . ."

He murmured the name of an unknown publication.

"Rather than condemning our young friend, you would do better to instruct him," said the bishop, visibly moved to pity by the wretched man's embarrassment. "As far as I can see, his fault — if there *is* a fault — is a very slight one."

He turned toward Pernichon again.

"These gentlemen only want to be of service to you, my son, so please try to keep calm. Since the President of the Council, in an honorable gesture, chose Baron Dufour as Secretary of State to the Ministry of Labor, it is possible, and indeed probable, that our eminent friend will need to maintain a certain reserve with regard to a venture that is in fact Christian in inspiration, given that its aims are charitable . . ."

"And is also subsidized by the Minister himself," Jumilhac noted.

"I knew that!" Pernichon cried, "but the Italian charity the Nuncio is sponsoring . . ."

"We should leave that aside," Catani cut in. "One thing at a time, dear colleague."

He shrugged in frustration.

"The charity you are alluding to, or more exactly its French section, will shortly be the subject of a major report by Monsieur Petit-Tamponnet to the Académie des Sciences Morales. That is universally known. Nevertheless, Monsieur Lavoine de Duras . . ."

"Quite correct," said the vicomte. "I would also like to say that what my colleague Monsieur Petit-Tamponnet is doing is extremely ingenious and bold. I haven't the honor to be exactly what is known as a politician, since apart from youth, an ambition I no longer have is called for. But I take note, I observe, and I like to keep an eye on what is going on. You're smiling, my dear sir," he said to Guérou.

"With pleasure," the invalid answered almost tenderly, moving his enormous chest with difficulty. "It's always a good thing to listen to what you have to say because you have the secret of what I thought was a forgotten art, that of being frivolous in serious things and serious in frivolous ones."

For a fraction of a second, Lavoine de Duras looked rather worried. Realizing that he could not find an impertinent answer on the spur of the moment, he simply shook his empty, noisy little head, as if to chase away an invisible insect and, as a precautionary measure, nodded with ironic complicity in the big man's direction.

"There's no merit solving such a simple problem. Any child could have done the same. It's simply a case of flattering Monsieur Le Doudon's self-esteem which, if you'll allow me, I'll describe as 'academic.' He's done a great deal for the Franco-Italian charity in the hope that the Nuncio will support his candidature for my late friend de la Baconnière's seat on the Senate. That candidature has become undesirable since the Republican bloc gained an undersecretaryship in the new government."

"And for another reason too," Jérôme remarked mysteriously. "Father Hochegourde's lack of success in the Creuse was due to the opposition of *The Christian Sower*. Father Hochegourde belongs to the most advanced group of the Secular Democratic Federation, which has a program that is no doubt excellent in parts but could perhaps compromise us a little with the right wing of the Catholic party, which is developing very slowly and is prudently sticking to the radical-socialist, almost chauvinistic, tradition."

Bishop Espelette gestured with his pale little hands, his amethyst ring doubly gleaming.

"Spare me, dear friend, have pity on an old man's weakness! I know what the needs of the times are, I envy the boldness of the young militants who dream of leading the course of events rather than following it, I can see them moving to the head of the great democratic masses with all their diverse ideals and their innumerable flags and bringing them one day quivering and tamed to the feet of the Vicar of Rome, I can see . . ."

"*We* can see nothing at all, Your Grace," the former member of the Consistory cut in drily. "The future will be what it will be, and we serve it as it will be. Democratic development is a law of nature, not only a political fact that anyone can feel free to interpret or woo as he wishes, one way or another. If only we had reached that stage! The enormous movement of liberation that came out of the Reformation . . ."

"Please calm yourself, my old and dear friend," the bishop begged. "We shouldn't be talking about what divides us. Can't we concentrate on what brings us together? I was a passionate democrat even in my young days, when it was still rather a dangerous thing to admit to. No social reform disturbs me, and yet I think that I've always been beyond reproach as a priest, in terms of my own strength and lights . . . it's such a joy, and so simple, to live in peace with men. All one needs is an unshakeable belief that they are all sincere. No doubt that means running the risk of one or two inevitable disappointments, but there aren't too many of those! I'm reaching the end of my active career, at least, and I think I owe it to my fellow men to tell them that I've known very few insincere people."

For a moment he half-closed his eyes the better to hear the discreet ripple of sympathy that always made his heart miss a beat.

"My dear Monsieur Jérôme," he went on with real tears in his eyes, "please don't take a spontaneous adverse reaction too seriously. I know the precise concrete sense 'chauvinism' can have in your technical vocabulary, and that you use it objectively, without hatred or contempt. In the lofty, humanitarian, universal sense of the word, you're no less of a real patriot than I am.

Nevertheless, I grant, for this once, that the worthy Father Hochegourde does frighten me a little."

Jérôme, furious at the interruption, made a vaguely courteous gesture while Lavoine de Duras and Catani were both speaking at once. The former prefect's quavering tone, however, was soon overlaid by a gentle and patient voice.

"It seems to me that we're tackling a great many very serious problems concerning no one but Monsieur Pernichon, who will not, I trust, be angry with me for regretting that arguments we had tacitly agreed to drop seem to be surfacing again . . ."

"I apologize," said the bishop with great dignity, "for my little outburst of bad temper . . ."

"Nothing in the world," Jumilhac cut in, "would make me risk compromising without good reason a good and cordial understanding that has lasted for several years. For all of us, trying to cast light on each other's opinions in free discussion is an honorable thing to do. As far as I'm concerned, I'm aware that I've never abandoned, even out of simple courtesy to opponents I respect (he bowed to the bishop) sacred rights . . ."

"My dear Jumilhac, all rights are sacred to the person claiming them," Catani resumed in the same level tone. "I'd rather congratulate our eminent host, who has brought us all together, on his extremely tactful way of avoiding discussions of principles that would soon have put us on opposing sides. Heaven knows what services his amiable skepticism has rendered us in that respect! I admit that in spite of my preferences I have often been inspired by it, strictly within my own modest field of action. It's to be hoped that young men like our friend here aren't carried away by their zeal to the extent of endangering results it's been so hard to achieve!"

"I don't know what you're alluding to," said Pernichon, who could feel Guérou's pitying gaze on him and already sensed that he could read his fate in it. "I must tell you that I've acted with the greatest possible prudence. I still can't see how my efforts could endanger the expected effects of a report by Monsieur Petit-Tamponnet aimed at very different readership. And in addition, with regard to Father Hochegourde's opposition to Monsieur Le Doudon's candidacy . . ."

"There *is* no opposition," Jérôme remarked more drily than ever. "I am amazed that you can use such a ridiculous word in such an important matter."

"My dear sir, I'm not a child!" Pernichon cried. "I'm quite aware of how important Father Hochegourde's mission is."

"Another rash statement, my dear colleague," Catani began.

"Please remember that I'm speaking absolutely frankly and for your ears alone," Pernichon retorted. "In truth, for two months now, it's been impossible for me to take a step, utter a syllable, or write a line without encountering a kind of hostility . . ."

"Hostility!" Lavoine de Duras yelped.

"Yes, that's the word!" cried the unfortunate journalist. "There's more to the whole affair than just solicitude."

"You're unfair to those who wish you well," Catani said, his icy face with its lustreless eyes reddening ominously.

"I wasn't directing that remark at you, monsieur," Pernichon stammered.

Far from calming him, the look on Guérou's face and the kind of compassion he thought he detected in it, even though he could not understand its true nature, now seemed merely to make him obstinate.

"Please, my friend, my dear son, you're terribly overwrought," said the bishop in an attempt to reassure him, not understanding what was happening.

"For the last two months I've been unable to do anything that's not been immediately condemned or at least severely criticized. Only yesterday, Madame de Pontaudemer decided that she was gravely offended by my silence regarding the campaign against her brother by certain reactionary newspapers. Well, I had taken advice. It had seemed advisable to let the detraction die down naturally. So what did I do? I sacrificed two articles I had already finished that were promised to my paper and had to replace them at the last moment with an account of the Siena festivities."

"It was a good subject, brilliantly handled," Catani said gently. "That kind of thing suits you marvelously. Why haven't you produced more material in the vein of your early *Letters from Rome*?"

"I asked nothing better," Pernichon moaned. "Imaginary mistakes are being held against me, or mere slips anyone could make. My editor's furious. I think he's ready to scrap his religious column out of pique. He agreed only reluctantly, after I'd pleaded with him, to find room for our news items in his paper. I'm not looking for praise, but after all *New Dawn* has a bigger circulation than any other publication of its ideological shade, and Têtard's political influence is considerable, especially since the Mongenot government was formed. Why the determination to destroy my standing with an editor who may be a communist, a Jew, and a Freemason but has the most broad-minded and incisive views on the religious question?"

"We know how great your responsibility is," said Catani mellifluously.

"So do I," cried Pernichon, with a moving sincerity based on great hope, for he had just understood the influential sage's words in a favorable sense.

"It's too great for you," Catani went on imperturbably. "Your first mistake was to accept it, or rather to have sought it. A more serious one — please excuse my frankness — was engaging in an activity out of keeping with your abilities and above all your experience."

He broke off for a moment, wiping his pallid forehead with

a small handkerchief. In the silence, his rapid, consumptive breathing sounded like tissue paper rustling.

Pernichon gazed at him in fascination. Until then, through the endless weeks when he had felt his luck slowly, gradually, and mysteriously running out, he had been counting on this final support, against all the evidence, as superstitious and stubborn as a gambler. Very probably no one had ever been stupid or fanciful enough to hope to win the friendship of such a man, for his well-known patience and gentleness were unassailable and ruthless, as firm as a wall of brass. Yet it was not impossible to benefit in some way from his indifference, or even from his scorn, as he had been known to make use of such harmless fools, associating them for a time with his undertakings or at least his preparatory obscure machinations, since his hate was very slow to erupt.

"I didn't believe . . . I never thought," the mortified young Auvergnat stammered, "that I deserved anything from you but criticism or observations, and I was quite prepared to take heed of them as a respectful junior colleague. Yet your blanket judgment, your condemnation of my past and all I've written . . ."

He looked all round the room, his face swollen with tears, and jumped to his feet, still grasping the back of his chair with his trembling hands.

Guérou yawned loudly.

Madame Jérôme stifled a giggle, which all present took up at once, although as a chorus of respectful teasing.

"You were dozing, *maître*, don't try to deny it!" the bishop cried.

"That's quite possible," Guérou answered, running a huge, soft, pink hand over his face. "My disability used to be merely ugly, but it will become discourteous and repulsive. I can feel fat-laden blood flowing in my veins, and my poor brain can no longer cope. I'm falling asleep as one drifts off into death."

He groaned and turned to pick up a glass of ice water from the occasional table, drank it straight down, and tried to push his inert body forward, his gaze sharper than ever.

"My dear Pernichon," he said, to everyone's surprise, as if he had not missed a single word of what had been said, "You have a great deal of knowledge, much talent and goodwill, and many excellent and useful connections. But, if there's still time, you must cure yourself of a vice that threatens to nullify all those valuable qualities. I can see that you want to be liked, that you're thirsting for it. That kind of sickly obsession is more dangerous than any vice. It has reduced people better equipped to resist it to despair, even brought them to the grave . . ."

Apart from the bishop, who was gently nodding his approval with a rather fixed smile, everyone heard the words with some trepidation. Catani turned pale.

"I, on the contrary, admire this great desire to be praised," he said. "I've never known it *myself*. It's simply that my circumstances, my love of history, a certain knowledge of men, and of course my indifferent health, have always led me away from the sound and fury of life, pointless arguments, great and rash undertakings. All I've wanted is to be merely a publicist putting my experience, rather than any talent, at the service of a forward-looking Church."

"Just as I was saying," was Guérou's insolent reply. "There you are, Pernichon."

"If you don't mind," went on Catani, still smiling, "I'd like to ask Lavoine de Duras something. Is it true that His Holiness received Noualhac in a secret audience at the beginning of the month?"

"I can confirm it," answered the vicomte. "We've already known it for a week."

"The Holy See judges certain bold initiatives, which are perhaps even to be condemned, quite severely and takes no pleasure in the space allotted to our religious columns in one or two very advanced journals. I have the information from an extremely reliable source."

"That's so," said Jérôme. "So much so that in my last column I deleted the paragraph on Syrian affairs."

"So would that mean," sighed Catani, who was now breathing only with great difficulty, "that we should be mortifying our young friend again if we were to point out to him how untimely the new inquiry into the development of religious awareness in France and Germany he is considering publishing would probably, and very likely certainly, be?"

"My inquiry!" Pernichon cried, as if from the depths of his being, like a man being stabbed to the heart.

"But gentlemen, why . . ." the bishop made a final attempt to protest.

"My inquiry!" repeated Pernichon, now grotesque and formidable.

His breathing was difficult and painful, and he pressed both hands to his chest. Then his jaws worked violently, although he was making no sound.

"Ah, the young!" said Guérou.

"All I said was 'untimely,'" remarked Catani, scenting from afar, rather uneasily, his prey's final attempt to escape. "Probably, if he were patient . . ."

"Patient!" Pernichon thundered.

He tried in vain to swallow his saliva. His throat was as constricted as if he had lockjaw, and in it he could feel his heart beating powerfully. Finally, the words found a way out, and his anger erupted like a flow of blood.

"Untimely! Patient! So I'm supposed to watch the fruit of eighteen months' work disappear in a moment!" he cried. "Don't you remember, Monsieur Catani, that just last Sunday you yourself were correcting my notes on the Haguenau affair with your own hands! Patient! What a disgusting joke! As if you didn't know better than I do that inquiries like that, which call for an enormous effort, have to be published at exactly the right time and are closely linked to the events that inspire them! As if . . ."

"But publish it anyway, young man," grated Lavoine de Duras in the uproar. "What an incredible fuss!"

"Publish it?" said Pernichon, "where can I publish it now? I can see your game. I've been used, crippled. Because my editor won't put up with this latest disappointment. My column will be dropped from *New Dawn*. I shall have been deprived even of my living. Oh, yes. While I was being encouraged to undertake something so bold and dangerous, something that would either make or break me, every step was being taken to make sure that publication would be delayed and then, at the last moment, made impossible."

"I forbid you . . ." Catani began, but was immediately forced to press his handkerchief to his mouth to stifle an ominous gulp. Fear made him look awful.

"Gentlemen, I no longer really understand . . . gentlemen, I beg you," the bishop implored desperately.

"Why are people determined to destroy me?" Pernichon went on in a heartrending voice. "I've had some success, and it's been due to my work, or good fortune, I must suppose. It's never harmed anyone. But since Father Cénabre sent me away — for that's what he did — I feel that people have decided to ruin me . . ."

"This is madness," Jérôme threw in so coldly that everyone was suddenly quiet. Only then could Catani's voice be heard.

"I forgive you for your . . . so unexpected . . . and so unjust attack on me," he breathed. "I've always liked the young. But you must agree that no one here can now be in any doubt that I've seen clearly what was happening. You're not self-sufficient enough. It's a quality we need. Without it, we can never learn what the least of us should know . . . the man not in possession of himself . . ."

"Yes, let's talk about that!" Pernichon shrieked so stridently that Madame Jérôme put her gloved hand to her ear.

"I'm sorry . . . please excuse me . . . my apologies," said Lavoine de Duras, waving a hand trembling with weariness and disgust at his host. "I'm afraid . . . I can't possibly approve of the tone that a . . . discussion . . . is going to take. And the provocative and personal turn it has taken . . ."

"Sit down," Guérou replied impassively. "You don't understand. What can it matter to you, dear friend?"

He was much paler than usual and although he was still smiling vaguely, from force of habit, a certain whistling in his nostrils and the folds in his huge, flabby cheeks, with their blue and red streaks, suggested that he was powerfully clenching his jaws. No one seemed to notice his overwrought state. Lavoine de Duras sat down.

"Don't persist, Pernichon, you can answer later," said Jérôme. "You can explain . . ."

"I approve, completely, paternally . . ." the bishop began, pink with embarrassment.

But the young journalist, still on his feet during the rapid passage of arms, had simply turned his pale face toward each of his interlocutors in turn, like a cornered animal. Catani shifted restlessly and painfully on his chair, then calmed down, seeming to be resigned to hearing everything. The silence was so deep that Pernichon could be heard getting his breath back.

"No one will make me keep quiet," he said at last. "My inquiry will be published, come what may. I will defend myself."

Catani looked questioningly at the bishop, Guérou, and Jérôme in turn. Only then did he murmur, barely audibly, "Against whom?"

"Against you!" yelped Pernichon in the voice that had caused Madame Jérôme to cry out. "Tomorrow would be too late; I should never find you all again. And perhaps what I'm doing is pointless. But it doesn't matter! Your Grace, Your Grace," he went on, turning right around toward the bishop, "I swear, I swear that for a year I haven't taken a step or written a line without his permission. Only the day before yesterday . . . oh, I've been rash, I know! I've displeased powerful people! Whose fault was it? He was behind me. I swear it. He told me that he wanted to lead me like a blind man. Didn't you?" the wretched man howled.

"This is *incredible*," Lavoine repeated, "intolerable."

"Shameful, absolutely shameful," Madame Jérôme added.

"Please be calm," the bishop begged, even more beseechingly than before. "I must say that the misunderstanding . . ."

Even Guérou made a gesture like a spectator disgusted by a clumsy toreador.

Pernichon scarcely heard the muttered disapproval, but through his tears of impotent anger he caught sight of his opponent and realized what was happening.

He understood that he was too late, that the man in front of him was no longer anyone's victim, and that if he insisted on trying to bring about his downfall he would harm only himself. It flashed upon him that the massive and profound indifference of the people around him, who had been polished like pebbles on a beach by stupidity, illusions, or lies, was insurmountable. No revelation of cowardice or betrayal could awake in them, even for an instant, what they had gone to such lengths to destroy, the kind of human pride that they despised in others as if it were some kind of coarseness, alternately dangerous and ridiculous.

Far from arousing their emotions, his desperate efforts and exacerbated sincerity would chill them and cut them off from any sense of pity, and for such people, so calculating in trivial matters, he could be no more than a disgusting spectacle. At once so unconscious of their own weakness and so skilled at hiding it, it would have been impossible for them not to recognize it, with shame and anger, in the turncoat who had just broken out of the magic circle of decencies and gone his own headlong way, in public, like a mad actor.

"I've tried to be useful to you," Catani breathed, more and more livid. "My . . . my great experience probably gave me the means of doing so . . . I regret that I failed . . . but you've been cruelly unfair . . . in truth, it's less possible than it ever was to take you seriously!"

He pressed his hollow chest with his hand, shiny with sweat, as an indication that he was feeling ill.

"You've done something deeply wrong," the bishop burst out, turning toward Pernichon. "It hurts me to say so in public like this, but I no longer have the right to be indulgent."

For a second, all could see the wretched Auvergnat bobbing like a cork on the ensuing silence.

"You know the man I'm talking about!" he howled. "There's not one of you who doesn't know . . ."

But suddenly he seemed to lose courage, and they breathed again as his voice weakened.

"Your Grace!" he begged, "don't condemn me. Understand me! Please understand me! I don't hate Monsieur Catani, not in the least! I hate myself for having offended him, but you *must* see that I'm struggling to save my job, my means of existence, my living! My means of existence! The attack didn't come from *me!* I asked nothing of anyone, my ambition was modest, and I did my job honestly! Why did that man ruin me? Because he *did* ruin me, skillfully and treacherously! I'll give you proof! Yes, I will prove it! I . . . I . . . will pro . . ."

He was stammering frightfully and deliberately to gain time, for in his disordered brain he was gradually beginning to see clearly just how futile his desperate accusation was and how impossible it would be to furnish proof, which in fact nobody would accept. He had lost. Even if he could show how despicable the dying man was, it would not put off the impending disaster for one minute. The investigation would not and indeed now could not be published. What was the use? And yet . . .

Then he made a supreme effort to stand up to his enemy, hurling his words at him.

"For years you've used your young colleagues like that, making use of them and then discarding them one after another. Has anyone read what you've written? No. What rights have you? None. I challenge you to name anyone established able and willing to act in public as a referee for you. Your 'experience' is a mystery for everyone. But you've never lacked fools like me to compromise: Erlange, Rousselette, Dumas-Mortier — I could name a score of others. *You* ruined Father Delange and then made me execute him in the *Montmédy Bulletin*. Everything you've undertaken, all you've tried, to get your envy-ridden self out of your obscurity and stop being a kind of mediocre go-between, has cost a disaster like mine . . . which will be as pointless as all the others, do you hear? Pointless, perfectly useless. You'll never ever force your way into the press. You've stolen my place, but you won't get it. Nobody will offer it to you, and you won't dare to ask for it. Will you? You *will not dare to ask for it.* You want to know why, eh? You want to know? It's because people fear you less and less and despise you more and more!"

His furious words were, of course, not heard in silence. With the exception of Guérou, each of those present had tried to interrupt on several occasions, and for the whole time the bishop had in fact been alternately whining sharply and moaning gravely. Finally, as the author of the *Letters from Rome* was reaching the end of his outburst, the disorder was at its height, and, if the burning desire to learn more had not carried the day over ingratitude, there would no doubt have been a riot, for all eyes were fiercely and impatiently fixed on Catani.

Nothing can trouble such hard hearts more, for their triviality is proof against the worst surprises their inconsistent lives can throw at them, provided that a certain indispensable agreement, a certain rhythm, is preserved and that at least certain mysterious rules that in their weakness they instinctively follow are obeyed. Their artificial little society lives and thrives in a hermetically sealed world, and the passions that develop in it, however violent they are thought to be, are expressed solely in conventional signs and submitted to rigorous control and a formal discipline that rapidly modifies their nature and symptoms. Ultimately, nothing is less like an open and intrepid vice than the same vice changed by dissimulation and cultivated in depth. The phenomenon can be observed anywhere, but never more effectively than in those strange men living equidistant from the religious and political worlds, patiently and diligently acting as intermediaries between them, kept in the background by the very nature of their perpetually secret maneuverings. That group of semiofficial and constantly disowned go-betweens, the natural slaves of circumstances and situations, shameful demagogues and suspect believers, have nothing of their own, for even their doctrine is naively borrowed from winning parties and their language is a strange pastiche of the style of reports and pastoral letters, with the priceless turn of phrase a certain kind of literature has spread. When apostolic zeal is no more than a sacrilegious sham, what a challenge it is to serve inordinate ambition and envy raised to the status of a sickly hatred of the whole human race and to deprive human life of all its spiritual nourishment. How can one help pitying those individuals whose almost unconscious professional hypocrisy has made them so sensitive to fresh air and the slightest upset, who can only go on by dint of meticulous precautions and care, and who would no doubt be destroyed by the first burst of sincerity, as they can no longer tolerate such an enormous outpouring of their being? And how can we withhold all admiration for the close sense of solidarity that brings them together like a wretched flock throughout a hostile world, despite all their many hidden rivalries?

Pernichon's first cry of anger had initially stupefied and then appalled them. Normally, stony silence or tacit reproof would have been enough to make the offender see the error of his ways. This time, however, he was beyond the pale. The group had therefore felt threatened and faced up to a common danger. However strange it may seem, not a single one of them was any longer capable of paying the slightest attention to the proofs furnished by the plaintiff (if in fact he had provided any), and a rigorous demonstration of the infamy of the accused would have convinced no one and would not even have been heard. For them, any violence was outrageous, setting them so to speak outside themselves in a kind of sacred madness. Like dogs going for the throat of the noisiest enemy, their first reaction was to hate and crush the dangerous, crazed upstart, and they were all waiting with a mixture of curiosity and fear for Catani to restore order and deal severely with him, ready to accept anything, any answer, as long as the tone was appropriate and conducive to a return to decency and gravity.

"The incident is closed," the Vicomte de Duras was muttering between his teeth . . . and Pernichon's very name was to be banished forever and wiped out completely.

Catani alone, however, was in a position to bring about such a happy ending, and there was immense disappointment, for the gloomy journalist had clearly been thrown off balance by the barrage of insults and was struggling and looking for help. For a moment, he gazed with such sadness and distress at the bishop that Espelette was shocked and looked away in shame, eventually managing to stammer:

"We've never seen anything like this . . . can this really be happening? After so much has been done for the young man . . . such intemperate language . . ."

Catani, vaguely aware that he had disappointed everyone, and as mortified as an actor who has just botched his part, seemed to pull himself together and answered in a soft, failing voice:

"My past, the dignity of my life, and Christian charity have obliged me to let pass a slanderous accusation, picked up God knows where. People have criticized me for producing my work in silence, never any seeking public honor . . . all of which is true. For the sake of my religious faith, my sense of the past, and my faith in the future, I've refused to compromise, I've refused to seek formulas for unity, agreement, and balance because, given my liberal beliefs, the excessive publicity they would have attracted would have done us more harm than good. The limited influence I've had . . ."

"You've turned Father Cénabre completely against me!" Pernichon cried.

"A name like his shouldn't be dragged into an argument that . . ." began the bishop, wringing his hands.

"*I* wasn't the first to mention him," the Auvergnat broke in. "Father Cénabre was my greatest support, my mentor, my *friend*, even. What lies and insinuations . . ."

"That will do," Catani suddenly moaned pitifully. "I . . . I'm not in a fit state to answer you."

He suddenly put his handkerchief up to his teeth and abruptly yanked hard on it, tearing it from top to bottom, hiding it so quickly and furtively in his cupped hands that no one except the astonished vicomte saw the strange and totally uncharacteristic action or heard anything but the sharp tearing noise of the cloth.

There was tremendous agitation and complete disorder around the antagonists. Pale with fury, Madame Jérôme was ordering the former president of the Consistory to intervene, while her husband, leaning on the back of the armchair, was shouting something brief and cutting to Pernichon, who was too busy with the Vicomte to hear him, as the latter was tugging his sleeve so roughly that he was almost pulling him over. Eventually Pernichon managed to break free, bawling out in the tumult:

"Remember Father Dardelle! Remember the fifteenth of June!"

He did not manage to finish, as Madame Jérôme's hand, still in its glove, was being forcefully held over his mouth. At once, a strange and stupid silence fell. Nothing in the world could have stopped the spectators from turning toward the victim to see if the blow had struck home. The Dardelle incident had in fact been both the most tragic and the most incredible episode in Catani's obscure career. The columnist, known at the time chiefly for his maneuvers concerning an unfortunate and subsequently ruined bishop, had been rightly or wrongly supposed to have persuaded the young priest, a harmless writer of lyrical poetry totally out of his depth in the modernist controversy, to put his name to a poisonous little pamphlet secretly published in a very small print run and sent only to totally reliable friends. This had led to his public condemnation and dishonor and eventually to censure and suspension. The humiliation had been too much for the feeble and unattractive little cleric, who had fled to Belgium, compounding the disaster by marrying a hard and ugly Wagnerian piano teacher twenty years his senior with whom he had fallen in love. After spending some months teaching in a people's University in Liège founded by Vandeverde, the apostle of socialism, he had shot himself through the forehead on the fifteenth of June 1907, leaving Catani, it was said, his books, the manuscript of a thesis, some unpublished verse, and a mandolin.

Saluting Guérou gravely but from a distance, Lavoine de Duras slowly crossed the room and went out. Pernichon, aghast at (or relieved by) his own boldness, followed Madame Jérôme passively, as biddable as a little child. A thin silver thread of saliva hung from his brown beard.

The violence of the attack seemed, however, to have restored something of Catani's famous impassivity, on which more powerful hatreds than the unfortunate young columnist's had come to grief in the past. Or, at least, his former friends could hope that it had. A tiny pink spot spread out a little on his cheek, and his thin face twitched once or twice and then became frighteningly impassive.

"I'm not seeking any revenge," he said. "I'm sorry for you. You're not mature. That's the word. What do you hope to gain from your childish attack? I'm afraid it has compromised you quite fruitlessly this evening. Anyone would prefer an enemy who comes out into the open to a friend like you. I'm not forgiving you, at least here, in public. At a time like this, my forgiveness would be the last straw that would break your back without, I hope, soothing your troubled conscience . . ."

There was a universal murmur of admiration.

"I know young men, and like them," he went on, with a deathbed smile. "Once they give way to unjustified anger and lose their sang-froid and the respect of their elders, and even the ability to see where their own interest lies, the odds are that they will take the shame they feel so keenly out on others. They heap all their faults on us because at that age, faults really are very hard to bear, and it's impossible to live at peace with them. My dear Pernichon," he went on, pushing out his lower lip oddly and running his tongue over it, "My dear Pernichon, your failing was that you were too eager to enjoy certain worldly goods. In perfectly good faith, you thought that it was your intelligence and talent alone that produced the small success that, in the judgment of your best and most perceptive friends, was more the result of your reputation as an excellent, well-behaved, serious, and thoughtful young man. This evening, you have just squandered part of that priceless treasure, or at least of what was left of it, for one or two of us know . . . are aware . . . the fact of the matter is that you had been dreaming of a splendid apartment. That's no secret. The name I will not utter is on everyone's lips. Hoping for so much has turned your head . . . I think, Pernichon, that your youth authorizes us to speak here, among ourselves, openly, freely, and paternally of your little concerns. The estate of an inexperienced young man is to some extent everyone's concern and is under the control and protection of people of property. When one is almost home and dry, and money worries are the only squalid obstacle, they harden the heart and make people capable of very rash and perhaps even shameful actions, such as . . . well, we won't talk of that. Anyway . . ."

"You are the noblest and most forebearing man I have ever known," cried the bishop, carried away to the extent of taking the speaker's glistening hand and holding it to his breast.

Catani, however, did not even look up, and his words came out with great difficulty and weariness, as if he were reciting a boring lesson he had been made to learn and was anxious to get it over with as soon as possible. Although his answer had been precisely what was expected, there was no trace of the tone, the accent, that mysterious quality that gives our treacherous innuendos the edge that cuts to the quick. The bishop's ardent words did nothing to dispel the strange uneasiness.

"Anyway, you're wrong to think I've ever said anything even slightly unfavorable about you. Nor have I ever been asked for my opinion. Indeed, there has scarcely been any occasion for me to express any reservations — in agreement with your eminent friend, Father Cénabre, to whom I had mentioned my scruples with regard to the temporary difficulty I spoke of a moment ago—about the excessive spending, for which there was no compelling reason. . ."

"My excessive spending!" groaned Pernichon. "No, no!" he cried, breaking roughly away from Madame Jérôme's hands. "Leave me alone, leave me alone, all of you! It's too much! I know what he's been up to for the last five minutes. At least you must allow me to . . . first, I'll explain to you . . ."

"Oh no, it will be time to explain yourself a little later," said the bishop, relentlessly gentle, before adding a few words whose cruelty he was far too innocent to perceive:

"You're shouting before you're hurt, my son."

"Nevertheless," Catani went on, clearly at the end of his tether and letting off a poisonous parting shot, "I think I gave proof of my goodwill by lending you sixteen thousand francs."

A unanimous cry, or perhaps merely a deep sigh or gasp, more decisive than any cry, immediately rewarded his efforts. In the circumstances, no revelation could have been so skillfully prepared or so damning. Pernichon, who had in fact been expecting it, moaned horribly. A shudder ran through his unprepossessing body, and he burst into sobs.

"You offered me the money! You almost forced me to take it! Yes, he did! He told me that I should leave my room in the Hôtel Léo XIII, get somewhere appropriate to live, and buy some furniture. He said it was a sacrifice I absolutely had to make, that my career called for it, that it was time to make an impression, and he gave me a whole host of reasons. Please, put yourselves in my position! My investigation had been accepted for publication, Fides had decided to bring it out, and I was committed to paying the money back by the end of this year. What was he risking? He'd got me in the palm of his hand, and when he closed his fist he broke me. And in addition . . . in addition, my entry into . . . a certain family . . . oh well, what does it matter? You all know . . . into the Gidoux-Rigoumet family would have meant that I could be of use to him. Oh yes, you've been plotting to get the Comte de Verniers to take over *The Universe!*"

"What utter rubbish!" was Jérôme's sole response.

Then Guérou's voice was heard again, thin, throaty and shaking as, confused and muddled, he turned his mind momentarily away from his imminent and insistent death and expanded and swelled.

"May I say something, young man? Any such attempt by a writer we know to be the stuff statesmen are made of is no more than right and proper. And in any case, if it's true that he needs you, why should he be plotting your downfall now?"

"I don't know, I don't know," stammered the wretched man. "I only know that he wants to ruin me. For me, that's enough. But can you imagine . . . ?"

He mopped his brow.

"Sixteen . . . thousand . . . francs . . . sixteen . . . thousand . . ." said Catani with an icy laugh.

The bishop and Jérôme looked anxiously at each other.

"Our respected friend can't go on," Espelette declared. "The incident has been too much for him. Monsieur Pernichon, I beg you . . ."

"Extremely rash . . . dangerously . . . really, enormously rash," Catani went on in the same tone. He jerked convulsively on his chair as if his old body, faced with the collapse of his soul, was summoning up all its strength to make a last stand against a treacherous mind about to reveal a secret it had kept for so many years.

Madame Jérôme pushed Pernichon toward the door, came back, sat down beside the sick man with authority, and took his hand in her own.

"He had a very serious hemorrhage last Tuesday," she confided to the bishop. "We can expect anything. What a hideous scene that was!"

"I'm going to call for a car at once," said Guérou, "but in any case loosen his tie and give him a whiff of ether. Here's the bottle."

"Leave me alone, leave me alone, no questions, please," the dying man was murmuring. "You're tiring me horribly . . . it's pointless, absolutely pointless . . . I shan't reply. Must be completely discreet . . ."

He thrust his open hand out, seized the bishop's arm in the process, and laid his face on it.

"Hear me," he said.

Almost immediately, however, he closed his mouth so violently that his jaws clicked audibly as they snapped together. Then he started nodding increasingly slowly, like a man beginning to fall asleep. His bottom jaw dropped to his chest, and his eyelids opened, gradually revealing a staring, tearful gaze, full of a secret inner vision of himself. A clot of blood shot out of his mouth onto the carpet.

"He's dying!" Madame Jérôme cried out.

"Be quiet, *please!*" ordered Guérou. "Dying's not as simple as that: I know something about it. Look, he's much better already. Move back! It was the clot that was suffocating him."

The color was in fact coming back to Catani's face, and suddenly, without the slightest embarrassment, he said very gently:

"I may have worried you. The first hot weather of the season bothers me greatly, and I have to be more careful than usual at this time of year."

"There's something lying in wait for us, Catani, yes indeed!" Guérou cried jovially. "For both of us, life's a perpetual ambush, and we have to get out of it as best we can. The poor old body's reaching the end of its tether. We can't trust anything!"

"I'm much better, much better, a great deal better," the dying man protested. "The summer months are the best. Come autumn, you'll see me leaving for Corsica to visit Count Sapène, who honors me with his friendship. I shall be busy next spring. There will be a move to the left in the elections, and from now on we shall have to maneuvre very cautiously. We're within an inch of achieving our aim. The socialists are extremely well disposed. Monsieur de Reversot's speech at the last Youth Congress has had wonderful results. My greatest consolation will be to have perhaps not dictated the wording but at least to have inspired the best turns of phrase, those opening up the prospect of a magnificent future and heralding the great revolution of the new age, the imminent overthrow of parties and alliances."

"Rest, rest now," begged Madame Jérôme, almost tenderly.

Never, in fact, had Catani spoken at such length, and more than anything else his feverish, breathless prattle showed just how weak and anguished he was.

"The greatest mistake of some — a few — of us is to let hotheads take part in these delicate discussions . . . like the young man you have just heard . . . who has been *such* a disappointment to me over the last few months . . . they all tend . . . to some extent . . . to rush in and upset things. Ah, it's too true, only too true. I like the young, and this young man isn't the first to make me do something stupid, really stupid! I've tried so persistently, so stubbornly, even, to find a keen young man I could work with. They all let me down. Anyone else would say that they had *betrayed* him. You've just seen the proof of it."

He stirred uneasily in his armchair, clenching his teeth in an attempt to hold back his moans, gently scratching the velvet arms.

"I've been properly punished, Guérou, for trusting others . . . I've hated pushing myself forward, quarrelling, living in the public eye . . . and my health hasn't been good. I've waited for a great many years! I'm biding my time . . . that's the secret . . . it's what you have to do. In the end, people will see that my humble and very concrete policy was the right one. By next spring . . ."

"The car's waiting," Guérou announced.

The bishop was the last to leave. He was still in such an emotional state that he dismissed his chauffeur and decided to walk to the rue Bellechasse, where he was staying with Pupey-Gibon, a radical deputy from the Côte-d'Or, a former minister and an old comrade from his Ecole Normale days. A vulnerable man permanently given to painful scruples, he was reproaching himself for not having acquitted himself more vigorously, although he was not sure on whose behalf he should have done so, as Pernichon's despair had affected him profoundly and he still felt the same mixture of esteem and fear (or perhaps a secret repulsion) for Catani. He felt that he could have influenced the younger man in time, calming him down and showing him how immoderate he was being. Strangely enough, he naturally assumed that the wretched columnist had been speaking the truth and yet found nothing upsetting in Catani's betrayal. The foolish bishop's lack of passion was scarcely distinguishable from the blackest kind of pessimism, and he despised human beings as a policeman or lawyer might. Despite real moral probity and strict self-control, he had found different and more reassuring names for falsehood, duplicity, ambition, envy, and hatred and been the first to be taken in by them. What in his own case, if he had been base or bold enough to be guilty of it, he would not have hesitated to call betrayal, he would have used euphemisms to describe in others ("mild deceit" or "excessive cunning"). In the same way, certain provincials feel that an elegant Parisienne can only be immoral. In his mixture of complexity and naivety, he was therefore completely convinced that a man of letters, a journalist or a deputy even of the right-thinking kind, *must* be assumed to be an upright man, be entitled to special treatment, and cannot be expected, like lesser mortals, to keep the elementary rules of mere honesty. Given his knowledge of and close acquaintanceship with such privileged people and his opportunities for making use of them, he felt the same ambiguous pride as a decent young man from a respectable family having a good time in some dive and finishing up as the friend of Greeks and whores, whom he points out from a distance to astounded girl cousins. His smiling indulgence and the skepticism arising from a gullible nature meant that his curates admired him, and in the small town of Paumiers he passed quite honorably for a kind of democratic Talleyrand whose compromises and audacity were deplored by the (no less gullible. . . !) director of the major seminary and one or two old and old-fashioned priests. For such reasons, the rather simple old man had achieved the almost impossible feat of both remaining blameless and losing, like an adventurer, a decent man's sense of what was right and proper.

Given his personality, he found it impossible that evening to admit to himself that he was glad that he had finished with the whole business, but as he walked along he enjoyed the happiness of having done so. The next day he would be in Paumiers and would not be back before All Saints. By then, the young Auvergnat would have been forgotten, like many worthier men. There is a high rate of loss in all parties in the vanguard of progress . . . or perhaps Catani? . . . but he was one of those who are perpetually at death's door without ever going through it. He started with a mixture of disappointment and anger as he heard Pernichon's voice.

"Your Grace, forgive me . . . I've been following you for a short while. I beg you to listen to me. You're my only hope. I can't count on anyone else."

"I . . . I was on my way home," the bishop replied sadly, quickly suppressing his initial irritation. "What an adventure, my son!"

"I've lost everything, haven't I?" the wretched young man asked.

He walked on a little in silence. He was no longer furious, but as calm as he could be in the circumstances, since for him indignation was an intolerable overreaction. His whole being, the indescribable look in his eyes, his very body, cried out for forgiveness, any kind of forgiveness.

"I went too far . . ." he murmured.

"My son," the prelate responded, "I'm happy to see you so sensible and well disposed. Your frame of mind is excellent, edifying and truly Christian . . . I thank God for it."

"I'm going to . . . all that's left is to kill myself," Pernichon replied.

The bishop stopped dead, stunned by what he had heard.

"You can't be serious, surely? How can you say such things to me? I . . . you've grieved me enormously, my son. What you have said is blasphemous . . . you, of all people!"

He had started walking again, quickly now, almost fleeing the scene.

"Why did I go to Guérou's today?" he moaned. "My place wasn't there." He took the columnist's arm paternally. "My dear friend, no doubt you spoke in a fit . . . a slight fit . . . of madness, perhaps. You're already regretting it . . . oh yes, I know you are! And that confirms what I have thought only too often for some time now — that political and social struggles have become bitter and violent, even among people like us, full of zeal and goodwill. Look at yourself, my young friend, so passionate . . ."

"I've ruined my career!" cut in Pernichon, who was paying no attention. "I'm finished, absolutely finished. And it was all decided long ago. I was lukewarm and overcautious at the last election to the Senate . . . I wanted to spare myself. I thought I could be a useful go-between when the time came . . . a certain adverse reaction was perhaps to be expected . . . Cardinal Riccoti . . ."

He bumped into the stone parapet, staggering like a drunken man.

"There's something to be said before you go on," the bishop interrupted with a note of great authority in his voice. "Withdraw *immediately*, in my presence, your pitiful and blasphemous words."

"What words?" Pernichon asked in astonishment.

"You see, I was sure of it," the bishop shouted triumphantly. "You were never seriously tempted to take your own life, to commit the crime of crimes. God never abandons us! You can finish what you were saying now. I'm listening to you," he finished, in a discreetly superior tone of voice.

"What?" Pernichon said.

"You mentioned Cardinal Riccioti a moment ago . . ."

"I expect I could make my excuses," the author of *Letters from Rome* went on. "But what good would it do? There were too many witnesses. And Catani knew very well what he could expect from me . . . he'll have to look after himself, in his own interest . . ."

"Do you feel that I could perhaps usefully intervene?" asked the bishop. "I'd willingly delay my departure. You see, my son . . . after what has happened, I feel I have the right to talk to you as a father . . . there's nothing more dangerous and clumsy than to irritate an enemy for no other reason than the pleasure and joy of humiliating him. God alone is the judge of our intentions. Our duty is never to condemn an enemy for his intentions, at least up to the point where goodwill becomes ridiculous blindness . . . I can try to make Monsieur Catani see that you were carried away by an impulse forgiveable in a young man and taken in by certain unfavorable appearances . . . or perhaps had bad advice? Who can say?"

For a minute, Pernichon had been staring at him oddly, sadly and wildly. He snatched his arm away.

"Your Grace," he gasped in a horribly broken voice, "you can't help but despise him. At least tell me that you do, that you despise him. If you do, I can bear anything! Please, I beg you!"

"And what good would that do you? What benefit would you get from something that my inclination, my habits, the very cloth I wear prevent me from saying?"

"I'm exhausted," sighed Pernichon, "worn out. I've no idea what's wrong with me. I think I'm going to die."

He ran a trembling hand through his beard.

"Don't leave me alone this evening!" he cried suddenly.

"That is pure childishness," the bishop said, after a long silence. "You *are* a child, a grown-up child. It will pass. By this evening, I promise you, you will see things much more clearly and be a lot calmer. You simply have to get through a bad patch. That we can agree on, I think. But reflection and determination can get you through anything . . ."

He took Pernichon's arm again, stroking his overcoat sleeve with his own fine hand, crooning slightly.

"I swear to you," the journalist went on, "I need . . . what can I say? . . . I need, really need, sympathy, your sympathy! For some weeks now . . . I shouldn't tell you this . . . you'll lose any respect you might have for me . . . for months, it has been absolutely impossible for me to pray!"

There was sincere feeling, and perhaps something more, in the prelate's sympathetic gaze.

"You must open your heart to some thoughtful and conscientious priest, but a clear-sighted one who knows the world. It's far from easy to find one. Why is it that so many of the clergy, including the most zealous priests, unfortunately often lack the vital breadth of mind for such a task? Before I advise you, I need to collect myself and weigh the arguments for and against. It's a delicate undertaking. You must agree that I couldn't have expected . . . our talk has taken a turn . . ."

He smiled, gently shook his companion's trembling arm, and touched his thin wrist with his outstretched index finger.

"You've got a temperature, or at least you're in a feverish state . . . it's madness! How could a mere argument have upset you so much? Don't take misunderstandings so tragically. Yes," he added at once, reddening a little, "I'm also thinking of a more personal kind of misunderstanding, the bout of spiritual aridity that turns you away from prayer . . . there is a danger, my friend, in allowing ourselves to be obsessed by these tiny episodes in our interior life . . . it's one of the forms of temptation that . . . No, no, you can believe me when I tell you that I'm not one of those cranks and visionaries who see the devil in everything and can't stop talking about him. That kind of thing needlessly makes us a laughingstock for the leading modern psychologists, not all of whose theses I would be inclined to reject, by any means . . . the weaknesses in our nature are enough, in most cases, to explain . . . incidents. Moralists and theologians are at one there, as they always should be! Work, exercise, carrying out our duties as citizens . . ."

"What duties?" Pernichon asked. "I no longer have any. I've nothing at all now. What's just happened was to be expected, of course, and was certainly predictable. It was a crisis that had to come, the material and concrete form of . . . oh, I was already lost . . . people no longer like me because I'm no longer any use to them. I've absolutely no standing . . . that's it, exactly . . . none anywhere at all!"

"Oh, come along," the bishop remonstrated. "Gidoux's support . . . how could Catani's resentment . . . between you and me, what does *he* matter? . . . have any effect on your standing with an eminent professor of the Collège de France?"

Pernichon looked at him wildly.

"But there's nothing, nothing," he declared, with something like hatred in his voice. "I've no real reason to suppose that there was any such honorable or profitable project for me . . . hardly even a little fellow-feeling . . . my relations with . . . oh, it was no more than a dream! A week or two ago I was mad enough to let Catani think . . . I could feel that he was turning away from me, escaping from me . . . and that lie, Your Grace, has cost me a great deal! From that moment, he really took quite violently against me. I was told that he was negotiating a marriage between Gidoux's daughter and Jean Delbos!"

"Well, that really is amazing! So you sacrificed yourself . . . made yourself a burnt offering . . . for the sake of a bit of harmless boasting? For nothing?"

He stared in total amazement at the shell of a man, the wraith that would disappear without ever having had anything of its own, not even this final totally unnecessary disaster, and would not even be a nine-days' wonder in Paris.

"My child, my poor child! But why. . . ?"

"Don't ask me why!" Pernichon answered wretchedly. "It wasn't the only lie . . . I'd left Aurillac with all sorts of illusions . . . I wanted to be a journalist and, who knows, perhaps even a writer . . . I had a recommendation from the Vicar-General . . . I arrived when the elections, and all the intriguing that goes with them, were at their height. At Châlons-sur-Marne, I supported a moderate radical candidate at the polls quite brilliantly, to keep the conservative out. I succeeded, and that was my downfall. I'm afraid that now I can see myself as I really am. I've no talent, none at all. If it hadn't been for all the intrigues, I wouldn't have offended anyone . . . but I'm outstanding at writing a report, that's the whole trouble . . . people like that spend their time making reports . . . oh yes they do, as you well know! . . . but they rarely write them and never sign them. Their world's a *very* complicated one! I'm too tired to start anything else. I'm finished . . ."

He bowed his head, seeming to doze as he shuffled flatfootedly along, indifferent and defeated . . . on their left, the Seine was bathed in a glistening golden light, which died away on the banks in a double fringe of blue foam, and the air was filled with the shriek of swallows.

The bishop found the silence intolerable.

"My friend," he said at last, "may I . . ."

But Pernichon cut him short abruptly:

"What do you think of Father Cénabre?" he demanded.

"He's a quite exceptionally intelligent man," the bishop began, "worthy of the highest respect, even though he arouses a great deal of often bitter controversy. As a historian, his conscience and talent . . ."

"That's not what I'm asking you," cried the author of the *Letters from Rome*, holding back his irritation.

He walked on a few steps, gesticulating wildly, and suddenly called out:

"I'll go to him and beg him to help me! Since he abandoned me . . . I'll get him to speak to Jérôme! A word in my favor from Jérôme in the *Bulletin* can save my poor old inquiry! I'm sorry! I'm going at once!"

"Be careful!" Espelette called almost reluctantly. He was already regretting his rashness but knew that he would never forget the look Pernichon gave him.

"Oh, he's in it as well, is he!" said the journalist heavily.

"Please be quiet," the bishop begged despairingly. "You're not yourself, my son. You're overexcited and exasperated. You're infuriated by the slightest thing anyone says to you. I beg you, don't read things into my words, just listen to them. You seem to be highly upset and ready for anything . . . I was afraid you would be disappointed. Father Cénabre is, or at least seems to be, cold, very cold, and rather unsympathetic—or that's how I see it—toward misfortunes like yours. That's all I meant."

"It's enough," said Pernichon icily. "I understand."

"No, you don't. Your wound is still very painful. And what a wound it is! Is there only one? I'm afraid that like some injured people in shock who can't say where it hurts them, you're not in a position to explain the true state you're in to anyone, least of all my eminent fellow priest . . . you know, I think that primarily you feel yourself slighted in your legitimate ambitions, but your conscience is also affected," he concluded, looking wise.

They crossed the Boulevard Saint-Germain in silence.

"I think we should say no more about your fit of revolt or your meaningless words. Yes, I think we should forget them. I shall not mention them again. I urge you to ask God to forgive you this very evening. You see, my son, it's only in Heaven that He is served by angels, pure spirits. On earth, we have to take certain social and political necessities into account . . . in that sphere, I'm obliged to be very circumspect, and I choose my words with great care, but when all's said and done . . . in a situation like mine, there are serious responsibilities. I hope that's some consolation to you in your present troubles . . . we have to fight against prejudice and distrust . . . Veuillot and his like have done so much harm. Lay apostles are scarcely what we need. Everyone should stick to his place. What we've tried to set up, to gather together, is a small band of serious, prudent, level-headed men, as free from all suspicion of class or ideological prejudices as possible, in favor of modern, even passionately democratic ideas, who can be of use . . . how shall I put it? . . . as unofficial intermediaries between us and power. And we should have no illusions. The fact of the matter is that the state is more powerful than ever before . . ."

He had taken Pernichon's arm again and was holding it tightly to his chest.

"In such circumstances, my poor son, it's not reasonable to be surprised and shocked by certain imperfections. And, you know, I see them in much the same way as you do. They're specks, spots that will be invisible in the blaze of light once our task — finally reconciling the Church and modern society — has been fully completed."

He lowered his voice.

"According to certain sections of the press, I have a reputation for being a prelate with advanced views. That may be so, but if you knew how very happy I always am to get back to Paumiers, among those simple — very simple — old parish priests . . . Ah, that gives me an idea. You should make a retreat for a month or two, in Auvergne, where you come from, with your own dear family . . ."

"A month or two!" Pernichon replied bitterly. "My beloved Auvergne! My dear family! And what would I do at the end of the month or two? In the first place, I no longer have a family. Where could I even get the money to pay for my travel and accommodation? Settling in Paris has cost me a fortune . . . I owe Catani nine thousand francs, true, but I've also signed an agreement with a big furniture company for almost eleven thousand francs' worth of goods. Leaving the paper and being unable to publish my inquiry are the end. I can't afford debts . . . without people's good opinion of me, I'm nothing . . ." he stated, fiercely and solemnly.

"Listen," said the bishop. "Here we are, already. We shall be separating . . . oh, for no more than five or six weeks," he immediately corrected himself, naively. "Just let me give you a final piece of advice."

He reflected for a moment, and then smiled.

"At the moment, I can only think of one man . . . his very special situation . . . his complete independence from the people we have just been talking about . . . a certain liking for paradoxes and challenges . . . even his skepticism — which, I can tell you, has been greatly exaggerated by malicious gossip — my old companion at the Ecole Normale, whose house you have just visited, Guérou . . ."

"Oh, him," Pernichon snorted.

"Yes, yes, I can see what you don't like to say. He's a little . . . mysterious . . . enigmatic . . . nobody has condemned more forcefully than I the immorality in his books . . . but he hasn't written a line for years now. He deserves our pity and respect for his illness, patience, and what, I fear, is no more than purely human resignation. He is also extremely interested in the religious question and the newest solutions to it, and he is so influential. In my view, he inspires a kind of fear . . ."

Pernichon gestured, and the bishop reddened slightly and continued in an offended tone.

"I've no intention, if you don't mind, of referring to certain slanderous accusations against him . . . I'm thinking only of you, my son. Never take well-informed people simply at their word. As you know better than anyone else, until a few weeks ago Guérou was living a very withdrawn, private, and apparently even austere life in the country . . . I saw him five or six times last year and there was not the slightest sign . . . when I left Paumiers, I discovered that he was back in Paris . . . to my mind, that was the action of a man who knows that his days are numbered and is facing up to the fact that he will very soon die. other words, is in a sense facing God. But that's enough of that!"

He stopped at the entrance to the Pupey-Gibon townhouse, quivering with sympathy, goodwill, and impatience. With a wave of his gloved hand he wafted away, like a wisp of smoke or a disagreeable smell, the drama he had almost been caught up in and from which he had closed himself off. Pernichon's tragedy was no longer his concern.

"A short while ago you rushed out of the room like a madman, without a word of goodbye to anyone, after a regrettable scene that our host was quite right to find quite out of place," the worthy prelate concluded. "I consider it absolutely essential that you go back and apologize as soon as possible . . . that is an excellent reason for calling there, and for the rest, my son, I rely on your natural honesty, intelligence, and tact."

He took both Pernichon's hands a final time, shook them with all his strength, and disappeared beneath the empty, echoing doorway with a scent of verbena and incense.

The younger man walked quickly down the street, but he was going nowhere, and even Guérou's name had slipped from his mind without a trace. He felt marvelously empty, for the bishop's presence, although he had not realized it, had become intolerable. His despair no longer needed a confidant: what he wanted was an accomplice, and that accomplice was inside him. As he moved away, he carried the thought he had never faced up to in his unhappy heart, clutching it to himself as if it might escape, like a poacher hiding a stolen bird under his jacket and feeling its fluttering wings. He was walking far too quickly, but he was delirious enough to try to escape the feeling as he escaped everything else — by hurrying. Eventually, totally exhausted, he came to a standstill in a deserted street. The asphalt that had been a dazzling white not long ago now looked black and shiny. He wondered why his shoulders were icy cold and why he was in the dark and deserted street. Immediately he realized he had been soaked to the skin by a heavy shower and that he was outside Guérou's door.

Scarcely had he crossed the threshold when he vaguely sensed that he had been wrong to come. He had been taken into the salon that an hour earlier had echoed with his feeble outbursts of anger, and the memory of the one great effort in his life was too much for him. He did not have the faintest idea why he had come to that place rather than knelt before Father Cénabre, in whom he still had faith. He neither understood nor wanted to understand anything about it, being at that final turning point where the force of circumstances begins to seem benevolent and sweet and pure chance is invoked like a god. Never, indeed, had he felt anything but fearful admiration and a great deal of distrust for the great man, the distrust of a plodding little provincial for an affluent writer universally seen as a morally suspect connoisseur of sexual pleasures.

Rarely had an ambitious young man been as fortunate as Guérou, the son of an obscure magistrate, unsuccessful in the *agrégation des lettres*, given bad marks by his teachers, virtually excluded by his peers, and then suddenly made famous by one strange book published at just the right time and attracting the kind of unstinting fame that gives itself unreservedly once and for all, like a girl. By some mysterious encounter the young man, at the time so insolently occupied with *living*, had found, without seeking it and as if it were his own by right, the lost and deadly secret of defamation, so calculatedly perverse that there had been no parallel since the obscure minor eighteenth-century masters. The *roman à clef*, that strange and infamous type of entertainment that had become the preserve of purveyors of the most brazen kind, was suddenly rehabilitated by an unknown young man who knew nothing of society save what was to be learned in fashionable bars. To it he brought a greed, or more exactly a voracity, that was nevertheless so frank, honest, and good-natured that it won all his readers over. At the same time, however, he was writing several very clever gastronomy columns, which brought him in an income sufficient to cover his expenses.

When *Maecenas and his Handmaidens* appeared two years later, there was no unfavorable academic reaction, and the reading public held back for a week or two after the publication of the disreputable book, watching carefully before deciding which way to jump. There was little movement until the summer holidays, when the enthusiastic mood of the casinos and fashionable resorts finally triumphed. It was an illuminating book, almost, but not quite, a major satire (which the author, because he was impervious not only to indignation but even to disgust, never achieved) that was praised to the skies. Indeed, it would be fair to say that it finally freed its readers from their abject slavery to an old man obsessively wallowing in nauseating lechery adapted to academic tastes by a scholarly apparatus of notes and references combined with cheap malevolence, and its tone was raised by a judicious use of mythology. In a few months, the book had sold three hundred and sixty thousand copies. Guérou became a fashionable author and at dawn every day was to be found dozing in one of those expensive brothels where all the demons of boredom hold their sabbath. The former columnist now laid down the law in cabarets where he had once been no more than tolerated. There was no appeal against his decrees, and his belly was already swelling under the table linen.

At that time, the strange man began to give the first signs of weariness, and the appearance of a second book staggered his acolytes and created a void around him. On the basis of his greed and the frank laughter in which no one had yet detected the frantic whinny, he had been taken for an entertainer with an endless supply of facetious mischief, and now suddenly he was offering himself as his subject matter. His book, in diary form, described with matchless precision, authority, and cruelty, not what was happening in Paris but the events of his own personal life. It was all done so meticulously and with such cold effrontery that the sequence of nicely calculated, pitiless, and frighteningly monotonous confessions — which were inescapable, as the reader was caught up in their logical unfolding as if in the events of a nightmare — created the kind of unease that few of his readers were able to bear . . . his illustrious publisher, who had been counting on a triumph, was crippled by a contract heavily loaded in the author's favor and had to resign himself to a disaster. Guérou, however, lost little, because although his readers had deserted him, a new troop immediately gathered around him as its leader. He was enormously successful, particularly in Germany.

His third book probably decided his fate. It was a masterpiece of spiritual aridity, a piece of frenzied and rather heroic research by an intelligence which, when left to its own devices, was nevertheless reduced, like the legendary beast, to devouring and exhausting itself as it progressed, coming to a halt and dying on the terrible road that leads simultaneously to perfection and nothingness. The vices that had played such a major part in his preceding book were now mentioned only warily and allusively. Guérou seemed to despise that still-too-positive part of his life, letting his readers know only the intentions involved, which led merely to a futile engendering of further intentions doomed to disappear into the void.

And that was it forever. He never wrote anything else. People were surprised for a time and then accepted his silence as the inevitable outcome of introspection pushed to the level of total sacrifice, the point where the observer absorbs the observed. At that stage, he received the universal veneration so rarely granted to living artists and was able to bear his fame spiritedly. He was wealthy, no doubt as a result of some undivulged legacy, treating his guests magnificently and acting as a discreet but beneficent providence for starving foreigners, who would carry his fame to distant regions. He managed his formidable pride with consummate prudence and, too clever or indolent to compromise himself in any way, gradually saw the most varied guests seated at his perfectly sumptuous and bountiful table and sent them away replete. Not one of them, however, could boast of knowing him thoroughly. He was assumed to have vices, but none could be proven. Yet the silence he suddenly kept about himself, after a double scandal, was never forgiven. The dignity of the apparently purely public life, although it revealed nothing of either his pains or his pleasures, seemed to be a challenge to the curiosity he had once so skillfully aroused and which now devoured what it could of its difficult and reserved victim. That same curiosity pitilessly followed his constant deterioration as fat invaded his body and his monstrous obesity suffocated him, impatiently awaiting his death in order to open his desks and ransack his drawers. Not once, however, did it learn anything.

Pernichon was kept waiting for twenty minutes. There were still signs of a recent and rather hasty moving-in in the color of the wallpaper, the smell of paste and fresh paint, and the thick material of the new draperies in the enormous flat, which Guérou had just rented. The drawing room was still just as the guests had left it as they hurried away, and the total disorder seemed about to let slip a secret, as if the inanimate objects, malign and motionless, had precisely and mercilessly repeated one or two of the fleeting gestures which, whatever people say, really do show us what is in the minds of our fellow human beings. Although the wretched journalist's confusion and embarrassment stopped him from saying anything important, and he was quietly and mechanically repeating to himself word for word the excuses he had thought out on the landing, he was nevertheless vaguely aware that his final effort had been merely another, and probably an irreparable, mistake.

"Monsieur Guérou asks if you would be kind enough to see him in his room," a voice said. "He's too tired to receive you here."

The words seemed indistinct to Pernichon, but he did as he was asked, blindly crossing a much darker room, then a gallery, and finally entering a farther room where he saw his mysterious host. Guérou, his eyes half closed and his mouth drawn in by approaching paralysis, raised his hand slightly, as if in blessing, welcoming him with a barely audible mumble. Then, suddenly, what seemed to be a corpse in a shroud of fat moved, and his swollen fingers grasped Pernichon's with surprising vigor.

"*Maître*," the author of the *Letters from Rome* blurted out, "I've come to say how deeply and painfully sorry I am for having unintentionally caused a scene that was tiresome from all points of view, and to ask you to forgive me . . ."

"Forgive you!" cried Guérou. "You're offering me an apology! I was thinking that you'd come to be congratulated."

For a moment he contemplated the little man trembling before him, holding his nose as he caught the smell of the soaked old overcoat, and took everything in at a glance.

"You staggered them!" he said. "Today, they learned who was master. You did very well!"

Pernichon was stupefied, and bowed his head without saying a word.

"Do you see," the invalid went on with atrocious irony, "every man worthy of the name has the chance, the heaven-sent chance, once in his lifetime . . . you jumped at it, rather brutally, I must admit, and could easily have spoiled it. I like boldness. At your age, it's almost a kind of prudence . . . and now, what are you going to do?" he asked, in a fatherly way, after a moment's silence.

Pernichon's face reddened. He was fairly sure that he was being made a fool of, and was already ashamed. Nevertheless, for all its ferocity, Guérou's curiosity touched him, and he almost felt like thanking him.

"I'm not joking," the writer went on, as if he could read what was going on in the mind of his tearful victim. "I'm quite aware that we have to recognize that chance and circumstances played a part, but that doesn't detract from your achievement. Have no illusions, my dear young colleague. You struck home. Are you going to finish your man off, or not? As you see, I'm speaking frankly."

"Finish him off, *maître?*" said Pernichon. "Are you laughing at me? I simply wanted . . . I certainly bear Catani no ill will, and in any case it would be very hard for me to do him any serious harm."

"No harm? No serious harm? What do you know about it? A single word in the right place and at the right time can do everything. Between ourselves, my friend, the only thing people are afraid of is a scandal, and anybody reduced to despair by injustice can always make use of that fear. Of course, hypocrisy is something universal and solid you need a pretty powerful charge of explosives to shatter, and nine times out of ten the man using it blows himself up as well."

"I meant . . . that's why I just intended . . ." Pernichon repeated.

Then he stopped, his voice choking with fear. He was certain that Guérou knew what was going on in his mind, and yet he no longer had the courage to admit his weakness. Now, he knew, everyone would expect him to show it frankly. It was there, waiting to come out into the open. He could still feel the other man's eyes fixed on him, implacably demanding to see it, but he dared not avow it.

"So come on, tell me what you *do* want," Guérou exclaimed. "I'm pretty sure that you didn't come here just to apologize, as so many people have! But they rarely pay me the compliment of letting me see sincere, honest, straightforward pain, a totally intact, virginal pain, if I may put it that way. I think I can see that you're deeply unhappy."

He stumbled over the last few words, getting his breath back gradually and painfully.

"What I've just said may seem like a joke, a rather cynical kind of bragging. It isn't. Other people's suffering means nothing to me now, absolutely nothing . . . those who envy me — and there are still those who do — are stupid." He raised his torso with difficulty. "You know, it's impossible to discourage envy."

"*Maître*," Pernichon stammered, "what I was hoping you would be kind enough to do . . ."

"Don't talk to me about kindness!" Guérou cut in. "You came to me, as I well know, full of prejudices and in despair. I think I'm fairly safe in saying that Ludovic urged you to come, am I not? Ludovic, of course, is the bishop of Paumiers, my old classmate from the Ecole Normale. What a fool he is! My friend, it's no doubt a fundamental part of my nature that mediocre priests fascinate me in some way. They whet some kind of appetite, stimulate a brain that's probably now little more than a ball of grease. I say mediocre *priests*, for once they've escaped, become emancipated, between you and me, they're simply tiresome little men. Look at Loisy, for example, whom I once liked very much. He's now simply a ranting, boring, irritating pedant. But Ludovic!"

"Yes, the bishop did advise me to come here," Pernichon admitted. "He's always been very good and kind . . ."

"Oh, kindness itself," cried Guérou shrilly. "Don't make a drama out of a friendly joke! We should be talking about serious things. You want to get your own back on Catani? Well, in a drawer for you, and you alone, I have . . ."

He pressed a bell.

"I swear to you . . ." Pernichon protested in despair.

"Don't swear," Guérou went on peacefully. "Soon, you'll be thanking me. Our greatest pleasures, young man, are those that we reject at first, because we're afraid for our mortal coil . . . isn't it stupid, we're even lazier when it comes to our pleasures than we are with regard to our suffering."

He rang again.

"I'm ringing for my nurse," he explained, no doubt already disheartened at the prospect of the effort he was about to have to try to make. "For months now I've been completely dependent on him. He's a devoted servant."

As he was speaking, the devoted servant himself appeared in the doorway, and Pernichon was amazed to see a sturdy, strapping man with a thick jet-black moustache, a gardener's blue apron fastened tightly round him, and his sleeves rolled up over enormous hairy arms.

"Ask for Lucie," Guérou murmured softly and almost beseechingly to his strange caregiver. "She holds my legs when you lift me by my shoulders and it helps a great deal. You were very rough with me last night, my friend."

"The young lady's gone a message," said the giant, trying, however, to change the tone of his voice. "If you just get hold round my neck, monsieur, I'll do the rest."

"Perhaps it would be better to wait a minute?" the sick man replied almost shyly.

"She's gone a message to Saint-Leu," the man answered, "to your friend's, sir, to take him the letter. Naturally," he said in his awful accent, "she can't get back before ten or eleven this evening, if you can wait that long, sir."

Before Guérou could answer, he braced himself, and the illustrious author moaned as he put his arms painfully round his nurse's neck. The man stiffened his back, and on his swelling biceps Pernichon could see the dark outlines of a complicated tattoo, incompletely removed by acid . . .

Guérou gradually regained his balance, staggering on his short legs, his arms half outstretched and shaking convulsively every time he stumbled, his eyes darting anxiously in his swollen face. He was moving sidelong toward the window, trying to shift the soft bulk of his body step by step.

"The master's much better, monsieur," the male nurse said. "In six to eight weeks he'll be jumping around like a jackrabbit, you can bet on it. His leg's getting better, and his buttock's been much firmer for a day or two now, oh yes indeed!"

At a sign from Guérou, and with a final wink of complicity, he went out.

"He's a first-rate masseur," Guérou confided, with an embarrassing smile. "Please forgive me, he's dreadfully crude, but really sincere. He served in the Foreign Legion for eleven years . . ." He grasped the corner of the étagère and, still moaning, slid out the shelf, picked up a bundle of papers, and went slowly back to his chair. Pernichon felt that he could no longer bear the sight of the monstrous gray-haired child, whose every hesitant step was a kind of sacrilegious parody of childhood, and stood up jerkily.

"I would like . . . I probably have no right to accept a favor from you when I won't be in a position to make what you would consider proper use of it, at least for the moment," he said, without daring to look straight at Guérou.

The latter burst out laughing.

"Good Lord, I know quite well that you won't get any advantage from it!" he cried. "We don't understand each other. Let me do it all. I've got all my wits about me today, which isn't the case every day. Sit down or stand, it's all the same to me. It will take about five minutes. Are you going to listen?"

"Yes, monsieur," said Pernichon submissively.

Guérou sighed with obvious relief.

"I like your frankness," he said. "You're a good, an excellent young man of the most ordinary kind. It's refreshing to see you. In here (he slapped the bundle of papers with the flat of his hand) there's material to shake Catani—and one or two others—up quite a bit. Don't worry, it's nothing, the most insignificant of my little dossiers—a unique collection! For twenty years I've been filing away material and putting it in order, building up my mine of information. It's my whole work."

"I don't see why . . . what use . . ." Pernichon protested timidly, blushing with shame.

"We're coming to that," said the invalid. "You simply came at the right time . . . I have gloomy premonitions, young man. Things aren't going well. I won't live long here and should never have left Barfleur or broken with my habits. In short, I'm sorry for you. There isn't much I can still admire, but I do appreciate your boldness, and I've found you very brave."

"Don't laugh at me," Pernichon murmured. "I haven't been at all brave. I was simply carried away. I'm really deeply unhappy."

"When we're really brave, we're not aware of it," Guérou declared. "You're no judge of yourself. *I* can see what you're thinking. You can't go on, you're at the end of your tether. Isn't that right? You'd go and kiss Catani's hand and crawl to him, I expect. You would, wouldn't you? It would be good. But you've got to start the struggle all over again, take an eye for an eye, be a brave man."

"I'll do nothing of the kind," said Pernichon, "as you well know. Even if I could use the weapons you're providing me with, it wouldn't be hard for people to take them from me. And it's too late to ask Catani to forgive me. I'm a man who needs a job, a position. I've lost it, and without it I'm nothing."

Guérou picked up a newspaper from the table and twisted it carefully into a kind of torch. He then lit it, snatched up the bundle of papers, and threw the lot higgledy-piggledy into the fireplace. The flames leaped up and roared. Only then did Pernichon's overtaxed nerves give way, and he burst into dry-eyed sobs.

"There's nothing to hold you back. It's better this way," said Guérou calmly, with an alarming look in his eyes. "No, nothing will stop you killing yourself, however little you feel inclined to do so. And you *have* the inclination. By the way, circumstances are absolutely no justification for suicide. Most of your troubles are imaginary ones, and you seem to take pleasure in exaggerating them. Now it would take less effort to kill yourself than to admit that you panicked for nothing. You're vain. Any passion can make us pick up a revolver one day, but in the end what makes us pull the trigger is vanity. If *I* were vain, I'd have been dead long ago. And, after all, perhaps *you* won't kill yourself, as you're free. But of course I could read all that on your face as you took your first step into this room."

Each of his loaded words in turn struck exactly the same spot in Pernichon's mind with deadly accuracy, seeming to numb his anxiety. Despite his initial terror he had heard, with growing and indescribable relief, his deepest and most secret thoughts being expressed by someone else. The look he gave Guérou was that of a slave, but it was Guérou who turned his eyes away.

"I said the same to Laudat in 1918," he said, with a forced laugh. "Do you know him? He's none the worse for it now . . . But I should have been very sorry to upset you."

"You didn't," muttered Pernichon, lost in his thoughts.

"You'll come out of it, young man!" cried Guérou cheerily. "A thorough investigation is always helpful, even if it hurts . . . but I was only joking. Do you see, I'm amazingly sensitive to certain states like yours. I could point you out in the street from twenty yards away as a man whose morale and ability to resist are low, who's going to give in . . . the night before a decisive battle, it's a safe bet that I could pick which of the two generals is going to lose . . . it's not funny! And now, please, would you be kind enough to half open the window . . . on your left . . . yes, there . . . just stretch your arm out . . . I'm not feeling well . . ."

He was sweating heavily.

"You see the little heap of ash?" he asked, pointing to the fireplace after a short silence. "I'm glad I've destroyed it. I'll burn all the rest as well. I've had enough . . . can you believe it, I've written — I must own up to it — my memoirs! A pretty stupid thing to do. And I've destroyed those, too. Who will know?"

He stole a glance from Pernichon, as if he were someone he had written off and banished from the land of the living.

"What are you going to do when you leave?" he suddenly asked.

The wretched man could not have thought up the tiniest lie. Fascinated, he answered:

"I think I shall write a note to Father Cénabre."

"That really is an excellent idea!" Guérou exclaimed exultantly. "A first-rate idea! He can be of great use to you."

For some time he muttered other words it was impossible to make out. The sweat was still flowing steadily from his forehead, which he mopped jerkily from time to time. It was tiring to watch him. Something gradually seemed to be overcoming his relentless curiosity, which so few people had suspected that it would remain his secret for ever. At length he shrugged, saying immediately and almost tenderly:

"Why in heaven's name did you seek me out this evening?"

The Auvergnat was distinctly calmer now, however, and gave himself up, without further resistance. The anxiety of the preceding weeks had prepared his exhausted psyche, finally broken by the enormous effort he had made that day, for his present tender and caressing distress, and he handed himself over to the strange being who was speaking to him in a new language and treating him as an equal. The past was a dream, and even the present was fading away. Never had the idea of suicide been vaguer, flimsier, or less clearly formulated in his mind, but neither had it ever been so very alive. His brain scarcely understood it, for his whole self seemed to be brooding. His conscience had already been defeated and remained silent.

"For the reason I gave you: Bishop Espelette urged me to . . ."

"I thought as much!" Guérou cried. "It shows how sensible he is . . . did you know Father Dardelle?"

"No, monsieur," Pernichon answered.

"He was like you. I keep thinking I can hear him talking . . . he was one of the worst kind of weak people, the ambitious ones who need sympathy, not health . . . another Pernichon. I saw him before he left for Belgium, one evening . . . no, wait! It was an evening in December, a winter evening. Why do people like you always stick your heads in the lion's mouth?"

He stopped abruptly and listened. In the silence, not too far there was a sharp cry, which stopped at once. All Pernichon could hear was the invalid's now hoarse and rapid breathing.

"Jules!" Guérou suddenly thundered, making an enormous effort to reach the bell, which was a few steps away. As he was reaching for it, however, the door was half opened softly and the ex-legionnaire's face, transformed by a mixture of insolence and fear, appeared in the gap.

"You lied to me!" Guérou shouted again.

He was so extremely agitated that Pernichon thought at first that he had gone mad. Reluctantly, he looked at the male nurse to see if his reaction had been the same, but was astonished to see only cringing submission on his face. He was seized by the disappointment that fills us in dreams when passing faces show no reflection of our own anguish.

"Here I am, monsieur," said an unknown voice behind him.

What had just appeared was something rarely encountered in broad daylight in a fashionable Parisian apartment. Perhaps the incongruity itself was the only strange feature of the sight, but the contrast was too stark and heartrending.

Guérou's neck turned crimson, and a pale white patch spread out around his mouth.

"Get out! Who sent for *you*? Get out!" he thundered again.

In order to get away faster, the little girl lifted her thin leg in its dirty stocking over the table where the teapot was still steaming. Pernichon glimpsed a pathetic face with the color of dead skin, the eyes wild and shining with terror. Was she ten or fifteen? She disappeared.

"What have I told you?" Guérou shouted. "How can you let that little obscenity run around like that?"

"There's no controlling her since the bachelor flat in the rue d'Ulm was closed up!" was the reply.

For the first time since the beginning of the strange scene the nurse seemed to remember that Pernichon was there and merely shrugged nonchalantly.

"It's your fault, monsieur. You thought I'd hit the young lady," said the masseur in the blue apron. "She's downstairs, as I said. You know, I've never even touched her. She's making it all up. I can't cope with her. She's eaten a pound of sugar. You can be the judge of it, monsieur."

"That's enough!" Guérou broke in. "I'm sick of it all! Get out!"

He dropped back into his chair, crossed his hands over his stomach and let his head sink low on his chest. Clearly, Pernichon's silence was infuriating him.

"What about you? Have you any vices?" he finally burst out.

"Have I?" Pernichon stammered in horror. "Er, yes . . . no . . . I mean . . ."

"The good thing about vice," Guérou went on, suddenly calm, "is that it teaches us to hate human beings. Everything is fine until one day we suddenly hate *ourselves*. And, my young friend, let me ask you this. Hating the human race in oneself, isn't that what Hell is? Do you believe in Hell, Pernichon?

He did not wait for an answer.

"*I* believe in it. All you need do is look around you. My house is a hell. As you can see, I won't even have the consolation of dying in Paris. I should go back to Barfleur, where people take more notice of what I tell them. The kind of thing you've just seen happens every day. Since I've been unable to move about because of this dreadful bloated state, my wretched life has been flowing back to the surface, like a blocked sewer. Jules is too soft-hearted, he isn't in control . . . and, my friend, the letters I receive are atrocious!"

He stopped and looked at Pernichon in amazement. Some of what he had said no doubt meant very little to the younger man, but he had realized that the invalid, who now seemed to epitomize, so to speak, the image and spectre of interior collapse, was also living through one of those moments when the most tenacious and cunning of men give up the struggle. His enormous head now seemed to be rolling slowly from one shoulder to another, like a wreck in dead water. Briefly, he even gave the impression of being lost in some kind of grotesque meditation, which was even more marked when his facial muscles suddenly relaxed, forcing his mouth outward and his bluish lips into a kind of smile. The illusion was short-lived, however, for his mouth suddenly opened a little, emitting, on a flow of saliva, a mere burble rather than any meaningful words. Pernichon stood up, touched Guérou's motionless chest, and rushed straight to the door. Once his hand was on the handle, he hesitated, went slowly back toward the table, and rang the bell.

"*Merde!*" the legionnaire shouted, and in a flash Guérou had been pulled up and thrown down, rather than stretched out, on a wide leather divan. Within seconds his clothes were torn off and scattered all over the floor and his naked body was being vigorously slapped with a damp towel.

The nurse persisted, grunting at each blow. On his face, which he had earlier turned away from in disgust, Pernichon could see genuine concern or perhaps even something more. The concern intensified into anxiety. Then, to Pernichon's surprise, his features were suffused with a kind of serenity, like some kind of frightful tenderness . . . Guérou had started breathing again, feebly.

"He'll be OK," said the masseur, wiping his nose with the back of his hand. "By God, that was a close one!"

He looked gently at the resuscitated red-streaked mass of flesh with water and sweat steaming on it. Pernichon's surprise turned to dread when he saw a meaningful grimace twist the black moustache . . . Jules was weeping.

"Christ, what a constitution!" he went on, after a cordial wink. "There's never been anything like it since time began. Strong as a cart-horse. Trying to grab everything at once, ready to die for anything, for pleasure. What a temperament! I hope you don't mind me saying so, monsieur, he could get through ten or twenty women. There was nobody to match him. I'm telling you, I knew him when he was as strong as an ox and really good-looking, a real handsome, strapping fellow. I was fifteen at the time. I'd have given my life for a bloke like that . . . and he goes and lets females ruin him — hope you don't mind this, monsieur — under-age bitches, real little sluts. God knows how many he gets through, and they're not your run-of-the-mill type. Ah, monsieur . . ."

He wiped his eyes on a corner of the towel, turned Guérou over onto his stomach, and started slapping him again, but un-hurriedly now.

"You can see my method works," he said. "It's tough and bru-tal, but it's dead simple and always works. In five minutes, he'll be on his feet and as good as either of us. He's pretty strong, but he can't move easily anymore and his blood's sluggish . . . it's his circulation you've got to keep going, with massages and every-thing. And it's donkey-work . . . I've had rheumatism since I was in Morocco, and some days I cry out like a kid when I'm working on him. God, he's damned heavy, but it doesn't matter. As soon as I'd done my stint out there, I came looking for him. I'd have walked on broken glass. I was a medical orderly in the Legion, and I learned massage on purpose, to . . . well, there we are. Oh, he's a dangerous man, and he's got a way of keeping his own people round him. You can't do without him . . . he's got lovely little vices and he's really intelligent!"

He threw the towel down, went out, and came back at once with a flannel dressing gown in which he wrapped his master like a mother caring for her child. Pernichon dared neither answer nor even look up. Eventually, Guérou sighed.

"If you wouldn't mind," the masseur said, "could you help me a bit to sit him down gently? When he's coming out of these attacks, you wouldn't believe just how touchy he is."

He arranged the cushions round Guérou's shoulders, sliding one or two behind his neck, picked up the towel, and, looking oddly at his employer, turned and slipped soft-footed out of the room.

It took all Pernichon's courage not to follow him. Shame alone, rather than any pity, held him back for a moment. The big man was breathing slowly, his arms lying stretched out as haphazardly as those of a child's who has fallen unexpectedly asleep. His face was so calm and familiar and the surrounding silence so undisturbed that Pernichon would have liked to forget what he had seen and heard. And after all, what did he know? What had he learned? But he felt overwhelmed by disgust, and so very, very weary.

At last the invalid stretched, moaned softly, and murmured, without opening his eyes:

"You thought I was dead, young man. Don't worry. In fact these episodes are welcome. I sleep so little and so badly. Sleep has to hit me suddenly, like a merciful executioner, spontaneously, without keeping me waiting . . ."

He ran his hands over the dressing gown, feeling the soft flannel, and trembled.

"Aha, I must ask you to forgive me," he said. "It must have been worse than I thought."

But as he was opening his eyes fully, he saw that Pernichon was no longer there.

At that very moment, Cénabre was leaving the Bibliothèque Nationale and walking down the rue de Richelieu in slanting sunlight and a golden mist. For the whole day, the city had been stifled by a merciless fog, as searing as a blast of air from an open oven, and was now relaxing like some mythical beast, growling more gently and investigating the twilight with uneasy and secret distrust, for cities both welcome and fear the night, their accomplice. The priest, however, was walking at his usual measured pace, as indifferent to the coarse tranquillity as he no doubt would have been to the blaring chaos of the afternoon or the heartrending purity of the morning air as the sun rises, losing itself among the stones like a wounded bird. For a long time, in fact, his thoughts had been locked inside his head, and he was savoring the harmful effects of it to the full with a strange and cruel joy.

Six months earlier on his return from Germany, where he had fled once he had overcome his initial anxiety, he had slipped easily into a deeply peaceful state. That, at least, was what he had called it, because it gave him the illusion of final stillness, the absolute calm after the storm. Obscure forces, whose strength and number he scarcely dared estimate, had clashed in a fearsome chaos into which he had felt his soul sinking, and now both had subsided and, it seemed, combined in some kind of monstrous alliance. Just as the wretched human race pitches its pathetic tents between hills thrown up in some terrible ancient cataclysm and scratches around in the cooling outer crust of a world that still has a raging abyss at its center, so he too had found a resting place at the very center of all his inner contradictions. He was living there in solitude, cut off from civilized life, all human contact, and his own terrible past. He had miraculously broken away from it, but it was now more mysterious and threatening than the future, and he could still hear it growling outside his shelter like a wild beast claiming its prey. Nevertheless, the break seemed complete.

Such breaks are not particularly uncommon, but in most cases they come about as a result of a specific set of unforeseen circumstances, a revolt of our senses, our pride, or our reason, which suddenly destroys our resistance, leaving in its wake such an overwhelming sense of emptiness that the will is weakened forever and secretly cherishes, as it might a death wish, the memory of the part of the self that has been torn out. So insidious doubt is reborn, more tenacious than before, since it thrives in this most favorable medium where everything is decomposing. At such a juncture, few men escape the double snare of either an ambiguous and nostalgic tenderness for what they have renounced or a sterile hatred, which is merely another form of remorse and completes their moral and psychological breakdown. No one is deceived by their violent behavior, and everyone sees them with spittle on their lips, begging the bread they have just thrown away and eternally hunger for. The fact that in their pride they now claim to be emancipated, unique, and alone hardly matters, for in reality they have an immense need of other people. They are merely dispossessed.

Father Cénabre, on the other hand, had taken chaos properly into account, like a commander making an orderly and safe retreat. His senses and his inaccessible and hitherto unshaken pride were unaffected. Even the acute anxiety that had marked the beginning of his slow and almost methodical separation from his fellow human beings he now saw as something no doubt decisive but in itself insignificant. He had quickly faced up to, and eliminated, his initial shame. Similarly, he was extremely careful to avoid seeing, as so many others had done, a tragic crisis as a source of pride, and he would certainly have been incapable of seeing it as matter for literature. Instinctively and from the depths of his being he detested Renan, or more accurately, despised him, as one species hates another.

That particular fact may be surprising, but it is also revealing, and to those who do not seek the hidden reason for such disdain Cénabre can only remain an enigma. The contradictions in Renan, his feminine sensibility, coquetry, unavowed egotism, and sudden emotional outbursts, all indicate a soul deliberately using distraction as a means of evasion. The perpetual equivocation bears witness to God in the same way as the twisting and turning of a hunted animal indicate the presence of an unseen hunter. Father Cénabre's life, however, was one of the few examples of absolute refusal, and perhaps even the only one. Nothing less than a reflection on Hell, where despair itself is static and the shoreless sea has no tides, can help us to begin to understand that kind of spiritual emptiness. Nor could it be the case that the strange man had been born under the sign of some terrible curse. Whatever part falsehood might have played in his youth, there had been one particular occasion when indifference had become a willed, lucid, and deliberate renunciation. No one knows when it was.

Nor did Cénabre himself. Along with the most painful symptoms of his affliction, the anger that he so violently displayed on one occasion had apparently disappeared. It was in fact dormant. His conscience did not reproach him, and he still felt no remorse. Once he had had the courage to take a hard look at his inner reality and establish a definitive self-concept, the wound had closed. He no longer believed. He had totally lost his faith. Where he had been most skillful (for his cunning matched his strength) had been in resisting the temptation to put off what had to be done for as long as possible by not wholly rejecting symbols now stripped of all substance. He had broken contact in such a way that any return was impossible and indeed inconceivable. "My sense of the metaphysical," he declared one day, "has completely disappeared." It was more than that, however. A handful of those like him have managed to break away from a mellow and highly nuanced spiritual view of life, reach the wilder shores of agnosticism, and still unknowingly live among familiar faces. Father Cénabre thought that he had emptied himself of all belief and hope at one bold stroke. At the far edge of all his struggles, there was nothing. The thought elated him, haunting him like a delightful memory known to him alone and recalled again and again. His soul, which his old offense had long ago condemned to solitude, finally surrendered to it and sank into it forever. "Between me and nothingness," he would say to himself, "all there is is this flickering life, which can be blown out or destroyed by a tiny blood vessel bursting," and he would immediately feel his heart encircled by flames.

More often than not, nothingness is reluctantly and despairingly taken to be the only hypothesis possible when all the others have failed, since by definition it cannot be disproven and is beyond the scope of reason. Cénabre, however, gave it his faith, his strength, and his life. He wanted it, and it alone, as it was. He was unaware of the part played by long years of bitterness in his extraordinary and heroic option. Realizing it would have humiliated him deeply. In his own mind he was quite convinced that he had acted without violence and accepted the unavoidable like a man, and he scrupulously refused to recognize any debt, of hatred or love, to anyone.

Nevertheless, he knew that he was guilty of one single and still incomprehensible act of weakness: his appeal to Father Chevance. Now that he was the only captain of his soul and the only source of his own pain or joy, the memory of it was unbearable. Like a miser who can no longer enjoy his treasure because some of it has been stolen and wastes his rare and exquisite pleasure in desiring what is lost, Cénabre could not forgive himself for having inadvertently let part of his life be taken from him. There was still a gap, and one particular premonition made him angry.

Apart from that anxiety, he felt sure of himself, since he had never left anything to chance or been guilty of any serious folly. Once he was back from Germany, he had remained indoors and spread the word that he was ill in order to make sure that he had a day or two to think things over. Even the very few close friends who came to see him would certainly have suspected nothing. From that moment, his mind was made up. He would not change the outward organization of his life and would live and die as a priest.

It may well seem strange that after champing at the bit for so long he did not think it the right time to free himself totally, claiming indeed that it was from himself alone that he had broken free and consequently no longer needed to justify himself to himself. Once he had rebelled, the duplicity he still had to engage in, far from not diminishing his newly regained freedom, made him more aware of it because of the sharp contrast. He would certainly have been astonished to learn that his decision was to cause several tragic events that his normal prudense could not have foreseen and that common sense would have considered impossible. Since he had come to terms with his pride, he saw nothing dangerous or shameful in his pretense. Indeed, he punctiliously fulfilled all the obligation of the priestly state with pointless zeal, greater dignity, and a seriousness, or indeed even a sadness, that would have deceived the most perceptive observer. Every day, for example, he said mass in the chapel of the Sisters of Mary, and the old sacristan who had assisted him for many years had never seen him so rapt in prayer.

The fifth volume of *The Florentine Mystics* had just been published, and nothing marked the book off from its predecessors, except perhaps that it was more cautiously critical and more scrupulously objective. A certain mocking tone in the discussion of disputed points and a somewhat impatient, insolent, and rather darkly comic vein were now absent. The imprimatur had been granted very promptly, yet the volume had been praised by a great many young priests fired by the author's reputation for boldness and what, in their naive and skillfully circumlocutory jargon, they called his "modernity." The truth was, in fact, that he had written the final chapters in great haste, wanting only to get them finished. His love of controversy had disappeared as if by magic, along with his remaining scruples. He intended to remain purely a sober historian, using his notes. He was waiting.

But not, as might be thought, for one of those unforeseen events that suddenly reestablish the balance of a life thrown into disorder, make appearances match reality, and sanction a lie. No, nothing like that. In fact, he was very proud of having so easily managed to return to his old habits without breaking any of the delicate interrelationships between them when very many others would no doubt have yielded to the blinding desire to smash everything around them to have their revenge on their anxiety once they had overcome it. *His* fate was now sealed and the course of his life established until his death, which he neither feared nor desired, for already in some strange way its image lay within him and was his certainty and his repose. What he was expecting was not easy to define, or at least he was a long way from imagining that the undertaking was scarcely underway or that it probably had neither a beginning nor an end. Discovering the solitude he now lived in had at first delighted him and filled him with confidence, strength, and disdain. All it required of him was a complete break with the rest of humanity and a choice to live for and through himself, and he had sincerely believed that he would never be able to come to the end of such a rare, bitter, and voluptuous experience. Already, however, it had to be constantly sought out and tested and provided only grudging and reluctant pleasure. He was beginning to feel that disdain in itself was not enough and that he needed to immerse and renew himself in some as yet unknown and more absolute emotion. He could almost guess what it was, but resorted to all sorts of pathetic tactics to avoid naming it, for he was afraid that all that the strange and monstrous creature now inside him needed in order to grow horribly and take over his shattered soul, like a cancer assuming the exact and repulsive shape of the limb it has eaten away, was to be perceived and looked upon fondly just once. He could not yet account coherently for his vague fears and premonitions or all the blind and crawling things in the depths of his consciousness, and he thought that all he had to do to free himself of them completely was to make one final effort. Whether things were really as he had wished them or he had reached the end of a slow and unbelievable collapse, he liked to think that his whole life had been firmly and securely based on pride. The strange mistake was that of a man not yet aware that pride has no intrinsic substance, being no more than the name given to the soul devouring itself. When that loathsome perversion of love has borne its fruit, it has another, more meaningful and weightier name. We call it hatred.

Just like a lover suddenly and fearfully realizing that once what he calls ecstasy is over, the empty and abandoned body he is clasping has nothing else precious to give him and he is empty and forsaken, Cénabre sometimes glimpsed for a moment just how precarious his triumph was and how futile his possession. At such moments, the calm that had washed over him was astonishing rather than fully reassuring. When he watched himself leading a life so like the one he had led in the past, a scrupulous and painstaking priest, visiting the same friends and still making all the same comments on things, he felt distrust rather than remorse and was aware that such facile duplicity might be no more than a respite. He would have preferred not to have had this initial success to have been forced to learn his new role painfully and diligently. Instead, he was at ease in it and seemed never to have known anything else. The strange scruple was mostly no more than a kind of vague unease, but sometimes it also welled up to the surface of his conscious mind, and he felt that he had been attacked in some vital part of his being. It could happen, for instance, at one of the early-morning masses he usually said with complete indifference, paying attention only to his actions and words, articulating the latter carefully and in a low voice, as if anxious not to demean himself by stooping to a pointless deception, giving the congregation their money's worth. After hesitating for a day or two, he now uttered the words of consecration not (or so at least he thought) from a secret taste for sacrilege, but because he judged it unworthy of him to deceive, even by a harmless omission, the old women who would shortly come to kneel at the altar rails . . . And suddenly he would experience a moment of acute suffering that stopped him dead and nailed him to the spot for a long minute, sometimes in the most inconvenient position, with his arms raised to present the Host to the Cross or his hand stretched out in blessing. He would come around as if from a dream, watching himself act not in terror, but with an enormous, undefinable curiosity, so pathetic and subtle that it cannot be described in any way that would not distort it. There was nothing less like any sort of even a rudimentary repentance, a movement of grace, or simply fear. Quite the contrary, for on such occasions it seemed to him that anything painful or sensitive still left in him suddenly closed up, and he felt petrified, suspended in some strange kind of expectation. That is indeed the right word, provided it is used in an absolute sense. He was both an actor in and a spectator of the strange phenomenon, awaiting something, something perhaps to be born out of his acute and agitated pride, which was as tense as a straining muscle. And so the rebellious, staring priest, face to face with the God he had betrayed, awaited a new and imminent revelation, but this time from within himself and not from the cold, silent bronze figure or the frail white disc through which he could see the candle flames dancing . . . what revelation? Why, at such times, did he hate the outstanding calm and the lucid indifference that normally filled him with such pride? Why was he, against his will, so angry, and what did he really want? Anyone watching his features attentively would no doubt have answered the question.

These strange, sudden, short-lived crises were so increasingly violent that his voice, if he suddenly heard it as he was halfway through reciting a versicle, scarcely dropped. And he forgot them, thought no more about them, unconsciously enjoying the exhaustion that followed them, the blessed weariness that made his knees tremble beneath his soutane. He also watched, uncomprehendingly, the perspiration streaming along his hands. The sacristan, folding his alb before putting it away in a drawer after mass, was astonished to find it soaked in sweat.

Crossing the Carrousel, he sat down for a moment on one of the stone benches carved into the wall, but there were too many passersby for comfort so he set off walking again almost at once, although more slowly this time. For six weeks he had been gathering his index cards together, taking notes, working with difficulty, setting out the plan of his book chapter by chapter, with all his usual attention to detail. It all now seemed a tiresome and deeply unattractive chore after his expectation that it would provide months of peaceful labor and a mild success very different from previous triumphs spoiled by fear of scandal, theological arguments, and censure. Suddenly, he was discovering that the fear involved had been part of both his life and his joy. Much more than that, in fact. The need for constant stratagems, for carefully calculating his chances, for attacking obliquely, for breaking off a potentially revealing polemic at the right time, the simultaneous pleasures of the hunter and the hunted, all these had been as dear to him as fame, and once again he felt a fierce desire for them. At the same time he was certain that he himself had destroyed all that forever.

He was hurrying now, almost running along the deserted quay, and he felt his delirium increasing. He was as painfully impatient as a man who has long been unconsciously seeking a forgotten figure or word and who suddenly realizes that it is going to surface from the depths of his memory and that his life depends on it. An immense wave of conflicting ideas burst chaotically over him and he seemed to realize, *did* realize, that once the question he had asked was answered, the confusion would disappear as if by magic. At virtually the same time he was ashamed of such agitation and, with one of the sudden changes he alone was capable of, he stopped and made himself stand perfectly motionless for a long time with his arms crossed on the parapet, looking like a tranquil passerby watching the muddy water flow past on a summer evening. In order to try to overcome the nightmare by dragging it out of the darkness and into the light of day, he began quietly to ask himself questions and then answer them, as if he were having a discussion with a friend.

the IMPOSTOR

"It's quite simple. I'm certainly abandoning the book, giving up the historical investigation, and to begin with I'm burning my notes this evening." "What on earth for? You're mad!" "Obviously there's no shortage of the subjects I was interested in a month ago. There are more than enough of them. And why am I mad? Why do I have no heart for it any longer? I don't believe, right. It's true. I no longer believe . . . I no longer believe in anything . . . I no longer believe in anything . . . I no longer believe in anything . . . I no longer believe . . ." He caught himself uttering the stupid phrase mechanically and repeatedly, and ten paces away an old man looked sadly at him with his head on one side and then immediately walked away, red-faced.

Cénabre hid his face in his hands and tried to resume the discussion where he had left it off, constantly muttering reproaches and then trying to encourage himself with childish phrases ("Come on! Come *on!*"), finding again, in the deepest places of his memory, the tricks a good pupil uses when trying to concentrate on a difficult text. If only he could have looked at himself in that way during his crisis. "Come on, come on, let's really get to grips with the problem. I've written quite a lot of books happily, haven't I? Yes, I certainly have. That's one question settled. And why did I force myself to give up my subjects, this rich and inexhaustible field? Be careful now, that's another delicate matter. If you take it for itself, study it from the outside, in a totally disinterested way . . . sanctity for example . . . no, never," he shouted aloud now beating his fist on the earth. "It's impossible to be detached. I've got to choose!"

He looked furtively right and left to check that no one had overheard him. As far as the Pont-Neuf the quay was deserted. A tugboat's siren moaned funereally, at first softly and then more loudly. A final heartbreaking note, lower now, marked the onset of twilight.

He gestured impotently and came to himself. The sky was pure and very close, covered from east to west by a sulphur-colored vapor. The boughs of the huge plane trees on the riverbank were swaying gently in the breeze. In unison a multitude of windows facing the setting sun shone with a red glow, which disappeared almost immediately. Only then did the wind freshen.

His watch showed ten o'clock. He put it back in his pocket, as an embarrassing witness is kept very much in the background. Already the argument he had taken part in so anxiously was no more than a vague memory fading like a dream, and all he was clearly aware of was the time that had been wasted. Although the same had also been true of each of the earlier crises, none had been such a severe trial to him, led him so far into his inner darkness, or made him so bitterly angry and disillusioned.

He crossed the Pont des Arts, set off along the rue Bonaparte, took a deserted road on the right, and then another and another. His nightmare had gone and no longer filled his mind. All he felt was the need to walk off his painful and uncontrollable anxiety, and, as he moved along, he instinctively chose the narrowest and darkest back streets for his pointless ramble. The first ran into the already deserted Boulevard Saint-Germain. As he turned into it, he bumped into a wretched old man standing in the corner of a doorway, no doubt asleep. For a moment, he stood still in surprise and then asked, angrily and roughly enough to make him feel ashamed, "What do you want?"

The other man, no doubt an old hand at such encounters, coolly replied, with the presence of mind beggars always seem to have, "Ah, Father, the good Lord's sent you. *Ave Maria! Dominus!*"

He put his hand in a hole in his jacket and pulled out a dirty piece of paper.

"Here's my certificate. *And* I used to have a certificate from the commissioner as well, with my discharge from hospital pinned to it. But just my luck, for Heaven's sake, I went and lost 'em, Father. Y'can see how lucky *I* am! It shows I'm a decent guy. Only scum and parasites have any luck, to my mind."

He put his hand half-heartedly in another hole, drew it out empty, and said, with a mixture of resignation and bitterness:

"That's enough. I'm only asking for ten sous."

Cénabre could see the small gray eyes gleaming in their rolls of dirty flesh and he felt his stomach turn. To his astonishment, however, he replied, almost in spite of himself, in a strangely gentle voice:

"Are you hungry?"

"Hungry? I'm always hungry! I was born that way. Don't ask me if I'm hungry. Yes, yes, I'm damned hungry!"

Raising his arms and opening his filthy hand, he asked Heaven to be a witness to his innocence, putting on a marvelous show of bitterness, but with the whole of his old face alight with some inner amusement. "A priest for down-and-outs. That's a good 'un."

"I'd like to do something for you," Cénabre replied gently. "What good would giving you ten sous or ten francs do? You'd be no better off for it. We've got to find something better, my friend."

The only expression on the old man's face was one of total distrust.

"I've got to work," he feebly tried to explain, "but first I've got to set myself up a bit. I'm as weak as a baby, Father. No strength left. Beat. I'd rather die."

He disappeared back into the corner of the doorway. All Cénabre could see was the lower part of his face, lit up from below. His lower jaw, so thin, was chattering with disappointment and anger.

Cénabre looked like a terrier that had lost its prey . . . for a moment he hesitated, ashamed but unable to extricate himself from the situation, then gradually yielded to an irresistible temptation. Day by day, and almost without his being aware of it, he was finding such sudden weaknesses more familiar and less painful and mentally disturbing to him. His life followed their strange and unchanging rhythm. The first unpredictable and overwhelming shock of a sudden and apparently harmless but in reality implacably persistent thought would bring the normal flow of ideas and images to a dead halt, like a piece of grit stopping delicate machinery. Then his whole being would be attentive and absorbed, like a man staring stupidly at a corner of a wall, afraid to look away before he has remembered the word he is looking for. Finally, deliverance would come in the form of a fit of rage, the savage easing of his humiliated soul.

Once he had calmed down again, he would tell himself that such events were merely peripheral and insignificant. In fact the simplicity, regularity, and indeed the willed and deliberate monotony of his everyday life supported the illusion that disorders of that kind were no more than the aftereffects or final symptoms of a long-standing condition. They were, however, his life itself relentlessly following its course, seeking its direction and outlet like an underground stream. The meditation begun in his period of anguish and then abruptly broken off had been banished from the high ground of his inner life but not defeated. It had continued in darkness, pushed down deep into the life of the senses, suddenly reappearing as if every other roundabout path had been closed to it, tracing its unseen yet painful way along his skin, following the mysterious networks of marrow and nerves, finally taking the will by surprise and breaking through into the conscious mind.

Once again the same stupid stubbornness kept him looking at

the down-and-out, whose eyes he could not see, as if he were waiting for some decisive response from the wretch. The old man, unnerved by his silence, drew back carefully into his refuge, pushing his hands deep into his trouser pockets and holding his breath, thinking philosophically to himself that the Father was mad. Cénabre, however, was so close to him that he could hear his heart beating. Suddenly he reached out, felt the cloth of his sleeve, stiff with grime, took hold of it, and gently, slowly, gradually pulled the old man out of his hiding place and looked at him again with increased curiosity. The old body weighed no more than a sack of feathers, and he could feel the skin sliding freely over the bones. His eyes, which the priest could now see, were both mocking and fearful, and they looked strangely naive and even childish, seeming to beg humbly for forgiveness. At the same time, his legs twitched comically in an impotent gesture of self-defense, as if they too wanted to be part of the great joke. "I give up, Father. I'm not playing anymore," the bag of skin and bones said with a frightful laugh.

Cénabre's motionless features turned scarlet with what might have been shame, anger, or, most probably, disappointment. He had already caught himself out in the kind of semilucid frenzy in which his words, actions, and even intentions seemed to have a double meaning, like those texts whose apparent banality hides a higher, secret meaning known only to initiates. His brief spell of madness would always clear up too soon, brushing against the absurd without entering into it and leaving only a vague, confused, and utterly enigmatic memory. This time too, reason, temporarily failing and, as it were, taken unawares, tried to pick up the threads again and build up its reassuring hypothesis like a spider weaving a web around a suspect prey. What could be more natural or understandable than a beggar disturbing his meditation and himself giving way to impatience or even unintentional cruelty? So spoke an inner yet apparently alien voice, which he despised as he heard its all-too-familiar insincere tone telling him that such distractions are far from rare, and all dreamers know them well. He did not believe it or even pretend to. He still did not have the courage to reformulate the pathetic lie that a different experience would no doubt soon demolish. What did he want from the ridiculous old man? What was he expecting from him? He had no idea at all and knew only that he had drawn the old puppet from the shadows as he would have liked to drag out from his own heart the living anguish that he could feel was slowly killing him, and that he was now looking at him as greedily as he would have looked at his own conscience. And, as with that conscience, he would have liked to cast it out, come back to it, trample on it and destroy it . . . the whole incident was over in a moment. He let go of the old man.

"Hell!" the old wreck said. "Hey, I've never come across a grip like that before."

He gave a tiny snort of frightened laughter, a child in his fifties, humbly turning to look at Cénabre, who found the appeal in his eyes intolerable. He turned away and moved off, slowly enough that his companion, whose footsteps he could hear behind him, at first hesitant and then firmer, could catch up. Suddenly a shadow was dancing comically before him on the asphalt of the pavement.

"No nonsense, and give me my ten sous!" it called in a resolutely brave voice. "Just ten sous, Father, and away I go! Ten souls for the big kid who knows what a joke is. Then don't you worry, I'll be off. I'll keep my own company."

"No, come with me," Cénabre answered. "I'd no intention of sending you away without help. As we walk along we might agree on some way of doing something useful for you. I'm expected somewhere myself, my friend."

He was speaking softly, almost smiling at the anxious face gazing up at him. The street they were turning into ran obliquely down to the Seine. The only person they met on it was a sleepy policeman, but the sight of him filled the old clown with bitterness. As he limped and puffed along, dragging one leg, he was already confiding in his companion, explaining his character, lining up enormous half-sophisticated, half-naive lies punctuated with phrases like "You're the kind who can understand," "I'll tell you straight out, no kidding," and "No need for smooth talk with you." Above all, he blamed his family for having been cruel enough to call him Ambroise, which had caused all his misfortunes. "A rotten name, father, a swine's name, a damned ridiculous name, fit for a jerk whose wife's cheating on him. You can't even be respected with a name like that. At school they called me Framboise, and the teacher couldn't stand me, and I lost my mother and father. Same old story at work. In the markets you couldn't mention me without them all falling down laughing. My father was a good worker, but he didn't have any judgment. My mother was bright but a bit of a slut. One day she ran off with a high-up cop, and to get rid of her he got her run in by the vice squad. A real cow."

He found it hard to keep up, as Cénabre was striding out without answering or even turning round to look at him. "God, I thought I was stringing him along, but the asshole's making me sweat," the poor devil thought, bravely trying to work off his sciatica without groaning. "Damned fish-face!" Nothing, however, would have induced him to let go without getting it all off his chest, no doubt from an obscure desire to do a good job, a sort of professional conscience bequeathed to him in his destitution by his unknown ancestors, tenacious peasants from the Beauce, the yokels that as a fully fledged con-man he thought he despised.

It would be hard to say what ancient servile instinct or sinister insight enabled him to guess what the grave priest, whose serious eyes he could scarcely meet, was secretly asking for and expecting from him, the very thing a beggar usually hides from his customers, his dreary stock in trade. He had in fact very quickly moved away from his usual repertoire of touching stories and was now holding forth, apparently delighting in demeaning himself with an obscure coquetry and a mendacious cynicism that would have broken the hardest heart. To encourage himself between one outburst of his terrible hilarity and the next, he told himself that the Father was laughing "deep down." He went on with his foolery, sleepless, weary, imprisoned in the part he was playing, like an exhausted whore falling back on her stock of perversions. "He's tight-fisted," he was thinking, "and if I rub him up the wrong way, I've had it. There's guys like that. I've known a few."

Cénabre was also letting him see that even if he was not exactly pleased, at least some interest had been aroused, and he encouraged him from time to time with a short reply or a vague, fleeting smile, which delighted the poor wretch. They were walking rather more slowly now down the quays toward the distant PLM station and could see its lighted clock face like an enormous eye in the fog. The hands were already past midnight, and the priest had not yet decided to break off completely with his strange companion. The dreadful chattering formed a not uncongenial background to his own meditation, and he would gladly have taken that congeniality for pity, although he had never in his life been less capable of such an emotion. But the severe self-discipline he had been practicing for so long had just been relaxed without his knowledge, and he was savoring what tortured pride seeks greedily—a sweet and fleeting renewal of shame. For humility, contrary to what fools believe, is by no means a purely heavenly good made for ideally noble men. Fallen nature, for which it is an object of hatred, can never dry up its wellspring in the deepest parts of our nature without condemning itself to sterility. It is like those elements of living matter of which only imperceptible traces can sometimes be discovered by analysis. No sooner does it seem to have dried up than it is there again, unexpected and unrecognizable, like a thin trickle of water breaking through the earth and making a muddy puddle for the poor wretch dying of thirst to thrust his mouth in. Perfect and absolute remorse would bring hell into man's heart and consume him on the spot.

Father Cénabre savored and gently abandoned himself to a certain kind of painless shame. He took unreserved pleasure in it, rejoicing in his momentary escape from the silent and tragic confrontation of his perpetual inner conversation with himself. Now, for the first time for many years, he had broken his self-imposed, severe, relentless external discipline. He was barely aware of, and hardly surprised by, his boldness. He was no longer even seeking out dark streets, but drawing his companion out into the light as if he were meeting some challenge, and it was now the poor wretch who was keeping himself out of sight as best he could, hugging walls, stifling his laughter, and wanting the whole adventure to come to an end, even if it meant losing the possibility of a full belly, a hope that was gradually deserting him. That night, however, it would have been unwise to contemplate upsetting Cénabre or playing on his feelings.

It reminded him so powerfully of another night that had been pushed into the depths of his memory but could not be forgotten, bringing back the memory of it so vividly that the two scenes were almost juxtaposed, with the present exactly covering but forever distinct from the past, like those subtle drawings that, by an imperceptible shift of lines or their relationship, make a tragic or comic version of the same face. Looking round over his shoulder at his companion, Cénabre thought of Father Chevance and his sad eyes, saw him rolling on the ground and picking up his worn out neck bands. The same mad laughter rumbled in his throat.

Imperceptibly, the blind curiosity that had initially drawn him into his strange adventure was giving way to another much deeper feeling that was unmistakably and irresistibly pulling him along. He was coming near to achieving a new goal, exacting his revenge, it seemed to him, on an innocent victim for having believed or hoped against his own better judgement that he was still the same man. He had already told himself a thousand times that all he had lost was God, therefore nothing. But, he knew, his life had been based on the hypothesis that there was a God, which had given it its point and purpose. It was clear to him that God was indispensable for his habits, his work, and his priesthood, that he would go on as if He existed, and that it was a once-and-for-all decision. He had taken it, and, to his great astonishment, the attitude he had adopted so simply and kept so easily and which neither his reason nor his sensibility had balked at had gone hand in hand with an inexplicable inner change, a slow and gradual transformation of the secret powers of his being. He was emptied of all belief, free of his whole past, without hope or remorse, at one of those special times in this earthly life when men find perhaps not rest but at least stillness because they have nothing else to lose and all their gains can be foreseen and anticipated to the last penny. Nevertheless, like a sailor sensing in the dark the strength of a current or the rising of a breeze from the tightening of the anchor chains, he still felt, or at least became aware of, an undefinable shift or displacement inside himself as a result of the strange tension in his will. God was not absent for him, for he was sure that he had not lost his faith, which had suddenly left him. What was it then?

Anyone else would no doubt have seen a walk with a tramp after midnight through an already deserted district of Paris as being of little importance. Most priests have been accosted and followed many times. Behind his arrogance, however, Cénabre had always been terrified rather than repelled by badly dressed people, a feeling common to many learned men, who see in every poor devil an animal of an alien species, always ready to burn down libraries, tear up notes, and kick laboratories to pieces with studded boots. In his mind, the studious lower-middle-class prejudice was accompanied by lasting hostility toward a degraded herd from which he felt he had only emerged by a miracle of intelligence and will and could never approach without an infantile fear in which all the humiliations of his deprived childhood were lived out again and he had a vague dread of being suddenly recognized and called by his name. In the greatest people, of course, pride is as disturbingly naive as that.

The man who at the age of twelve had begged to be allowed to spend his holidays in the seminary and invented ingenious and hugely edifying lies to get permission to do so, simply because he hated his home and once back inside it could never catch the lowly and unforgettable smell of rough corduroy and hot bacon fat without blushing with shame, had never really known poor people. He had moved on from the junior to the senior seminary and thence to the Sorbonne, escaping military service, and lived the life of a poor and hard-working student, intimidated by his rich contemporaries and despising the others (but carefully hiding his likes and dislikes and associating only with the most industrious and successful of his companions, whose rise he had prudently followed), respected if not liked, until his first major achievements had rallied the waverers. Every step forward had been a break with the past, his family (now reduced to a very few cousins whose names he had forgotten), his region (which he had never crossed, even by rail, without a great deal of painful tension), and the diocese he had fled, whose old bishop was one of his most dangerous critics. More deeply immersed in his austere and industrious life with every passing day, he had tried very hard not to arouse envy, always showing the same prudence and the very assured taste evident in the way he surrounded himself with almost invisible luxury in the shape of rare furniture and admirable pieces appreciated by a few cultivated friends and hardly noticed by anyone else. Every action had so far had something rather coarsely but patiently, purposefully, and methodically cunning about it, which had eventually overcome or at least worn out all distrust. The only weak points in his extremely clever defensive system had for many years been the deliberate ambiguity and the ever-deepening indifference to God, which he had finally dared to call by its proper name. He knew now what he was: a priest without faith. He was certain, and there was to be no further debate. A hypocrite is first and foremost an unfortunate person who rashly admits his own attitude toward others before he has the courage to define himself precisely, for he hates seeing himself as he is: he seeks sincerity, sacrificing real advantages to the aim he can never achieve, and eventually deceives himself. In order to lie to a useful purpose, effectively and completely safely, we must know our lie and strive to love it.

And so Cénabre had savagely ripped out that fallen, long-condemned, and now dead part of himself. His implacable and remorseless good sense, too strong to be completely destroyed by any anguish, had led him to take the experiment as far as possible and complete it in one go. He had often reflected on the plight of even the most illustrious of those renegades who finish up engaged in a monotonous argument they can never quite extricate themselves from and seem to be insulting the God they have offended, dragging Him along with them like a fellow criminal shackled to them. Consequently, he had vowed to remain inscrutable to the end, to death itself. He thought, not without some justification, that where such tortured and anxious nihilists had made their greatest mistake was in having freed only their intellects, leaving belief to go on surviving and festering in the most hidden and least accessible parts of their sensibility. Such a deep and hidden contradiction is all the more destructive because they cannot form a clear idea of it, or indeed express it, except in terms of stammering, repeated, pointless, and childish expressions of hatred. They no longer have any part in a faith that still holds them in abject and slavering thrall. It matters little that they think they have destroyed it. In Cénabre's scornful view they were still "tied to a corpse," for he liked to think that he would never have anything in common with such wretched pariahs, and in order to escape from himself to some degree he would take courage from the thought that in the Church there was no doubt a great number of people like him — watchful, strong, unbending, and capable of keeping a secret.

At that point, his pride suffered its worst blow, for strangely and unbelievably, the ambiguity came back, subtler and more perfidious than ever. In vain he tried to convince himself by all kinds of irreproachable arguments that having resolutely given up a certain now pointless interior discipline, both his self-interest and his dignity insisted that he should at least order his external life in terms of it. The constraint that had previously seemed to him so slight and so perfectly in line with his love of order, esteem, and work was now irksome, and he tried to escape it unobserved, at first by those apparently absentminded but in fact deliberate lapses that are, however, always noticed by servants or secretaries. Father Cénabre let his beard grow, neglected his naturally fine hands, and prolonged his meals and the nap he took after them. He sometimes dropped fully clothed onto his bed, which in the evening his housekeeper was astonished to find in disorder with the dark red counterpane smeared with mud and marked by his heavy shoes. "My master," she would confide to her friends in her Limousin accent and choice of words, "my master's getting dirty. Such a care he used to take of himself, too!"

What, he would wonder, was the point, not daring to admit to himself that the ominous phrase that lies behind every act of self-abandonment only half expressed the total transformation he had undergone. The common people say, in their own way of speaking, that someone who has given up struggling against the sickness unto death is "letting himself go" or "forgetting himself." Cénabre, however, was not *forgetting* but rather deliberately *deserting* himself, or at least gradually moving away from the image he had so patiently created. He was trying out, still with timidity, some confused pleasure and, with more curiosity than disgust, the disorder he had once thought he hated, like a chaste young girl hesitating on the brink of an impure thought before yielding completely to it . . . a day of idleness left him anxious, irritated with himself or contorted with scorn, filled with an absurd desire for the same painful relaxation the following day. He might have noticed other, stranger symptoms. For example, certain rare books that he had loved above all else had suddenly and inexplicably become hateful, as if their luxurious and splendid covers and white margins and the attractive smell of neat and untouched paper had somehow challenged him. One evening he had stupidly put his greasy thumb on some immaculate Holland endpapers, like someone squashing a harmless insect. Then, trembling with shame and looking like a murderer, he had rushed to throw the soiled book into the stove.

Those who — with admirable modesty — call themselves psychiatrists would no doubt have seen his actions as the preliminary signs of the great sexual upheaval we are threatened with in our fifties and would have recommended, in the time-honored way, a journey to Italy. In Cénabre's case, however, no other journey save that to the land from whose bourn no traveler returns would have brought him silence and peace. He moved around in a kind of confused murmur that even sleep could not quite still. It was now too familiar to worry him seriously, although it did help to keep him in a state of perpetual irritation, producing sudden outbursts of violence that he brought under control with enormous effort, albeit always too late. Such explosions of feeling would quiet the tireless murmuring for a moment, but it would begin again softly and carefully, like a well-rehearsed choir seeing the conductor raise his baton . . . and yet murmur is hardly the right word to describe something that the human ear could not detect.

In attempting to trace the stages of a slow, oblique fall and the gradual deterioration of a psyche, there is a risk of seeming to attach too much importance to certain material signs the patient is unaware of or which, at least, trouble him only to a certain extent. At that time Cénabre was quite incapable of paying any real attention to such varied episodes, which normally combined to form a single profound but bearable unease he found easier to tolerate as his resistance diminished. It is hard to accept that one has radically changed when the more or less unaffected will still controls the muscles and determines attitudes and actions. There was, however, another fateful trap, undetectable to even the keenest insight, since it was set in the most inaccessible and delicate area of his being, at the very roots of his life. In fact he was not changing but seemed rather to be going back to the past, to his very beginnings. It was not a new man he was discovering, but the old one. He was gradually rediscovering himself. Such had been the unexpected, unforeseeable, and eerie consequence of his total and definitive acceptance of falsehood. The powerful image, the artificial and fraudulent character that everyone, himself included, took to be the true, living man, was gradually disintegrating and coming away from him in shreds. It was as if the whole painstaking and industriously assembled creation was collapsing as it reached perfection, as if the kind of psychic force animating it so far had been precisely the trace of doubt, or at least hesitation, the hateful ambiguity he had dared to face and destroy. Just as during an evening of rioting we see forgotten men, disgorged from cellars and prisons, pouring out onto the streets, dazzled by the light, carefully, furtively, silently hurrying toward the clamor and the fires, so too Father Cénabre could have recognized and named, one by one, the sea of faces from his childhood. Pride and ambition had taken possession of this most fated of souls at too early an age, and his indomitable will had thrust the ghosts back into the shadows rather than overcome them. Every nook and cranny was swarming with ferocious embryonic life — thoughts, desires, barely developed longings — reduced to their basic elements, to the sleeping but living germ. The whole monstrous company, suddenly torn from the limbo of memory, was staggering to the edge of consciousness, as difficult to make out and name as the ageless and sexless fifty-year-old dwarfs that obsess haunted painters.

A man seeing brutal adolescence returning when he is mature or elderly at least knows the enemy he is dealing with and how strong it is. For the wretched priest, however, there was nothing for him to wrestle to the ground. Indeed, he had never previously been tempted, or the temptation had been as vague and indeterminate as the curiosity he had experienced as a child. His flesh, that highly sensitive, very accessible, and most directly affected part of us, which has such profound reactions that if our reason had the courage to make use of them they would put us on guard against all the most complex and treacherous works of evil, remained cold and indifferent. Even more than the hard-working life he led, his enormous pride had long stunned and numbed his sensuality. But it was waking now, although the first sign of it was just as enigmatic and obscure. Whereas in the past his boast had always been that he had never failed to exercise his higher faculties and was always arguing and meditating, even during his solitary walks, he now caught himself greedily or slyly letting his eyes rest on external things he had formerly despised. Sometimes, with a kind of nostalgia, he would seek out an undefinable tenderness, perhaps in the cheerful jostle of a working-class area at midday, with its close, rough contact and the ebb and flow of its coarse and fraternal life. Momentarily, he would want to lose himself in it, and then he would confront and challenge it with somber delight, for he had always dreaded crowds and noise, and having to overcome this absurd fear was a major element in his fickle pleasure. A distrustful look from a face on the street, an insult from a cheap eating place heard without turning a hair, a whore laughing or timidly accosting someone, all the hundreds of petty incidents of street life were extraordinarily exciting. Never was he more aware of his solitude, never did he desire more keenly to escape from it, to break the magic circle whatever the cost, to surrender completely, body and soul, than on such occasions. They were like a wind buffeting him full force, knocking every breath out of his body and making his knees sag. He wanted to shout out to those happy people, or to those whom he naively saw as such: "Accept me! Free me, or at least insult me! . . . " For every liar has felt the need to provoke abuse that is directed not at him but at what he seems to be, at the appearance he is now enslaved to, his mask.

"No, monsieur, I've had enough," the old wreck said. "It's mainly because of my pulled nerve. It's like a hot wire. You like a laugh, and I'm not against it, but I've got to say, no kidding, it's not very Christian to run me around like a thoroughbred with a leg like mine. I know what you're up to. We're walking around for a laugh, for something to tell your pals about for a joke. I can't go any further, boss."

His voice was trembling pitifully with fatigue rather than anger. Leaning on a wall, standing on one leg with his bad one folded under him like some malevolent bird, totally swallowed up in Cénabre's shadow, he looked at the priest humbly.

"You're mad, my friend," Cénabre replied roughly. "I never laugh at the poor. And I acted without thinking. You should have stopped me sooner, that's all."

"No offense meant," the man said. "Got to be honest, you always answered me nicely. Yes, I know what it's all about. A priest's educated, polite, he knows the trouble you go to. I'd like to have been a bit more amusing, but my heart's not really in it. Just my rotten luck. Usually there's nobody funnier than me. People only need to see my mug under a gaslight to come running up. Hey, last night, rue Richer, opposite the Folies-Bergère, I got two Yanks, absolutely pickled they were . . . "

"Shut up!" shouted Cénabre. "You're not to think that . . . "

He quickly pulled himself together, simply adding:

"My friend, I'm sorry you think I could be so cruel. I was wrong and stupid to tire you unnecessarily and to let you go on with your absurd comedy as if I was taken in by it or playing a part in it."

"Taken in? Playing a part?" the old wretch repeated, grinning idiotically. "You've got a real job there! As if you can tell!"

"Shut up, will you!" Cénabre cried, beside himself. "If you keep on, you won't get a sou, understand? For over three quarters of an hour now I've been trying to get a straightforward, sensible word out of you and all you've done is tell me lies that wouldn't take a child in or terrible jokes. I know what I wanted to know."

He pulled out his wallet and took out a hundred-franc note, crumpling it between his fingertips.

"I've no change . . . " the old rogue said, as incorrigible as ever.

He seemed to be trying to catch his joke in the air, as if it were a fly. When he saw the priest replace the note with a mere ten-franc one, however, he stared hard at him.

Yet it was only the kind of look a beggar might give after a long wait, cynical but without any cunning. Despite that, Céna-bre's heart jumped, not from fear but from what comes before it, rather like the sound of a gong in the middle of the night.

"There's nothing for you," he cried. "I'm giving you nothing." For the second time he turned his back on him. He almost ran as far as the rue de la Harpe, rushing into the shadows like a madman. The night was so mild that a bird in a chestnut tree behind a wall had woken up and was producing something like a song. The road was already getting rather steep, forcing the priest to slow down. He lowered his head a little. At the level of the rue de Luynes his harmless enemy was hurrying jerkily along, and then, no doubt in real despair, he broke into a sort of ex-hausted gallop.

With very little effort, Cénabre could have escaped, but he slowed down, merely taking care, as he had done before, not to let his pursuer catch up with him too quickly. His anger was still just as powerful, but mixed with it he could feel the frustration in his relentless curiosity. For a moment the hideous vagabond was the focus around which the scattered images of his anguish had come together and crystallized. Even more mysteriously, he seemed to have recognized one or two of his most secret and unformulated thoughts in the ignominious secrets he had heard. He felt eased by the torrent of filth, as if he himself had spewed it out. He wanted it to go on flowing, taking with it other admissions, other lies, hitherto inaccessible in the murky depths of his own mind. Although he could not admit it and was even per-haps unaware of it, he felt a shameful pleasure in his contact with the abject life that had just been laid bare before him. He had handled and weighed it with all the experience and confidence of a connoisseur and sensed the motives, intentions, and crude malice behind the idiotic bragging and boasting. He wanted it again.

From the way the old man's feet were dragging on the pavement, he could tell how exhausted he was and hear his furious, persistent panting. It suddenly stopped and, looking around, he saw the grotesque silhouette down on the pavement, motionless in a patch of shadow. Softly, he walked slowly back toward it.

"That's what you get for playing the fool," he said. "I'd like the lesson to be of some use to you, at least. All it will have cost you is a wasted bit of running around. That's not too high a price to pay for the advice to chatter less, be in less of a hurry to grab, and to be more polite . . . are you really so short of breath?"

"Yes, boss, I am," the rogue said, without a trace of resentment. "But my chest's OK," he said, tapping his skinny torso, "it's my nerve, always my nerve. Good God, the blasted thing gets right to my heart. Oh thanks, boss."

He took the hundred-franc note from Cénabre's hand and slipped it under his shirt next to his skin. Then he clicked his heels, gave a military salute, and called out "Atten . . . shun."

"I owed you something like that," the priest said. "Now we're calling it quits. You won't get another sou out of me, for any reason whatsoever, so don't forget it. There's no point accosting me from now on, because if you do I'll hand you straight over to the first policeman I see. Understood?"

"I've been around. I know what to expect," replied the old clown resignedly, with a grimace that said more than any words could.

"One last word," Cénabre went on, "just one. For once in your life, try to reply honestly and truthfully. Why do you play this idiotic game? Why degrade yourself like this?"

"I don't degrade myself. I just go through my little act."

"That's enough of that rubbish! Go through it all again tomorrow with someone else if you want. That's all the same to me. But just try to take an honest look at yourself for one minute, if you can. Look at me. We've spent over an hour together, I've listened to you patiently and even asked you a question now and again. You've said nothing, absolutely nothing, that could make anyone feel sorry for your wretched life. All you try to do is disgust people. You know I'm right."

"I know what's going on," was the reply after a moment's silence. "You're going to take my hundred smackers back."

"No. I'd even give you another hundred to get something out of you that wasn't completely abject."

"Abject, object, project," replied the fool with a giggle that would have discouraged anyone but the angry priest, who had been dragged willy-nilly into seeking his soul like someone hunting down an enemy but hoping never to find it, wanting desperately to be faced with no more than the bundle of rags, the corpse.

"What you deserve," he said, "is a good thump."

"P'raps," was the softly spoken reply. "How could I know what you wanted from me? You're a difficult customer. Some of 'em are OK, some aren't. My job's to keep you happy, that's all. But I ask you, can I force myself to be something I'm not? That's how I was born, and apart from it I'm no trouble at all, dead easygoing. I've always made people laugh, that's how I am. One night in Montmartre they poured my fifth of rum down my throat—one, two—and they'd finished by the time they'd counted up to six. Then I walked around the table on my hands with my legs in the air and a saucer in my mouth to hold what I collected. It's one of my tricks. Trouble is, I wasn't very well-fed at the time. As empty as my pocket and as hollow as a Louvre balloon. I'd've popped if they'd walked on me, my guts were like a fish's, honest. So I nearly died. Course, obviously, they're not good things to do. But nobody's ever seen old Framboise back out, there or anywhere else. I'm a nice quiet guy. Pimps, females, police, none of 'em mean much to me. I'm used to nice people and polite ways, I can express myself well. I like to do as I'm told. That's how it is. I get paid and that's that. Suppose somebody suggests a hundred kicks up my ass, hundred sous a go, I swallow my pride and let 'em get on with it. Hey, early one morning last summer, near the Porte Dauphine, in the middle of the woods, I was a real Aunt Sally for a guy and his two dolls. Tennis balls, they said. Wham, bam, in my face. God! You'd of laughed! My eyes were swollen up like big apples, my nose was bleeding, everything was bleeding. 'That's enough!' the guy shouted. Drunk as a skunk, he was. 'More, more!' the dolls was shouting . . . 'Give him fifty smackers . . . a hundred!' One of them — ooh what a little darlin'! all pink and lovely . . . melt in your mouth, she would, nice and young, curly hair, a kid, you know! She came over and wiped my face with her little silk hanky and then, wham, bam, all over again! She was throwing the hardest, and her aim was best. Said I reminded her of her dear departed dad when he was drunk after a bender with his pals. But what was really funny . . . "

"You're lying," said Cénabre in a slow, deep voice. "I could tell you the precise moment you started again. I've got your lies sized up, do you hear? I can see it in your grubby little heart, you fool. Keep your disgusting stories for someone else. Wait! I haven't finished with you yet. If there's still anything in there (he rammed his strong finger so hard into the hollow of the still-panting chest that the wretch could not help moaning) I'll drag it out."

He could feel the feeble, defenseless body trembling and felt no pity. He stared into and held the pale, imploring eyes, like those of a dog that does not know why it has been beaten and wants only to obey. The old drunkard's stupidity and appalling artlessness no longer struck him. All he was aware of was the degradation, the real and living form of an abjectness he had never known and barely guessed at or suspected and had finally discovered, whose imposing presence now filled him with dread. Faced with such a sight, his scholarly calculations, ingenious hypotheses, the painstaking work on the minutely dissected specimens of which he was so proud seemed irredeemably trivial. The same impatience, the same greed for knowledge, for reaching and possessing the most inaccessible part of the soul, the same passion that had so often driven him when, at the very end of his admirable deductions, he was looking at his men and women saints and finding no answer to his questions, unable either to condemn or to justify them, was now afflicting him once again. This time, however, the prey he had so long pursued and coveted was no longer outside him and outside his reach. He saw it as being somehow within the depths of his own psyche, and it fascinated him like a reflection in dark water.

"Oh, ouch, that's enough, that's enough. Suppose I did lie, all the same, the Aunt Sally's a real good story, no kidding, isn't it? When I've nothing to do, when I'm not dreaming something up, I tell it to myself, and it really amuses me. I'm a poor harmless bastard, there's no malice in me. What I do, I'll tell you again, is just what I'm told. Go to it, Framboise. With rich people, boss, you've got to be obliging. Can I split myself in two to give you a laugh, eh?"

He began to moan, sighing deeply and hiccupping like a child, and at the same time cautiously feeling the precious note under his shirt.

"Never mind making faces," said Cénabre. "You know quite well what I want. Answer my questions honestly. The first one is, why the tears?"

"Trouble is . . . trouble is . . . " the old man finally sobbed.

"Trouble is, oh God Almighty, trouble is . . . I can't — oh what a damned fool I am . . . I can't . . . any longer."

"You can't what?"

"I can feel the lies coming on," he said in his own inimitable way. "They come out on their own. It's like a spring, I can't hold it back. You could beat me up or take my hundred smackers back and I'd still tell you the same thing. I'm a dead loss, chief, a poor old sod. God's truth, you wouldn't find anybody else like me anywhere in Paris. Nobody."

He looked as if he were asking the whole of the huge city to bear him out, and at that moment his pale eyes, which could not meet Cénabre's, were probably filled with vistas of stone, of the innumerable streets where he had lost all he had, even his truth and his name.

"I'm going to try to help you," the priest said, his voice nevertheless trembling slightly. "Well, my friend, you were young once, a child, weren't you?"

"Course," was the reply, in a dreadful voice. The man's head was thrust forward, his shoulders hunched, and he seemed to be thinking deeply.

"Well," the priest went on relentlessly, "you haven't always slept on the pavement and eaten out of dustbins or been used at night as a plaything for drunken women, have you?"

"Somebody once pointed that out to me, one day," the down-and-out finally said, after a long silence. While he was looking as if he were struggling to collect his memories, his filthy monkey-like hand had already moved the banknote from under his shirt and pushed it down into his boots so quickly and expertly that Cénabre sensed rather than saw what he was doing. For a moment, he went on holding the boot indifferently and absent-mindedly with the tips of his fingers. The rustling noise the paper made was barely audible.

"You've just taken a totally unnecessary precaution," Cénabre said calmly. "I never take back anything I've given away. But listen: perhaps I'll give you another one, if you agree to speak like a man and not an animal."

"Fair enough," said the man, a kind of unexpected and frightening blush appearing on his forehead and cheeks and then fading away. He started moaning once again, softly at first but after a time increasingly loudly, and suddenly so noisily that Cénabre had to thump his shoulder roughly to make him stop. A convulsive shudder ran through his old body, but it was no doubt not quite involuntary, since it was accompanied by a grimace of cunning as much as of pain or fear.

"I'm undernourished," he moaned. "That's not work for an underfed man. Questions like that! . . . what on earth do you want me to tell you about my younger days? I'd scare myself to death trying to find you a story like that in a few shakes of a lamb's tail . . . God damn me! First things first, then. My late lamented mother was a . . . "

"The lies are about to start again," Cénabre said calmly.

"May I be . . . " the old wreck began, raising his hand as if to swear an oath. He did not finish however, and a look of genuine surprise lit up his features. His arm fell.

"It's possible," he went on. "I'll have to think about it . . . " He sniffed again loudly, spat out his last tears and began again, as if an enormous weight had been lifted from his shoulders.

"I was wrong to cry, I'm too sensitive. Anything that's outside my line of patter really upsets me. You understand, boss?"

He sighed again, a sigh of inexpressible relief.

"I've seen jokers, believe me, but you, oh you, my God. You seem to have ripped it all out of me. I'm a different man, like a new one."

"What's all that nonsense?" Cénabre demanded. "Ripped it out? What do you mean?"

"That story about my mother," the tramp began, with a huge grin. "It's all nonsense. I don't really know if she was a whore or not. She's dead. Died while I was still sucking my thumb. Only I've told the same pack of lies hundreds of times. It's all part of my bloody rotten patter. What's true, what's lies, you see, boss, I mix it all up. Even a professor couldn't get to the bottom of it. But you, oh you, you've pulled it all out like a back tooth."

He was quiet for a moment, then licked his lips greedily and tried to understand as he had probably never tried before.

"I think you're no more a priest than I am. Priests are all peasants."

"Just another minute," Cénabre asked. "You're not telling me you've forgotten so much of the past that you can no longer tell what's true and what's false about it. Oh yes, you certainly understand what I'm telling you, don't you?"

"Oh God, yes, of course," was the vague reply.

His face had also immediately taken on its usual stupid and malicious expression and he was pulling gently at Cénabre's sleeve, to get himself away.

"Answer me," the priest repeated, "slowly and politely. I've no intention of harming you. If your answers are satisfactory and completely frank, as if you were talking to a friend, I won't stop there. I'll look after you, you see. You'll have food and drink and a bed not once, or twice, but every day."

"Some hope!" the old clown said.

Nevertheless, his hands were trembling as he stroked his forehead and the nape of his neck. The tension in his puckered face that seemed to draw the network of wrinkles together at the base of his nose slowly faded. It was very probably the first time for years that his dim features had reflected such a concern. He seemed to be hesitating on the brink of his squalid past and then to slip straight down into it. Cénabre had the impression of smooth, dark, leaden water closing over the scrawny, feather-light carcass.

"I'll explain it all," the wretch was saying. "You must think I'm a real fool. I'm not just being awkward. It's my nature to be pretty smart, but I'm starving, that's the trouble. I've got a belly full of air and my guts are made of tissue-paper . . . but as far as memory goes, I can match anybody. But I've knocked about such a lot, all over the place. I'm a bit like my old jacket, I've changed color a bit. And . . . "

"How old are you?" Cénabre interjected.

"Fifty-eight. It's on my certificate."

The enormity of the figure seemed to have suddenly amazed him. He looked with a kind of fear in his eyes at his ten out-stretched fingers and then, shaking his head gravely, uttered a barely comprehensible phrase:

"No offense, but you're a real bastard . . . I hadn't thought."

"Can you read?" the priest asked brusquely.

The old man hesitated.

"Sometimes," he prudently answered after a time. "So-so. Don't get much opportunity."

Cénabre shrugged.

"Come on! Either you can or you can't. Stop waffling. And if you *can* read, you've been to school. You've been to school, you've been a child like any other. There aren't any savages in Paris!"

"Savages! That's a good 'un!"

He staggered away a little with his hands in his pockets once again, his head bowed, his back bent and shoulders thrust for-ward, strikingly thin, a shadow without substance, taking the first step toward a mysterious past just as for so many years he had moved along streets without beginning or end, full of the pitfalls of the city of underground noises.

"I know what it is," he went on ominously. "I'm not completely stupid. You're the kind who wants to steal my act. What the hell does it matter to you whether I've been young or not? And damn it, you'll get it. I can't look after myself, I'm not a man . . . to tell you the truth of the matter, I . . . I . . . "

He shivered as if an icy blast from the depths hit him, and neither Cénabre nor anyone else was ever to know the truth of the matter.

"School, eh, that was a real cesspit. I got nothing to eat then either, but I was already good at surviving. I'm not boasting, but I like being ill-treated, it's my nature. I don't want to be respected, don't give two farts for it. People make me laugh. Do I respect myself? No way! Supposing I had some self-respect? I could die. And it's not only for not dying, it's for enjoyment, isn't it? Eh? I like it. Eh, boss? All the time at school lads like me, poor little runts, kept out of the way, slipped between your legs like rats. They were all the same, both hands on their little butt because of the kicks, the little bastards. *I* stuck with the big lads, the smart ones, the jokers. With lads like that, there's always something to be gained, you can always get something out of it, you've got to know what you're doing and do what they want. I might have got slapped around, but you'd never ever have heard a whimper. They liked it. And then there'd be the good bits — you understand, boss? — a marble from one, a hunk of bread from another, and always another to give you something else. They gave me a girl's name and a nickname I can't repeat, no offense meant. And there was one called Poitrine, Amédée Poitrine, son of a butcher in the rue Haxo, a real smart lad. I used to take messages to the girls' school for him, and he always banged my head against the ground when the kid stood him up. Apart from that, he was as nice as pie. He used to pinch bits of meat from his dad, and I ate them raw, it's more filling. A real wise guy, let me tell you. The kind of lad you'd let walk all over you. Once, would you believe it, he made me drink ink, no kidding. The inside of my mouth was like a drain and my guts were all in knots. The teacher told a few white lies to defend me, so to speak. What am I getting mixed up in? I'm going to tell you about pity as I see it, boss. The only point of it is to slap poor little bastards down, that's what I think."

He spat on the ground in disgust. His strange words echoed in the silence and eventually seemed to fade reluctantly into it. The devouring curiosity and the pitiless, arid desire that had made Cénabre confront the terrible, grotesque man met by chance, now weakened a little, probably not from pity, but certainly from surprise and perhaps from fear, because what he had been listening to for a quarter of an hour, the confidences anyone else would have found ridiculous or detestable, had a more hidden urgent and profound meaning for him. He did not yet recognize anything of his own wretchedness in his ravaged and utterly deprived companion's insuperable misfortune, although the way in which it had suddenly been revealed had caused enormous upheavals in a hitherto calm and sheltered part of his soul. In its own form, his anguish was gradually taking it over, blending with it, extrapolating it endlessly and imposing its own shape and rhythm on it. The old man's last words seemed, however, to have broken the fundamental harmony.

"Well, was he your friend?" he asked quietly.

The tramp leaned his head to one side, raised and lowered his eyebrows twice, and said with a confidential smile: "A friend? Some hope!" and drifted back into his dream.

It was now Cénabre who was following, for he was moving away gradually, dragging his lame leg behind him, unsteady on his legs and stumbling along with no more noise than a shadow. With an immense bitterness the priest watched his wretched prey, flushed out from among thousands, now defenseless and very like any other exhausted animal when victim and killer, both exhausted, are trotting along and panting side by side across an endless plain at nightfall in a slow and solemn pursuit.

"I've never come across anybody like you, boss. I'm tired, boss. Why, why should I be dead beat? Fifty-goddamned-eight. If you look at it right, it's a helluva long time. Fifty-eight rounds at the bar, that's nothing, is it, boss? But they've gone straight to my guts, I've never even felt 'em."

"At least tell me what you know," Cénabre said. "You're right, I'm not like other men. It interests me, very much indeed. And in addition . . . "

For a moment he laid his hand on his companion's thin shoulder and felt it trembling and bending beneath his fingers.

". . . it will ease you, my friend."

"Might," was the reply.

He walked forward again as fearfully as before, sighing deeply with his eyes on the ground, perhaps to go on looking in the dust for one or two of the few shards of the past that had been so strangely destroyed, annihilated, sunk like a boat. Then, discouraged, he stopped.

"It wants to come out," he said, "but it can't."

Cénabre pretended to be surprised.

"To put it plainly, I can't climb back up the slope, it's too hard. I must've slid down on my ass, all in one go. You're laughing? If I'd killed or robbed somebody, I'd remember. That's something big, something you'd notice. But I've never been fit enough to try to be smart. I look for all my chances in the garbage, and as for fiddling, there's a damned snag. I do what's wanted and say what's asked for, I get fiddled about with like a putty doll, I'm always changing. You think I'm telling you a lot of nonsense? I've got nothing, honest. If you've got no strength, you've got to be crafty, let the others have their way with you. Some idiots try to make people feel sorry for them, but it's a rotten ploy, it never brings anything in. I don't feel like sitting around in drafts and pretending to be a simple Holy Joe just to get some old biddy to slip me a coin as she comes out of mass. Poor people, I'll tell you again and again, don't play friendly, they eat each other. You get nothing for nothing. D'you follow me?"

"I'm beginning to," said Cénabre, "but go on. I'll follow you better later on."

"I watch rich people," said the tramp. "I see 'em outside, in the open air. I never go out except at night. That's the only time you can get an idea of what rich people are like. That's when they eat the poor, to my mind."

"Eat the poor?" Cénabre asked.

The old man gave him a distrustful sidelong glance, and then laughed incredulously.

"Sometimes? That's good! And what are you doing, boss? Some people are satisfied with just my patter. But you need the real thing, the man behind it. Who are you? Where d'you come from? What d'you do? No offense, mind. I just want to please you. It's just that I'm not used to it, and it's hard. My God, it pisses me off. I can't manage to come out of my shell. But usually, I'm going to explain . . . "

For a moment his face lit up with a terrible joy.

"It's the first time I've taken to a guy like you. You've scared me. I prefer jokers. Daytimes I sleep by the Observatory and get moving around midnight. I used to move steadily up toward Montmartre, but now it tends to be down towards Concorde or somewhere else, anywhere. I don't plan, I've got a feeling. First I spot my types. Preferably ones with dolls. Even better if they're black! They come out of the dance halls, all nicely warmed up. The hardest thing, boss, is to get 'em hooked. At first glance, I'm not very appetizing. Early in the morning, you see, he's fed up of music, silks, gilt ornaments, smells at a hundred francs a

bottle; all that turns his stomach after a time. But somebody really poor's a tonic, sets him up. He's glad that God's given you
such a rotten hand and that you're taking it so well. It's better to
be disgusting than pitiful, right? And then it's such a surprise.
'Oh, darlin',' the whores say, 'what a dirty little man. He smells
awful. He's disgustin'.' So then's the time: I start my patter. When
I've shown 'em my line, I've got 'em. They're not leaving, they
want more."

"You're always talking about your line or your patter. What
do you mean?" Cénabre asked.

The older man shrugged his shoulders disdainfully.

"It's not an idea, it comes from inside me. I find words, stories, I'm never short, I can see from people's eyes what they
want. Packs of lies, you wouldn't believe how many, lies you'd
refuse to listen to, boss. But when I'm leading 'em on I can't be
too fussy about that. You need some of the old sordid stuff!"

He held out his filthy hand as if to settle some obscure deal.

"That's the job!" he said, and then fell quiet, lost in wonder.

For a moment, Cénabre looked at him with no desire to break
the silence. Despite the mixture of pride and shame in his eyes,
for some moments now the vagabond had been showing signs
of a kind of clumsy, feverish impatience rather like the uneasiness and vague fear of animals faced with an unknown danger or
death. For what was probably the first time, the degraded human
animal, like wreckage rising to the surface before being swallowed up forever, was wondering uncomprehendingly about
himself.

The priest, however, was in no position to insist. He was in
the grip of severe distress and said, articulating each word clearly,
as though speaking to someone deaf or mad, "You'd promised
to tell me . . . "

He was unable to finish. The tramp began to tremble in every limb, and with his face pressed against his tormentor's and his pale eyes dilated with a suffering for which he had no name, he cried:

"What do you want me to tell you? I don't know anything, d'you hear? I was ready for anything, nice and peaceful. Yes sir-ree, I'd have passed away a happy man. Tell you what, I've got right on my side. I've the right to be what I want, and my patter and everything, it's the law. A poor bastard like me, as you see me, hasn't got any story. Why d'you want to give me one, eh? What a horse's ass! In here (he half-opened his jacket, showing his wrinkled skin) it's swarming in here, nothing but lies. How d'you expect me to sort it all out? It's too old, it's all in one lump, it blocks things up, for God's sake . . . fifty-eight!"

He was clinging to Cénabre's soutane with both hands, yelling into his face:

"I ought to get you locked up. D'you hear me?"

The rest of what he was saying was lost in the thick scum on his lips. Epilepsy seemed to be already squeezing the small of his back in a vicelike grip. His pupils dilated even more and then fixed and turned slowly into his head. To his great amazement, the priest could see the man's soul, which he had hunted and finally tracked down, appearing and disappearing as if in deep, eddying water.

The light body fell into his arms, the head leaning on his shoulder and the back resting on the palm of his hand. Just for a moment he could feel the stiffening legs against his calf. The feet were resting on their heels, casting their double but dimin-ishing shadow on the ashen, empty pavement. For a long mo-ment the priest did not dare move and simply listened. The weak and almost childish rattle stopped suddenly, and all he could hear was the faint sound of bubbles of saliva bursting between the clenched teeth . . . two passersby who had been in front of them a minute ago had disappeared, and the street was deserted. Far away, deep in the Jardin des Plantes, an unknown animal uttered a ridiculous cry from time to time. Cénabre looked around one last time, then hoisted the light burden onto his back and went slowly away.

When he got home at three in the morning without having seen Guérou, he found an envelope carefully folded in a sheet of paper on which his cleaning woman had pencilled a message: *Brot to Monsieur by a Door Man at Eight (8) OClock. Ergent.*

First he turned the letter around in his hands. The envelope, one of the kind stuck into the blotting paper holders found in cheap cafés, was sealed with two small squares of gummed paper. The sender's name and address (Pernichon, 48 rue Vaneau, Paris), with the information that it was extremely urgent and for the addressee alone, had been hurriedly written on the back. He shrugged his shoulders and threw the letter onto the table.

He was no longer upset. Indeed, he had not felt so fresh and alert, so eager to examine himself and calculate his chances, for a long time. The meeting that night, with its dreadful chain of harsh and absurd episodes, had had a hugely liberating effect on him. The struggle with the vagrant, the furious, inexplicable, unsparingly frank and radical argument and pitiless refusal to leave any stone unturned now seemed like a victory over himself. Handing over the weightless bundle of rags, from which a childish moaning emerged, to an officer amid laughter in the police station, he had felt a terrible and undreamt of joy. The chief's secretary, who had been kept there by an urgent matter, his eyes swollen with tiredness and boredom, had recognized Cénabre before the priest had introduced himself. He had made a rather unsuccessful attempt to hide his stupor in a flow of commonplaces, deploring the fact that a down-and-out like that, so well known to the entire Paris police force, should have waylaid an eminent man with better things to do. "He's a wreck, sir, a real wreck. We pick him up two days out of three. He really is a problem — lost his papers, no civil status, and you know what all that means . . . your profession, or your ministry, I mean, has its own painful duties, but ours is even harder. And they seem to be taking it on themselves to make it more complicated. It's unbelievable."

Cénabre had not heard him, for he had been closely watching the still-wailing bundle of rags laid on the floor between a bayonet belt and an empty Camembert box, expecting some other sound to come from it, sharper moaning, perhaps, or an intelligible cry of pain. He had watched with half-closed eyes, filled with an overwhelming solicitude. He would have liked to pick the man up and hold him in his strong hands again and question him further, as if, like some frightful joker, the wretch had purposely drawn an impenetrable veil of shame over the rarest, most useful and magical part of their shared secret. At the same time, he had felt that the fear was futile and that there would be no further opportunity, if indeed there ever had been any, to discover it. There would be nothing left but the bitter, detestable, solitary joy of having plumbed the ultimate depths of his own consciousness and violated his soul . . . his final glance at his fantastic companion from the doorway as he was leaving had been not so much a look of hate or pity as one of assuaged desire.

He was reflecting on such matters as he lay stretched out with his heavy shoes resting on a silver lamé cushion and his fingertips just brushing the wool of the carpet. His weariness was very welcome, and he did not feel sleepy as he lay there with his temples throbbing with a slight fever, enjoying the silence and solitude of a return to a familiar security, as if he had been on a long journey. He seemed to be starting a new life and, over a few hours, to have cast off an enormous burden, like a debauchee joyfully gorged with pleasure after a long period of abstinence.

Within reach, in the half-open left-hand drawer of his desk, a suspiciously shaped and very familiar case containing his now harmless Star revolver could be seen between two piles of white paper. What a strange episode it had been. When throwing it away so violently earlier on that evening he had broken one of the pinions, and he had sometimes amused himself by trying to put the delicate springs back with his own clumsy hands. At each movement there was the click of nonfunctioning machinery, the trigger yielding to the pressure of the finger, the breechblock sliding to the end of the groove, and he would finally put the weapon back in its case with a shiver of pleasure. This time, he compressed his lips firmly . . .

Not even the memory of his earlier danger in the same place was strong enough to fool him: the image of death or crime could do nothing to hide the mediocrity of the tiny world in which he had wanted to enclose his life. Now he could defy it and feel in control. He was no longer taken in by *any* setting, and he saw his own, the delights of which he had by no means exhausted, lucidly and wearily. Closing his eyes, he pictured the vagrant alive and wandering within the stark walls, heard him limping across the polished wooden floor, and pressed the wretched burden against his chest once more. The hallucination was so compelling that he spat between his heavy, dirty shoes onto the silk cushion. Then he fell asleep.

The light at the windows suddenly disappeared, then came back with a livid double line that vanished in its turn. Thereupon the layer of gray that had immediately spread out began to move along majestically and extremely slowly, black toward its middle and with a wan light toward its edges. Almost at once, however, blinding spots appeared all over it, and it floated for a second, then began to whirl round furiously and opened up from top to bottom, showing once more the calm window with the same oblique ray passing through it as if suspended in the evening air. Father Chevance gently rubbed his eyes.

"What a nuisance," he said aloud. "What a disability. What's to be done?"

He sat down on the bed, simply because it was the nearest object, and sighed, looking randomly around, his eyes filled with the innocent sadness of a child, so artless as to be very like joy, and on his lips the same impatient pout that could herald either tears or laughter. The door opened suddenly.

"Madame de la Follette," the poor priest said, "I've just had another blackout. It worries me, you know. It is worrying, isn't it?"

The concierge merely shrugged her powerful shoulders.

"Monsieur de la Follette," she replied, "is working late at his office and will be dining out. I've warmed up the green beans and a little sausage. I'd like to bring them up now. It's already half past seven."

Father Chevance blushed furiously.

"I'm a little late," he agreed. "I was miles away. I really am indisposed. And I'd left the window open to hear the Sainte-Eustache clock strike."

"So?"

"Well, Madame de la Follette, I don't quite know how to put it. Towards evening I get a buzzing noise in my ears now. My head's heavy, if you know what I mean. In short, I'm not well, not easy, not in my normal state. It really is a nuisance."

"Whines and moans won't make old bones," said Madame de la Follette. "Fact is, for the last few days you've been looking like a turkey-cock after five in the afternoon."

She stopped, clutching the little whitewood table to her bosom between her huge arms, and looked her interlocutor up and down with an expression of disgust.

"Monsieur de la Follette," she said finally, "feels that the father should bleed himself every fortnight. Otherwise, you've got too much blood for your own good. And that's a shame."

"Oh, but I don't produce a lot of blood," Father Chevance protested. "You can see, can't you, that I eat very little? Perhaps I don't eat enough. But I force myself a lot."

"Eating without pleasure means pains at your leisure," was Madame de la Follette's simple observation as she unfolded the tablecloth. "I never interfere in other people's business. We're all free."

She turned her head, listening.

"Oh, damn the rotten alarm clock. Won't the blasted thing ever shut up!"

She ran into the room next door, returning immediately with a nickel alarm clock in her hand, which she hurled onto the bed.

"It's too much. I just can't stand hearing it any more. It goes right through me. I'll go mad if it keeps on like that. And the stupid thing still says quarter to ten."

"Madame de la Follette," Chevance said severely, "You've put it out of commission. We have to be fair, even to inanimate objects. Do you see that? The workman did his best, Madame de la Follette. He must have put it together with great care, with the greatest care. Neither of us two would do as much. So that means we mustn't despise his work, I assure you. Ah, madame, we're not good for each other, no, not at all. I don't want to upset you, Madame de la Follette, but we should all try to live and die in peace."

"You talk well," the concierge said generously, "but you go about things the wrong way. Monsieur de la Follette doesn't like priests. He's a self-made man. He was going to night school by the time he was fifteen, so naturally he knows more about things than you and me. And I also admire the way he puts up with colds and upsets and everything. Education does a lot, of course. But Monsieur de la Follette hasn't always been what he is today, at least his family hasn't. His great-great-uncle was a colonel or a captain in the days of the Empire. So it's in his bones, it's his nature. Whereas you, if you'll forgive the expression, you just moan all day long. A headache yesterday, blackouts today, it's like the vapors, no sleep, no appetite, and all the rest of it. With all those problems, you're not an easy man to look after! I can't go on. And for one thing, if you're not going to touch the beans, there's no point bringing them up to the fifth floor for you, not with my varicose veins . . ."

"Madame de la Follette, there's a great deal in what you've just said," the priest admitted. "I'm not well . . . I'm not my usual self at all . . ."

"There you go again!"

"Ah, yes, you're right," he said with an apologetic smile. "Let's say no more about it."

"Fine then. You're an open book," the concierge went on scornfully. "You may be just a simple ordinary priest, but when it comes to manners and politeness you're as good as a Jesuit. But you resent things, and I don't like that, to be honest. What are you trying to say? Let's hear it, come on!"

Never, or at least not for a very long time, had the former curé of Costerel-sur-Mer been able to resist such demands. Before replying, he gazed sadly at his shoes.

"In the terms of our little agreement, Madame de la Follette," he declared vigorously, "you were to be responsible for cleaning my footwear every morning . . ."

"Responsible!" she cried, "Responsible! Monsieur Chevance, your dishonesty is shameful! If I'm to clean your shoes, you should leave them outside your door, where you never do put them, either because you've forgotten or to make trouble. When I get there, you're wearing them. Monsieur Chevance, a poor upbringing isn't a sin, but I must point out that I'm not a woman to kneel at somebody's feet to scrape the muck off their shoes. Now, do you want me to bring the beans up or not?"

The poor priest was so taken aback that he had dropped the handkerchief he had been clutching and was looking gravely and attentively at his tormentor.

"It's true," he said at length, "you're quite right. I forget to put them out. Madame de la Follette, I'm afraid that so far I've lived in the world far too simply, and in the end it attracts attention. Really, if a priest is to be beyond reproach, he has to be unnoticed. In Paris the clergy have a reputation for being correctly and even elegantly dressed, but an old country priest has no business having an opinion on such matters. It's better to follow established traditions and customs. I'm not trying to hide the fact that it costs me something. So from now on I shall be shaved twice a week, and that's very expensive. I've often told you, Madame, that I'm expecting my appointment any day now. I shall soon be a parish priest. Perhaps I shall be responsible for a curate. I shall have to honor my little world."

"So you've told me, but I don't believe you," Madame de la Follette answered. "Somebody must have been kidding you. A parish priest in Paris is a different kettle of fish, you know."

"Of course," Chevance replied, "but there aren't enough priests to go round. Things have to move quickly. It's wonderful! And my parish," he said, in a tone of great tenderness, "is one of those tiny ones in the outer suburbs, absolutely new. Just imagine, it hasn't got a name yet! It's so, so poor, just think! It hasn't even got a name."

Without thinking, he crossed his arms as if to hug his treasure to his breast.

"They've obviously been kidding you," the concierge said obstinately. "You can't help thinking you've wangled it nicely. But Monsieur de La Follette is very serious minded and he made the same kind of mistake. He thought he was going to spend last year as the chief clerk in the pawnshop on the rue de Rennes, but nothing ever came of it."

"But Madame de la Follette, I can assure you . . ."

"Assure away, as much as you like. But at your age, people know about life, they use their brains. Well, between you and me, it's better to get our little affairs in order, because getting everything fair and square makes for good friends. If I'd just listened to Monsieur de la Follette, I'd never have rented to a civil servant, particularly a curé. But what's done's done, it's no good harping on it. Everybody thinks I'm a bit rough and ready, but you won't find anybody fairer as far as business's concerned. Asking for what's due to you isn't pestering your lodger, is it? So I'm letting you know that the first month, paid in advance — two hundred francs for the rooms and three hundred for board—expired, as they say, almost a week ago. Correct me if I'm expressing myself badly."

"I . . . you . . . ah, yes, you're expressing yourself very well . . . perfectly well, indeed," the poor priest stammered. "Madame de la Follette, I apologize . . . I'm sorry for being forgetful, absentminded . . . oh, I've taken on a lot, a great deal!"

He took a second handkerchief out of his pocket, put it carefully on the mantelpiece, opened his purse, and searched inside it very seriously with two fingers.

"I'll give you your money tomorrow," he said at length. "Tomorrow, without fail, Madame de la Follette. I'm a little short at the moment . . ."

He picked up his handkerchief and wiped his forehead and cheeks convulsively.

"It's just a shame that I'm having to ask for my money," Madame de la Follette finished. "Charity begins at home. A gentleman lives within his means. A word to the wise, eh? And now that's quite enough of running up and down your five flights of stairs till tomorrow, *gratis pro Deo*, as you say at mass."

"Stop, Madame . . . one moment," said the old priest, sighing deeply. "I know that I manage my little budget very badly. I've no order. I'd be very sorry if you were tempted to judge my fellow priests on the basis of what you know of me. In general we're good, even very good, customers. As for you, you're a sensible and thrifty woman. God has also blessed such women, Madame de la Follette. Don't go thinking I despise order. It's a very good thing. There's order in Heaven. As for me, I'm content with very little, I'm not what you'd call a moneyman. But I repeat, I have to do without a lot while I'm waiting for an appointment. Certain standards are expected, I've had very specific instructions about them, and it's my duty to conform to them. When my presbytery's built . . ."

"Oh, that's good!" the concierge remarked bitterly. "He talks about being a curé, and he hasn't even got a presbytery!"

"Of course, it's certainly a nuisance," the old priest admitted, still locked in a daydream. At least I've got *very* suitable quarters here, haven't I? I can see people in the room next door, it's my parlor. And we're a stone's throw from the Porte de Vanves — forty-five minutes on the tram and I'm ready for work. There's a small problem though, having to leave very early, as I can only see my parishioners either first thing in the morning or last thing at night because they sleep during the day."

"Sleep in the day! So what do they do for a living then, your parishioners?"

"They're mostly rag and bone men," Father Chevance admitted gravely. "Oh, not all rag and bone men are the same, you know, Madame de la Follette."

"Rag and bone men! I can see it already! A converted wagon out in the slum belt with a rabbit hutch and as many kids as rabbits and fleas everywhere.. I think it's best to warn you that Monsieur de la Follette married just an ordinary working-class woman, but if he ever meets one of them fleabags on the staircase, he'll boot him out onto the pavement with a kick up his you-know-what, as sure as God made little green apples. You just see!"

"I'll sort something out," said Chevance. "Where there's a will, there's always a way. I told you I was going to be appointed curé soon, Madame de la Follette. Not at la Madeleine, of course! I honestly don't think that I deceived you knowingly . . . I'm at a turning point in my life. If you can just be patient for a while, everything will be all right. The real drawback, you see, is my health . . ."

"Eight o'clock striking already!" the concierge interrupted cruelly. "The beans are sure to burn!"

"Please, please," said Chevance, "I'd like . . . well, if it's all right with you, I'd like to do without supper. No," he went on, suddenly discouraged, his trembling lips screwed up into a grimace of distaste. "I don't think I could possibly eat anything this evening. I feel too ill."

"Oh, you make as much fuss as a pregnant woman," said Madame de la Follette in a tone of absolute indifference. "People who get worked up like you don't make old bones. I've worked as an orderly at the Pitié, I've had experience. You're in a bad way."

"Do you really think so?" asked the priest, with tears in his eyes. "I ought to see the doctor, oughtn't I? It would be an expense, of course, but a necessary and useful one. I'm being severely punished. I'd find dying really awful, Madame de la Follette."

She covered her mouth with both hands, her cheeks swelling, reveling in some cruelly ingenuous inner laughter.

"Nobody ever finds it nice," she said. "It's a job I'd more than willingly give my neighbor to do. All the same," she went on after a silence, "you're a bit out of the ordinary. My husband sized you up right from the start. A bit of a kid, no defense, and no real reactions. It's right, and between ourselves I'd have thought a priest would know a bit more . . . and why should dying be such an ordeal for you?"

"Oh, Madame de la Follette, I'm not exactly afraid of death, if you understand me, but I was glad I had a lot of work to do, and I'd drawn up a little plan . . ."

He stole a glance at the narrow bedside mirror, running his feverish hand through his hair.

"Obviously, we haven't reached that point yet, but if I were ill it would have the worst possible consequences. I know that the diocese wants to be able to count on those working with it. In the situation we're in, there's no room for half measures. In war, harsh things happen. There's no room for the walking wounded!"

Once again he laughed like a child, a sound full of pain but with no suggestion of bitterness.

"Well, Madame de la Follette, tell me frankly how you find me then," he asked, moving over toward the window and trying to stand in full daylight.

"How do I find you?"

"Yes, physically . . ."

"Physically?"

"Oh, come along. You understand very well what I'm asking. Listen, Madame de la Follette, you're wrong to laugh at me. The sick certainly are to be pitied . . . oh yes, it's a very humiliating situation for human beings. It's impossible to do anything good, the desire to pray goes away. All you can think of is the work we need to do, the waste of time, pointless meals . . . I'm not talking about the odd ache and pain. Thank God, I'm hardly suffering, and I don't pay much attention to it . . . but there we are: I think I'm getting weaker. I'm beginning to go downhill, Madame de la Follette."

She was staring at him strangely with her calm, flat gaze, and her mouth was slightly tense, with just a hint of almost animal cruelty about it, an expression to be seen every Sunday at the boa's cage in the Jardin des Plantes as the huge snake watches the little rabbit facing the soft, enormous mouth with its fur standing on end.

"I've come round to thinking that there's no harm in you," she said pensively. "Why did you have to be annoying me all week with your illnesses?"

"I think that's a bit of an exaggeration, Madame de la Follette . . . I've only been really ill since the day before yesterday . . . no,

Tuesday . . . since Tuesday at most. I was taken by surprise, you see, shaken, unprepared. The fact is, the blackouts are particularly worrying, I can't see as well as I used to, and my hearing is worse. Could I even manage to preach or hear confessions? And perhaps I could be thinking that things are worse than they really are. So, I was relying on you. Someone who doesn't know what's been happening might be better able to judge from appearances, looks, things like that. Do you think that's possible, Madame de la Follette? I'm so unused to watching myself that my own face isn't . . . what shall I say? . . . too familiar to me. Until the last few days, I've rarely looked at myself in the mirror, in fact."

"What do you want me to say, Monsieur Chevance? You couldn't look any worse. There now, maybe you'll live a hundred years. Who knows? But, you know, you don't have much pride if you go asking for sympathy and consolation and information and all from a stranger who's never asked *you* for anything except what's due to her."

The poor priest quickly put both hands flat over his kidneys and, leaning back slightly, turned his wretched face, on which every line and furrow was suddenly etched, toward the wall. All at once he looked so ill and wild eyed that the concierge turned away and had the decency to pretend to be wiping a glass on the corner of her apron.

"As you can see, it's serious, Madame de la Follette, very serious," the priest said in his gentle country voice. "Ah, if His Eminence had seen me like this, there'd have been no hope for me. I've told them all so often that I'm as strong as a horse. It's my kidneys, Madame de la Follette . . . I wonder what it can be?"

He was gravely wiping his forehead with his handkerchief rolled and squashed into a ball.

"My guess is that you've been overdoing things, likely as not."

"Dear God, I would have thought so too," he cried piteously.

"But there are other symptoms . . . I have to tell you that my kidneys seem to be only working . . . with great difficulty and not very copiously . . ."

"You mean you're not peeing anymore?" she asked with a grimace.

The old man blushed and stammered.

"You're a bit forward, all the same," the heavily built concierge went on indignantly. "Talking to me about things like that, it's horrible. I've never heard of such nerve. And that's three quarters of an hour I've been listening to you going on. Well!"

She grabbed the door in a rage and jerked it wide open with her huge hand. Then Father Chevance's voice nailed her to the floor in the doorway.

"So far, Madame de la Follette, the only person you've offended is a poor creature of little or no value, myself," he said. "Now, you've just seriously offended God. You must make reparation, madame, and quickly. Ah, we're stupid and don't realize what we're doing. It's not always easy to take our share of our neighbor's suffering and understand it. But we may never deride or dishonor it, madame, never, never, never. In our poor broken world, suffering is the Good Lord. We pass Him by without noticing Him, of course. But once we've recognized Him, offending Him is a very grave, a very serious matter. You were hurrying out, Madame de la Follette, almost knocking the door down, and you thought that you were afraid of me. What an idea! You can see that it wasn't me you were afraid of, but *yourself*. You can see, I think, that you were deliberately cruel. It was as if you had killed your soul to get it over with. Yes, Madame de la Follette, I saw your soul die. And now you're ashamed. That's all to the good, but it's really no more than merely a natural reaction, is it? We stand before the angels with the corpse in our arms, embarrassed and confused. What else does God ask of us? Very little. Sorrow for having done evil, the desire to make up for it, sometimes the tiniest glance heavenward, the wish to be better, to know, to understand . . . we must all do what we can, given the strength, insights, and graces . . . and whatever else . . . we've received. As for me, Madame de la Follette, I bless you, I bless you with all my heart."

Sweat was streaming down his cheeks, which he was still wiping mechanically. An anxious smile puckered his childlike mouth and the golden evening light was catching his magnificent eyes obliquely. He was as frail and tragic as a heartrending note at the climax of a symphony, and his old, black-sheathed and apparently motionless body was somehow being raised from within by a more than human ardor, alternately leaning imperceptibly to the left or the right, now huddled into itself, now thrust forward, bearing a rapid and deadly accurate succession of invisible blows. What appeared to be a mysterious struggle, entirely subsumed in his elated and eager look, the silent prayer of his hands, and the almost frightening force of his thin shoulders, was so urgent that the big, dark woman in the shadows backed away slowly, her broad features twisted in a kind of melancholy. She vanished.

Chevance sat on the edge of his bed and closed his eyes. A slight breeze was coming through the window and, trembling with weakness, he turned toward it humbly, seeking its caress. The vague but deep-seated sense of being ill that he had had for some time, the feeling that his blood and lymph had spread the sickness insidiously throughout his whole body, was momentarily dull and quiescent, or perhaps merely less acute. Another man might have soon lost courage, used up in a few days the limited inner resources each of us has on earth, and given up the unequal struggle, but with miraculous meekness, submission, and gentleness, he endured. Like a child opening up his little arms to death in a gesture of sanctity he had resigned himself from the very beginning not only to suffering but, in his extraordinary simplicity, to petty and unheroic suffering and to being a scandal to his neighbors, since he could imagine no way of coping with such afflictions. He felt pity, not scorn, for himself and deplored his sickness as he would that of an insect or of one of the inoffensive plants he sometimes bought, which soon withered because he forgot to water them.

"I'm frivolous by nature," he would happily repeat in his grave, sing-song voice, no doubt meaning that he totally lacked the inner strength he admired and desired so much. "Our Lord," he would also say, "sends special sufferings to the greatest in His kingdom but anxiety and humiliation to the least."

When he was finally informed officially that he would very soon be appointed to a new parish in the outer suburbs (which was so impoverished that it had dismayed the stoutest hearts) he had immediately proposed to camp out on a vacant lot the archdiocese had purchased, intending to put up a temporary chapel and a tarred timber hut he would call his presbytery. His sponsor, however, Canon Mercier, soon dissuaded him by pointing out that such haste might embarrass and inconvenience His Eminence, wisely advising him to beware of unseemly haste and not to appear to be teaching his superiors their own business. At what Chevance saw as such an important and decisive point in his life, his greatest fear was precisely that he might lack prudence, a cardinal virtue he claimed to have great difficulty in acquiring, but which he was still secretly, patiently, and assiduously trying to cultivate despite his tormenting doubts and scruples. "A good parish priest has to be a good administrator," he would concede with touching seriousness every time he visited his friend the Canon, even though he had only the most bizarre grasp of administration and its mysteries. He was, however, known to be as good a money raiser as he was a bad bookkeeper, since he was one of those simple men whose humble path was destined to cross those of the wealthy and the sensual as he led Poverty by the hand.

He had therefore left his room in the hotel Saint-Etienne and taken the hideous (but in his view very decent) furnished apartment just near the suburban tram station. He was up before dawn and trotting round the flat, dry area festering in the August sun until evening. From the very first day he had been astonished to find that his strength was already failing and that his old body, taken unawares, perhaps might not be up to the task he had set it. If he had been capable of despair, he would have broken down at once. For him, however, despair was simply one of those vague and abstract words one did not dwell on. Souls like his cannot imagine themselves falling victim to it and are unaware of it, at least until hatred, with its patience and cunning, eventually finds some imperceptible chink in their innocent serenity.

What he experienced was not despair but bitter shame. He was convinced that he had never done anything good or even useful and was now going to miss his one unexpected opportunity. Confessing his weakness to his superiors would have killed him, and he could not think of doing so without feeling unbearably debilitated. He was afraid that it would be discovered too soon and that he would not be offered the last, magnificent opportunity of his wretched life. Consequently he resolved to receive no one and stay at home, dreaming of perhaps being able to come through his wretchedness in secret. It was a vain hope. Within a week his heroic solitude was too much for him. As he had never had any other remedy for his own misfortunes than lavishing, in the depths of his unhappiness, the consolations of his deeply paternal heart on other people, he found such withdrawal into himself stifling. He sometimes admitted as much to the ghastly woman with him during his last days on earth, trying to break her stupid indifference, lavishly and vainly offering his great fervor and charity and pouring out all the gifts Heaven had given him, emptying himself of his mystic blood.

He thought he was settling into a new solitary life and already sinking into the shadows. The flesh he had so implacably and gently defeated and tamed was already in the grip of eternal cold and moaning in anguish. Although his almost superhuman will still held it in subjugation, it was disintegrating and, for the first time, obeying the laws of its own nature and participating in its own death agony. The humble, continuous, plaintive, monotonous murmuring, like that of an abandoned flock lowing far away at night, weakened him, even though he instinctively shut himself off from it. Almost without realizing it, he wanted to see a friend's face.

Among all those he would have liked to see around him, Mademoiselle de Clergerie's would have been the most welcome. The daughter of the obsequious historian, who was to die in his late nineties, outliving many famous and hated rivals whose reputations he had tirelessly and painstakingly sabotaged, is now no more than a faint memory. The obscure drama that took her transparent little life covered it forever in a layer of mud and encapsulated it in a sordid little news item. The oblivion she so deeply desired and in which she must sleep in peace was granted her in a particularly gruesome form.

Father Chevance's tenderness for the only such girl likely to bring him honor in the eyes of the world was known to her father, who was somewhat worried by it. He first held up the old priest as a second Saint Vincent de Paul and then considered him eccentric. The former curé was fated to hold the interest and even the admiration of fools because of a simplicity they thought they could fathom. In their eyes, he was dewy and delightful, a wildflower from the Garden of Eden. On closer acquaintance, however, even the coarsest or most cunning of them suddenly had a stupefying or infuriating revelation of a mysterious force to which they scarcely dared give a name, even though the one they had carefully chosen was always wrong. To a man, they all realized, suddenly but too late, that he lacked breeding.

De Clergerie too very soon noticed it and did not hide his disappointment from his daughter. Then, with a certain paternal dignity, he complained about having to take sides in the matter, for he was in no doubt that his authority was no more than a purely internal one. He nevertheless decided to do so, and his mind was soon made up. Father Chevance, he thought, was an excellent priest, and his superiors held him in high regard and praised his zeal. What is praiseworthy, however, does not always deserve to be imitated without due care. Young girls need to be more reserved than anyone else, and the spiteful are always watching them like hawks. Choosing as a spiritual director a man who even innocently makes people laugh entails risks a twenty-year-old could hardly imagine.

"Your choice is rash, I'm afraid," he told his daughter. "Find someone else, at least officially. You can go and see Chevance, as he's harmless. But at least help me discourage malicious talk. Why should I blame you? I myself was once attracted by our venerable friend's extraordinary evangelical charm. I have a deep respect for him, and I'll always think highly of him."

She looked at him wide-eyed with a suggestion of laughter in her gaze.

"Poor Father Chevance! Things will be hard for him, as you'll see!"

"My dear Chantal . . ." her father began.

"Oh, I only mean that he'll be a little surprised when he's told. And, you know, he'll soon forget it all. He's very absentminded!"

"No, Chantal my dear," de Clergerie continued gravely, "you can't deceive me. The sacrifice I'm asking you to make . . ."

She shook her head again, laughed, and moved closer to him, putting a hand on each of his shoulders and gazing steadfastly into his narrow, blinking eyes.

"I never deceive you," she said. "You know I don't. I'm always happy as I am. Aren't you glad that I'm happy? I never find things hard, Papa. Don't you like me to be happy?"

He took her little hand, holding it docile and trembling in his own.

"You worry me, Chantal," he said sincerely. "I'm not sure I understand. I know that you never hide anything, so why do I feel that I never reach you, that I just miss you by a hair's breadth, as if I were dreaming? I miss you by a hair's breadth, that's it exactly."

She frowned slightly before answering.

"Perhaps you weigh things too carefully. I think historians are like that. So, quite unintentionally, I'm different from what you expect me to be. You think I'm all ship-shape, with a rich cargo and a terrific captain, and that everything is just as it should be, when really I'm an empty little boat that gets along as best it can."

"Oh yes, you *do* deceive me," her father answered. "You do it without meaning to, because not for one moment can you force yourself to see things through my eyes, speak my language, or explain yourself with reasons I can understand. How can I know anything about you, my dear, apart from the habits and tastes, the preferences, I suppose, that we all show in everyday family life! But you *have* no preferences. You seem happy with everything. Even that would be frightening in a girl of your age, but you can't even tell me *why* you're always happy. I just have to take it as it is. You're happy because you're happy."

"Good Heavens, just take it as I do, as it comes to me. I'm not so complicated . . ."

"Oh yes. My part's a very easy one to play."

The look she gave him was so transparent and sad that he turned his eyes away, blushing slightly.

"Well, at least you must admit that I have a right to be a little surprised. You've never lied, and you're the soul of loyalty. Well, let's suppose that . . . well, thinking in terms of your future, for example . . . I was asked certain . . . very simple . . . questions . . . I would be unable to answer them. What sort of woman will you be? Only someone very shrewd could say. Yes, you like being in the house and seem to be a bit of a stay-at-home, but if I announced tomorrow that we were leaving for India or Canada, I bet you'd greet the news with the same happy smile. Do you or don't you like society? That's another problem I haven't solved. When you're with people, you're charmingly lively and sensitive, just enough to be pleasing, not enough for me to be sure that you are really enjoying yourself. With your friends, you're perhaps too loyal even in small things, and yet you don't seem upset if they abandon you. You're good-humored and, one might think, disconcertingly naive if they deceive you. Sometimes we get a glimpse of your will, but it goes gently back to where it belongs, in the quiet places of your life. Where *does* it go, and where do you hide it? Because you *do* hide it. Only someone who didn't know you or had never seen you could doubt that you look like your poor mother and have the same feelings and passion . . . as I watch you coming and going I have a terrible premonition. I know very well that you aren't one of those women who avoid obstacles, or at least manage to get round them. Which one will break you, I wonder? . . . Chantal, don't cry," he suddenly burst out. "I'm just a pathetic old man."

She was not crying, although she was so exhausted that her lips were trembling.

"I'm not crying!" she said, trying to laugh. "I would so much like to please you, but you're always watching me and you see things in me that I can't. I'm not, I assure you!"

She laid her chin on her fist and said, with her eyes half closed and her fine features drawn by the effort she was making:

"I'm simple, very simple, that's all."

Then, as if the childish secret had been forced out of her, she immediately turned pale.

"Forgive me," her father went on. "Perhaps I'm hurting you. It's so hard to question anyone without offending them. Obviously, yours is a rare nature, but that certainly doesn't explain everything. You're eighteen now, and eighteen-year-olds have dreams. What are yours?"

"Dreams?" Chantal asked.

"Yes, dreams for the future."

"Oh, I don't bother about the future. You've taken care of it, so why should I?"

"So try to understand what I'm saying. You're not one of those flibbertigibbets who can't see beyond the next day. Not at all: you have the attitude, the look, the tone of voice and — how shall I put it? — the serenity of a woman who's made her choice and committed herself. So you see, the happiness has a meaning, but what is it? You say you have no dreams, but your silence itself is full of a dream that makes you smile without realizing it."

She dropped her arms, discouraged.

"What would you like me to say, Papa? That's how I am. Don't be angry, because I don't think I could be any different. I'm not afraid of the future, and I'm not longing for it. Outstanding trials are for outstanding people, aren't they? Little ones come and go quietly. Well, I'm not outstanding. As a ruthless old beggar I once met said, 'My vocation is to receive. I need so little to live on, so I stay in the church doorway and hold out my hand to God. I think he'll always put a couple of sous into it.'"

"Very nice," her father retorted. "That will lead you straight to the Poor Clares."

"The Poor Clares!" she laughed. "Where did you get the idea that I could ever be a Poor Clare, or even a Carmelite!"

He ran his fingers nervously through his beard.

"I won't contradict you at all," he said. "I think your piety is strong, perhaps even enlightened, but very calm and reasonable. That's another reason why we shouldn't rush to take up thoughtlessly a way of life made specifically for the mystics."

She was radiant.

"You're absolutely right. I'm afraid I only want my own share, the beggar's share. Do I look like the kind of young woman to seek out humiliation, poverty, and obedience? You can be sure that I'll never go out to meet them. I should be frightened to death as soon as I set off. What you call my serenity and happiness is precisely the certainty that I'm no good for anything and the hope that as such I shall get special treatment on the Last Day. I don't want to look after my own interests. Think of my dog, Tabalo — if I pretend to run at him, he runs away. If I really chase him, he immediately lies on his back with his paws in the air. That's how things are. I have no concern for myself, and I hope that that's all God will ask of me. I stand up to no one and nothing — pain, death, not even the smallest irritation — I'd be afraid to rouse them and make them angry. If a trial came to meet me, I think I'd probably retreat a little, which is natural. But I'd very soon convince myself that I wasn't strong enough and stretch out on the ground with my arms over my head and my eyes closed. Probably there's basically only one kind of heroism, but there are a thousand ways of being afraid, and I would want God to show me which of them would displease Him least. We're always strong enough to take blows without returning them, and once we expect nothing else or nothing more of ourselves we sleep peacefully. It's fear and calculation that keep us awake."

De Clergerie had listened to her without moving. When she had finished, he scrutinized her very closely for a long time and then nervously picked up his scattered papers from the table, as a lawyer who has lost his case might do.

"You're playing, Chantal," he said.

His venerable head shook slowly, as if he had answered himself with an anxious "No." Forty years of stubborn and empty work carried out through so many intrigues just as pointless as he himself was, the bitter experience of his own nothingness, his childish fear of all truth and simplicity, which to his distrusting mind were no more than a complex trick, a harder kind of lie to expose, and the unbearable mediocrity of his life flashed through his gray eyes, which he quickly covered. He sighed deeply.

"That's all very well, but extremely vague," he said. "It's certainly not a rule of behavior. And I must point out that you haven't answered the questions I asked you."

He looked up, sighing dreamily.

"Please note that I approve of . . . what I can. But, thank God, I belong to a generation that to a much greater extent than any other has proved just how excellent methods involving measurement, analysis, and checking are. I'm not against the supernatural, and even intend to remain an irreproachable Catholic, and yet I firmly believe that with just one or two exceptions — that is, the miraculous, which so far has remained inexplicable — we all — you and I, and everyone — depend closely on circumstances and situations, and your dream of purely and simply accepting things seems impossible to me. I suspect it does to you too, and that your attitude is something of an affectation. It is, isn't ?"

He struck the edge of the table lightly with the flat of his hand.

"I can't believe that you could so easily give up your spiritual director, for instance."

"Why?" she asked. "Oh, you've misunderstood me. You're talking about sacrifices. I haven't reached that stage yet, you see. I couldn't 'sacrifice' anyone. The trouble is that you take me too seriously, Papa. It costs me so little to obey that I'm really forced to think that my sufferings are as worthless as I am myself. I don't know how to suffer, and I'm ashamed of it. Perhaps I shall never learn?"

"And yet," he said, "you could have shown . . . it seems to me . . . it's unlikely, my dear. Father Chevance has always been affectionate towards you . . . I just wanted to beg you choose a better confessor, someone not as . . . colorful . . . but I had no intention of stopping you from seeing him . . . just spacing out your visits will be enough . . ."

"Thank you," said Chantal. "I'm happy for him . . ."

"You see!" he cried with a sidelong glance toward her, "you knew as well as I did that the break would be unpleasant and even painful for him . . . he has a great love for you."

She opened her mouth, moved her lips, and blushed. Then, with a mysterious touch of anger but still smiling, she said gently, with her voice as steadfast as her gaze:

"Oh Papa, he doesn't set much store by the things he loves!"

"Here's your meal," Madame de la Follette announced tranquilly, although with unwonted gravity.

Then, as she was quietly pushing the door shut with her large furry slipper, she saw on her right Chevance's body stretched out motionless, facing the wall.

"Oh God, he's dead, just my luck," the poor woman muttered through clenched teeth. "Course, he couldn't do anything like other people, the crazy old so-and-so. Enough to give you a real start, and me just at the change, too!"

The plate of beans was steaming on the cloth. The alarm clock, which had fallen into the space between the bed and the wall, was ticking as crazily as ever. She was already backing toward the door with downcast eyes when, as large as life, the man she had thought was dead raised himself up on his elbows, turned slowly around and eventually managed to sit up.

"What a stupid thing to happen!" he stammered. "I must have slipped on the tiled floor . . . stumbled, I suppose. I'm sorry."

"Oh dear, dear, so you slipped on the floor, did you?" asked Madame de la Follette, vexed and upset. "You think it looks as if you stumbled, do you? Just have a look in the mirror. You still don't have any idea where you are at all, do you?"

"Of course I do. I'm quite sure where I am," Chevance replied with a touch of sharpness. "It's hard to believe. It was no more than a dizzy spell at most. I didn't lose consciousness for a moment. And I clearly felt myself falling."

"Right," the concierge said. "Believe it if you can. It looks to me as if you got weak all over . . . you need to get some blood in your veins again. Eat that while it's hot."

He was standing up now, dazed, painfully moving his head. Eventually he moved slowly toward the table, clumsily grasped a chair, and collapsed into it with an awful smile on his lips.

"There we are, that's it," he said meekly. "Thank you, Madame de la Follette. I need to gather . . . gather my strength. It's getting dark, Madame, very dark. I can hardly see anything."

"So you say," she replied, still suspicious. "Don't make jokes, eat. It's better for you. I'll wait till you've finished before I go downstairs again. Monsieur de la Follette's out, but he'll be back any minute, and he doesn't like being kept waiting."

She was watching him stealthily, innocently enjoying the spectacle, which was like one of those street incidents in which even horrible things are funny. Chevance's glazed look, deliberately slow and clumsy actions, and shaky, suddenly suppressed movements gave him the grotesquely solemn look seen on the faces of pensive drunks laboriously making their way across the street through a frivolous crowd. At that very moment, as the steady noise from outside fell, there came through the window, suddenly huge against the evening sky, the crude chorus of a song from a café-concert rising from the street on a breath of cool breeze like a coronet of spray on a jet of water, muffled, barely distinguishable and indescribably pure.

"Madame de la Follette," the old priest said, "when I was about fifteen, in the junior seminary at Montligeon — excuse me — I was strictly ordered by the doctor to swallow large quantities of raw meat. Thinking about it, even now, turns my stomach. Horrible!"

He reached for the dish, piled his plate high and, holding his fork in his fist, began to wolf down the food.

"That's better," the concierge said. "That's doing you good. You look better already."

"I feel as if my head's absolutely empty," the Chevance said with his mouth full. "Perhaps that's why I felt faint just now. There's surely some weakness in me."

There was a kind of playfulness in his voice that Madame de la Follette found reassuring, even though she could not take her eyes off his dazed, glowing, gleaming face in which only the jaws were moving.

"I'm very thirsty," he added.

He poured himself two glasses of wine in quick succession, draining them at once. A thin red trickle ran down from the corner of his mouth onto his chin.

"Can you please light the lamp?" he went on. "Evening's here early . . . in the old days . . . oh, Madame de la Follette, on the pools in the area I come from . . . it's strange . . . the daylight never seemed to die away completely . . . and there's a cool time, very cool, as cool as it could be, when we took our beautiful cattle to drink. The house wasn't far away, at the end of the path that looks black in the trees, under the trees. It's paradise. I'll take my poor children back there. Just think, Madame de la Follette, I know women who give their babies soup made from peelings. They need milk, plenty of milk . . . there's milk wasted, Madame de la Follette, it runs down the side of the pail into the grass, a white froth, and the dew gradually washes it away. There's so much milk spoiled! I said so to Simon Clos's daughter, coming back from school. Sylvie, Sylvie, watch out, stand your pail up straight, girl! She went to the fountain, filled her clog with water and threw it in my face! There y'are! There y'are! It went all over my new smock . . . Your Eminence, Your Eminence, some of our people are starving! What can I say to people in that situation?"

He refilled his glass, lifted it to his lips with a trembling hand, sniffed it twice, and put it back gravely on the table.

"Hey, hey!" Madame de la Follette shouted.

She saw him turn toward her as if he had heard, or was trying to hear from an enormous distance, and caught the sound of his teeth gnashing in his empty mouth.

"Hey, come on , you're asleep, aren't you? What a nuisance!"

He gestured to her not to worry and to leave him alone. His old hand made a vague sign in the air, then fell gently back onto the table and snuggled there palm upward, like a dying animal.

"Madame de la Follette," he murmured, "don't worry, you can talk a little louder. The other day I was telling the Vicar General I need only a little sleep, very little. What time is it? Oh, I know you're worried over nothing. Yes you are, I tell you! I understand everything, absolutely everything. I can see you very clearly, and the table and the glass, and look, even the tablecloth I'm holding. So no more talk of my stupidity . . . don't tell anyone, I beg you . . . promise me . . ."

"His eyes!" she howled, for he had just looked up, and his wretched features and constantly working jaws were visible, and two gray globes swimming with tears turned slowly and majestically beneath their lashes and then came back, showing the wild, contracted pupils once again. "He'll drive me mad! . . . what on earth's wrong with him?" she moaned, filled with a curiosity stronger than fear, "what's wrong with him, for God's sake?"

She stepped back quickly, sliding her body along the wall as if glued to it, her arms stretched out, sighing huskily in her intense concentration. The unfortunate priest had grabbed the edges of the table and was bent double with his shoulders thrust forward, as if the pitiless suffocation had snatched him upward. His open mouth was trying to bite the air he could no longer breathe, and he was moaning and struggling desperately to stay alive. Beneath the sweat, she could see his gradually reddening skin, his deathly pale nose, and the ugly swaying movement of his neck. For a long moment, man and death met head on and looked each other in the eye unflinchingly, face to face. Then his old chest, as if finally exhausted, sagged and collapsed again beneath the black cloth, the rattling in his throat ceased, and a last burst of retching brought up a muddy, bloody gobbet onto the tablecloth.

"The pig! He's drunk!" thought Madame de la Follette, both hands pressed to her lips in fascination.

She must have spoken aloud without realizing it, for the voice that she would have recognized in any crowd replied after a silence.

"No, I'm not drunk, Madame de la Follette . . . listen to me, please . . . I'm better already, I'll be all right . . . go . . . go straight away . . . and call, book a fiacre, a car I mean. At once. There's something urgent, terribly urgent I have to do, something that absolutely has to be done."

"But just look at you!" she cried, red-faced and not knowing what to do. "Rest. I'm going to fetch Monsieur de la Follette . . . if he's not there . . . let's see . . . the concierge at 12a can't refuse to help me. Bed's what you need, that's for sure."

She waited three long minutes for an answer. Eventually it came, articulated so slowly that it was almost a murmur, but in the same gentle yet inflexible tone of voice.

"I'm not moving . . . I'm waiting . . . to avoid another attack . . . must be careful . . . do you understand? That's all . . . my strength's coming back . . . quickly, go and book my car, Madame de la Follette . . . Father Cénabre!"

"Now, be reasonable," she said. "It can wait till tomorrow."

He was still exactly where he had been when she had loosened his grip, with his arms crossed and his face on the tablecloth.

"No, no, not tomorrow, today," he answered patiently. "I might be in bed for four or five days or even a week, there's no telling. Are you getting worked up over such a small matter? Aren't you ashamed, Madame de la Follette? If you delay any longer . . . but you know, I'll go for the car myself . . . I'll be on my feet in five minutes . . . I know what I can do . . . it's old age approaching, Madame de la Follette, I need to be careful . . . otherwise you wouldn't have seen me in this state . . . I've had more of these attacks . . . than you think. I must say that I'm very surprised how long this one lasted. There, there we are, that's all right. I'm on my feet again now."

She backed away from him, shuddering. He staggered along, with one arm outstretched and the other motionless, his mottled face still streaming with sweat, his cheeks and neck covered with gray froth, his eyes half closed. As she moved aside to let him pass, she saw him stagger against the wall and steady himself with both hands. Then he moved straight toward her, caught sight of his face in the mirror, and smiled.

"I'm not very nice to look at. Good heavens!" he said. "Well, we can't judge people by their appearance, Madame de la Follette . . . a drop of water will soon clean me up. There'll be no . . ."

"All right, all right, ALL RIGHT!" cried Madame de la Follette.

The car suddenly swerved to the right, slowed down gently, and continued on its course again. Night had just fallen, and the car was running through the soft and gentle darkness that was still echoing with the daytime noise that lasts until the beginning of the muffled, fierce, night-long rumble.

Seen through the car windows, moving in and out of dark patches and obliquely struck by a double blaze of light at every crossing, the endless, almost deserted road was running unhurriedly past shuttered windows almost straight from the outermost suburbs into the old maternal heart of the city. All Chevance could make out, however, was a kind of futile and comical dance, strangely attuned to his accelerated heartbeat, since despite all his efforts to pull himself together, the monotonous, intolerable thumping had been the only thing on his mind for some time now. The last vestiges of his conscious life seemed to be dependent on the violent throbbing of his arteries. After a great struggle, he had just managed to impose silence on his confused brain once more, only to find that it was immediately dissipated, destroyed and shattered by the remorseless, painful cadence of the echoes his imagination was transmitting through his nervous system. He grasped his noisy chest in vain, for every last fiber of his exhausted body was vibrating, with strange silences and even stranger resumptions, black holes where the anguish would suddenly sink, a whole range of subtle tricks, abrupt attacks, deceptive remissions, catching out the will and exhausting it in pointless acts of violence, ripping it piecemeal from the soul. "It's only a palpitation, nothing more," he repeated aloud with the gentle stubbornness that had so often helped him throughout a lifetime of bitter experiences. No sooner had he put his illusion into words, however, than the obsession was back, stronger than ever, this time taking over each of his senses in turn. Sometimes it seemed that the ridiculous pounding was speeding up until it shifted from a merely serious to a more acute single buzzing that reached the limit of the scale of sounds and burst into a thousand blindingly red bubbles. The illusion was so cruelly convincing that the wretched man clenched his fists with all his strength to overcome the temptation to grasp, to feel and test the mysterious globes to see what pressure they could withstand. Then he thrust his head violently into the upholstered corner of the seat, moaning and begging for both silence and darkness. The memory of the resolution he had made and the deed he had sworn to carry out at whatever cost to himself was probably still hidden away in a corner of his memory, but it was now more like a veiled, motionless, barely recognizable shape in the sickening swirl of vertigo, which he hardly dared to wonder about in case there was no answer and it silently left him, taking away forever something more precious than life itself . . . the last chance was not to be lost in a single moment . . . but what chance? Whose chance? . . . for in his disordered reason a humble, angelic, heaven-sent consolation had come to him. He knew, he was sure, that it was not his own salvation that would be in his hands, but that of someone else even more wretched and forsaken. But who was it? . . . the answer, he knew, would come in time. He had forgotten the name and could hardly make out the face amid so many strange signs, but he was going toward him, running to help him, and would soon clasp him to his bosom. Strangely but not unusually, the partial delirium did not affect certain memories or recent images, or some fragment of the past, just as the crest of a roof, the corner of a wall, or a single window may be left visible in a thick fog. He felt, however, unable to link such memories to each other in any sort of familiar perspective. They came and went one by one, suddenly reappearing. In some cases words even preceded thoughts and he would say them mechanically and almost unwittingly. Much later —or so it seemed to him—the image would rise behind them, gradually taking a clear shape. "It was to be expected," he murmured. "I'm getting weaker every day, my faculties are going . . ." Then he saw Canon Degrais's green Empire salon, the table, the flask of ether that he had been hurried brought, the man's worried face, his look of sympathy . . . and felt again the agonizing cramp in his calf, the pain spreading like lightning to his hip, the noise of running water in his ears and then almost immediately the fall into darkness. Only at that point, and with a great effort, did he find the meaning of the words he had said a moment ago. They had been his answer to his friend's anxious question when he had opened his eyes again after his long fainting fit. And the specific image already belonged to the past. It was leaving his conscious mind, his heart was beating more strongly and furiously against his ribs, the hellish whirl was joining and separating sparkling rings, and his apparently almost weightless and empty body was floating like a rag, held to the ground by a huge, painful leaden head. He was lying at the foot of a poplar at high noon, barefoot, clogs off, grasping the whip handle, and Muguette the cow was clumsily muzzling his smock, her warm breath felt beneath the cloth. He stroked her and pushed her away, listening to her mooing, made out the staccato tone of the car horn, the purring of the engine, the window open onto the lighted street, himself dying wretchedly and being carried through the crowd of so many unknown faces. "I'll go to him . . . I'll find him . . . surely I've got the strength to tell . . ." The man was in front of him, upright, black, inflexible . . . the pity of it . . . what distress! It was time . . . if only his poor heart could stop racing so frantically for just one minute, or if he could only stop hearing it! "No, I won't stand before God without giving you the kiss of peace! I . . . I who know . . . I alone! I can forgive you in His name! Have mercy on yourself! I . . . I . . . ." The words merely came out in a jumble, however, and then disappeared into the air like a swarm of buzzing flies . . . "Tell me, what's expected of me?" he asked the man, with a friendly smile. Then he summoned the last of his strength and tried to force out a single cry from his constricted throat: "Your life! Your eternal life . . . !"

Sadly, it was his own life that he could feel slipping away through a thousand unseen channels . . . suddenly, an enormous awe and silence. The wild heart itself hesitated, and was about to stop, and did stop. Everything was silent.

"Can you hear me, monsieur?" the driver asked. "Can you hear me now?"

He had just come in through the front panel of the car, which had swung around silently on its hinges like any ordinary door. Chevance tried in vain to raise his head a little and look out through the window.

"Where are we, my friend?"

The man shrugged his shoulders without answering, took a candle from a mantelpiece, brought it close to the priest, and moved it from side to side in front of his eyes for a moment.

"I'd prefer to wait," he said. *"I'll try again shortly."*

"Don't wait," Chevance begged, "I'm in a great hurry . . . not a minute to lose. If your car is broken down, help me out . . . I can't quite make out where we are . . . Saint-Germain-des-Prés, perhaps? It is, isn't it? That's fine. Let me get out."

He grasped his interlocutor's wrist with all his might, but was gently pushed back onto the seat.

"I'm going to wash my hands. You can leave him be, but don't go away."

"Thank you, thank you," said Chevance, horribly confused. "But I'm afraid I also must tell you . . . my eyes are bad, very bad . . . I'm afraid I won't be able to see the figure on your meter properly. I've been asleep, and I'm scarcely awake yet . . . what do I owe you?"

He, or least a part of him, was waking up enough to drag along the remaining heavy, inert mass behind it. He was gradually leaving the nightmare and coming back almost joyfully to a real, effective suffering, as if he were sliding carefully and humbly back into it with infinite care like someone putting on an old and worn but faithful coat. Anyone else would no doubt have wasted the precious moments in struggling pointlessly, but he was careful not to do so. He had always patiently made the most of whatever came his way, good, bad, or indifferent. For him, what God withheld was unnecessary and what He granted was enough. . . . He was already on his feet at the edge of the pavement, facing the astonished driver.

"What do I owe you?"

"Eleven-fifty, monsieur. Night rate."

"Ah."

The pavement seemed to be sinking beneath his feet, and the road began to turn slowly from left to right then steadied imperceptibly in one position, like a ship held by its anchors. Eleven-fifty! . . . his numb fingers were feverishly searching in the bottom of his purse, and he was hopelessly adding up a string of numbers in his mind to gain time. Ah, if only he could rest his head in his hands for a few minutes!

"Here you are, my friend," he said, holding out his purse, "take what I owe you. I can't see anymore . . ."

"There's nothing worse than these convulsive forms," the voice answered, but distantly, as if from the other side of a partition. *"Please keep calm. I'm coming back."*

"Come back!" Chevance bellowed. "Call Father Cénabre! I want him! He'll come! I want . . . I demand . . ."

The driver, however, was walking unhurriedly back to his car and did not hear him. The poor priest was deeply ashamed of having shouted so loud. What in fact had he shouted? He could no longer remember.

For a long time, he stood still exactly where he was, looking like someone trying to get his bearings before making a decision, but out of the corner of his eye he was watching the car slowly moving off. He was so distressed that he would not have had the strength to answer any further question and would rather have died than try to do so. Perhaps for the first time in his life, there, in the middle of the intersection, the former curé of Costerel remembered the humble delights he had once enjoyed, left behind without regrets and now lost forever. Between two attacks of anxiety his old body was finally experiencing lassitude, not merely the weariness of extreme fatigue but a soft, irresistible drawn-out sloth akin to a collapse of the soul. Buses were arriving from Montparnasse station, some distance away, driving straight across the empty square and stopping a few feet away from him, their engines roaring. He saw again the ochre-colored presbytery door, the ruined dog kennel, the cool, dark, narrow corridor, but his chief sensation was the smell of cretonne and lavender from the big feather bed in the alcove, where he could have died so very peacefully. "I used to be the curé of Costerel . . ." he had said so often, as if reporting some unlikely fact he hardly expected anyone to believe merely on the strength of his word . . . and now, the same humble words were on his lips again and he hardly dared utter them for fear of bursting into tears.

He started off again, edging his way along the close, and disappeared from sight . . . the sudden solitude of the rue de l'Abbaye frightened him, however, and his long, thin, black silhouette was suddenly back in the rapidly moving throng. For a moment he stood lost in thought before the great church door, afraid to raise his eyes, anxiously and surreptitiously watching the shadows of passersby on the wall. His head was so heavy and painful again that any abrupt movement forced out a moan that he tried to bite back, fearing that he might be heard, noticed, even questioned . . . he reached the corner of the boulevard and slipped along the iron railing of the garden in the square until he reached the east end of the church, where, in a dark corner, he rested his chin on his crossed hands, summoned up the last of his strength, and noisily and slowly breathed in the silence of the little garden.

The powerful beam of a headlamp swept in full blaze across the stained glass windows in the transept for a moment, throwing up a shower of sparkling light. The huge stone wall seemed to shudder from top to bottom and then immediately steadied itself on its enormous base, turning disdainfully back toward the night, with which it resumed its awesome dialogue.

"My friend, my poor friend," Chevance murmured, "my poor unfortunate friend . . ." He repeated his words quietly, without perhaps giving them any specific meaning, but found them consoling and did not tire of hearing them. He was sure that eventually they would slowly and delicately waken the unconscious and recalcitrant memory he sought in vain. Nothing, he thought, must tear its delicate, fragile, gossamer fabric. Behind him, all was noise, light, and movement, but he tried to keep his eyes on a small dark area in a secluded part of the wall sheltered by a thin, sickly laurel bush. Around it, the earth was gleaming feebly, thin grass was growing between the pebbles, and a breeze at ground level was making a small, silent eddy in the dust . . . "My friend, my poor friend . . ." he was hiding away as best he could pressing his chest against the railing, trying to ignore for a moment the huge and futile city to which he had given thirty years of hard labor and which had just snatched away his humble death, all he had left and was not yet ready to relinquish. Indeed, he would not have thought of quarrelling about it, as it had been so long since he had ever had anything really his own, but this final gift was already earmarked for someone else, and he could no longer dispose of it without betraying that person. Someone else, someone else . . . his mind was a blank. Timidly, he tried to go back over every stage of the way he had come in the hope of perhaps finding, in some detour he had forgotten, the solution to the problem his exhausted memory could no longer even formulate. All the details of his pathetic adventure rapidly came and went on a single level with no chain of cause and effect unless, following the absurd logic of dreams, the flow was precisely the wrong way around and he had to force himself mercilessly to go against it. The least obstacle or unexpected difficulty made everything uncertain and meant that he had to spend a great deal of time on some futile point until a mad image suddenly threw his thought off the track and drove it into a new maze of far-fetched deductions from which he had to try laboriously to find a way out. But even then, when the very idea of an urgent and compelling duty for which he was going to give the last breath in his body was weakening, the strength of his pity still carried him toward the unknown friend who was in a peril greater than his own. The worst anguish did not break the fraternal link but made it closer. The old priest's final secret was a secret of love.

Eventually he abandoned the struggle, not so much because he was discouraged as because he was beaten. In his confusion, his overstrained will was also flagging and begging for mercy. Beneath the top of his skull he could feel his brain hurting, like the stump of an amputated limb, and he was extremely weak. To keep on his feet he had to let the railings take his full weight, and his knees bumped against the stone ledge. He was then able to free his left hand, which he put over his eyes. As quietly as he could, he wept, watching with terror the shadows of passersby growing and shrinking on the wall.

He wept as children sometimes do, not because they are tired or upset, but because they have to, since it is the only effective response to certain of the harsher contradictions and existential incompatibilities in life — in short because there is injustice and it is futile to deny it . . . his old man's lips slipped instinctively back into the same childish grimace and his shoulders into the same gesture of naive, acknowledged, unavoidable impotence. In fact he could do nothing more for either himself or anyone else, since he was using the last of his strength in a useless attempt to stop himself falling where he stood and to avoid the final disgrace of dying in public among curious passersby. A feeling of indescribable powerlessness and infinite humiliation flowed into his heart. There were no words to express it, no prayer, at least no human prayer, to carry its witness to God, for that kind of resplendent certainty only exists far above the slow and wretched body, beyond the world of symbols and figures. All he could still see between his fingers was a thin strip of pale light sliding over the stone; but the illustrious and indestructible church had already received him into its shadow and was familiar and near to him, its powerful roots plunging to the heart of the city. Many a time in the past, when he had been up before dawn, he had seen it with living and truly human eyes as it rose bare, golden, severe, and pure in the morning sunlight. But he was moving uncomprehendingly away, because however sure he might once have been that he was a clumsy and rather useless servant, he had still had his physical strength, but even that had left him. He was nothing now. He could slip straight into the great simplicity of God forever.

"Take the bowl away," said the man with red hands. "It's serving no purpose. The blood's stopped flowing now."

He wiped his fingers one by one and suddenly bent down and felt the sheet clumsily, looking for his pince-nez.

The window was scarcely any lighter, and a candle was still

burning on the mantelpiece. A slight murmur filled the room, then died away.

Father Chevance's knees were still bumping painfully into the stone . . . in vain he grasped one of the iron bars as he fell and clung onto it. A final jolt snatched it out of his hands . . . the immense lighted boulevard was slipping away from him at top speed but suddenly stopped, noiselessly.

The old priest rolled on the pavement, got up, and fell again. No one saw him. Just a slip? But who in heaven's name *had* thrown him to the ground so roughly once before? "I should have liked your blessing," he said sadly. "I should have liked to ask you for that act of charity before we parted forever . . ."

Oh, my God! He put his hand to his chest, trying not to faint with joy. Before getting to his feet, which he could now manage, he repeated the saving words, and each magic syllable brought air, light, warmth, certainty, and life back to him . . . "I should have liked your blessing . . . I should have liked to ask you for that act of charity . . ." They were the very words he had said earlier. He recognized not only them, but also his rediscovered self in them, intact, freed, still alive! A single recollection, sharp, lucid, surging whole and fully formed out of the dream, firmly fixed in space and time, was enough to tear the dream's dark fabric. It became a permanent part of his memory, immediately and seemingly miraculously balancing a painstaking and fragile edifice on that single fixed point, scattering the hallucinations into the darkness.

Everything was so much simpler and clearer. *He had been going to Father Cénabre's* when the attack came on. Indeed, he had never lost sight of the vital fact that it was the name alone that he had always been seeking but had never found. But the irrevocable decision had been made. Nothing, no power on earth, could have distracted him from the pressing duty. It was simply that the time had come. Why today rather than yesterday or tomorrow? Did it matter? He did not exactly know where he had been, but he did know where he was going. What more could he ask? He was sure that he had been and was being called. Certain facts that were still mysterious would be self-explanatory later . . . he could see the tall, commanding silhouette emerging from the darkness, the outstretched arm pushing him away and casting him down so roughly to the ground. "I should have liked your blessing . . . I should have liked to ask you for that act of charity." Merely at the sound of the humble but at least deeply charitable words, his reason, which was swaying at the edge of an abyss, suddenly stood firm, no doubt because it was God's will. "I was mad," Chevance muttered with a beatific smile. "I'd lost my head . . . what an adventure!" He was already slowly crossing the boulevard, carefully avoiding a car, amazed to find things looking so reassuring and plausible. Once he had reached the corner of the rue Bonaparte, he allowed himself a short breathing space. There was a small splash of mud on his soutane, which he wiped carefully for a long time. What a shame! When he had fallen, he had torn the sleeve just above the elbow. He touched the place and felt a sharp pain, which he pressed with his fingertips, moaning as he did so.

"Don't let him touch the dressing," a voice behind him said.

"He's a real pest," Madame de la Follette answered. "He won't stop fidgeting."

(Poor Madame de la Follette! . . . But, with her shadow, she was already moving away and disappearing. He was alone.)

On the deserted street, everything suggested rest and sleep.

The silence was so deep that he seemed to be walking on velvet and had to listen carefully to catch the sound of his own footsteps. Like a true Vosges peasant, he had always found that his legs and brain worked together automatically, but now, as his body was breaking up, his thoughts were becoming lighter, rising weightlessly and unexpectedly, like a wild lark . . . he could lengthen his pace without tiring himself and would have liked to run. So far, he had never thought of another interview with Cénabre without a pang of unease or, to be frank, a supernatural anguish. Perhaps no one could have kept such a secret without finding it repulsive or wanting to ignore it. "I am the only man," Chevance would say to himself from time to time, "in whose presence *he* need not blush," and he had waited days, weeks, even months with the ominous feeling that if he failed there would be no second chance, and a wretched and deeply mortified human being would be lost forever. Too simple to believe that he could try anything on his own, the poor priest, like many others, had simply waited for some mysterious and often prayed-for sign and had been naively astonished to find that pity remained dumb. Far from bringing his illustrious rival closer, circumstances seemed to drive the two men further apart when Cénabre had returned to society after a short retreat, as free and bold as ever but with that touch of melancholy gravity in which his devotees recognized the disappointment of a great soul. For Father Chevance, however, the person coming and going in this way, accepting his rightful tribute of admiration and honors, was nevertheless a futile simulacrum of a human being, a hollow man. The real Cénabre was his and his alone. To Chevance and no one else he had made the avowal, dragged out of his despair and shame . . . "I've lost my faith!"—which was in fact not so much a declaration as a cry from the heart. Was he not accountable to God for that cry? Almost every day, with the marvelous insight his charity afforded, he himself uttered those horrifying words, as if terrified that the last moan of pride brought to its knees, the kind of feeble prayer that might be heard at the gates of Hell, might be forgotten. Since, however, he dared not speak thus to his Master, he fearfully left the secret in the darkest corner of Our Lady's chapel, because the ineffable love in her mother's heart can refuse nothing. Sometimes, when overcome with sadness, he had dreamed that peace had miraculously come down again on the fine, once imperious and now bowed head. "I should have seen him again," he would tell himself. "I should have seen him again. He would have called me himself!" His experience with the human soul and his humble sagacity, moreover, could leave him in no doubt: the man he had seen that night was driven by no ordinary temptation, but fighting for his very life, and the outcome could only be clear-cut. "His first impulse," Chevance was still telling himself, "would have been to ask for my forgiveness," for better than anyone else he knew that it was almost always pointless to hope to take such souls by force or surprise. He had been the only person to see and share Cénabre's ordeal and had waited, at first patiently and then in anguish, struggling alone against the silence he could feel gathering again around the rebel, like a curse becoming harder to bear with every passing day. His great fear was that he might die too soon, depriving the defeated man of his last chance and the possibility of sanctifying grace. As his only friend, he was weighed down by the obvious solitude they both shared. The unsought and secret bond with his famous colleague, whose name he had never uttered in the past without feeling a childish admiration and the sense of sharing to some extent in his terrible fate, had long seemed to him to be a kind of nightmare from which he would wake. As a result, he had momentarily been in doubt about what he had seen and heard. He accused himself of being a crude and unsubtle man who had quite fortuitously become aware of a secret he was too simple to deal with. He threw himself into his daily tasks but was unable to stifle the humble inner voice with its insistent question: why had Cénabre, who knew he had wronged him, not come back? Then he had sworn to finish with the whole business, setting himself a deadline that was soon past, alternately trembling with worry and deeply ashamed at the thought of all the rash conclusions his fellow priest might see as so many insults. "At least," he told himself, "God won't let me die without seeing what my duty is and doing it." That single thought brought him some peace, but he felt that such a time was still a long way off. It had in fact come.

It had come and, after a short lucid spell, he was no longer aware of it. Of death, which had suddenly appeared like a bitter face seen through a windowpane, all he had kept was the vague certainty that any delay was now meaningless and that it was wise to move quickly and see the matter through at once because time itself was running out. He was probably aware that he had suffered to the limits of his endurance, but he could not say what the suffering had been and had no desire to find out, since it would serve no purpose. What did seem to have happened was that far from destroying him, his enormous suffering had completely renewed and purified him, as if it had laboriously emptied him, sucking out everything in a single concerted action. The past — it mattered little whether it was good or bad — had gone with it. There remained the present, which was strangely free, intact, as fresh and new as if it had never been part of a clouded and doubt-filled future. All it contained was Cénabre, toward whom his old legs were strangely and silently taking him.

At that very moment, Cénabre himself opened the door and smiled. In his right hand he was holding a brass candlestick, like the ones Madame de la Follette polished every week. His left hand, held out in a welcoming gesture, looked huge. The small dancing flame, flattened by the wind, made all the darkness in the room appear to revolve round his face.

"I was expecting you, Father," he said. "It's very late."

"Yes, and I was expecting you, too," cried Chevance, surprisingly sharply. "For a long time I've been waiting to take up with you again a . . . a conversation that was interrupted . . . but not through my doing. I don't deserve to be criticized, and I will not be, Father. I'm telling you that once and for all, you see . . . It's understood between us, something we've both agreed on. And if there were no witnesses here . . ."

"Are you mad?" Cénabre asked sharply. "We're alone. See for yourself. I insist."

He slammed the door, raised the candlestick above his head, and went into the apartment, drawing his visitor along behind him. The rooms were absolutely bare and echoing. Each step they took raised a little dust, which soon fell back to the floor. In the final room Cénabre leaned against the wall, silent and unmoving, for a considerable time. Then, in a sad, even voice, he suddenly said:

"If you wish, I can show you the very place where I threw you to the ground the other night. I know where it is. But you simply walked over it, although you are a just, exact, punctilious man whose accounts are accurate to the last sou. Nevertheless, please note that I owe you nothing. I defy you to get anything else out of me, whether you were hoping to or not . . . I've sold my furniture, carpets, even my books. Yes, my books! You won't find a single one here. I live in extreme poverty, Father, perfect and really evangelical poverty. Why are you persecuting me? Yes, *Quid me persequeris*, Chevance?"

"I've already forgiven you, Cénabre, as you well know. So how dare you speak like that?"

The famous historian shrugged his shoulders scornfully.

"I can see that we don't understand each other," he said curtly. "You're an argumentative little priest. I've wanted you for months. For you, I've done what I wouldn't have done for anyone else. To make up for a touch of prejudice, no more than a fit of bad temper, I've stripped myself of everything and condemned myself to destitution. I don't even have any more friends. I've just sent the last one away, last night, so that I could wait for you in peace. Now I'm just as I was when I was born. I have absolutely nothing. God is no poorer than I am."

He put his candle down on the parquet floor, then stood up abruptly and stretched out his arms, embracing the old priest with a sob. Chevance, bitterly disappointed, felt his heart contract painfully and turned away without a word.

"You hate me," said Cénabre with a bitter smile. "I knew it. You know, I was behind you not long ago, following you here and watching your thoughts. Yes, my friend, you're full of guile, but if I could only be bothered, I could quite simply mold you like a lump of clay, believe me."

He squashed the candle angrily with his foot, and the last sound he uttered was snatched up in the gaping maw of the night.

"No, no!" Chevance moaned softly, "I *don't* believe you. I'm dreaming, I know, there's no doubt at all about it . . . Madame de la Follette please . . . you must . . . I beg you . . . light all the lights, every single one of them . . . The packet of candles is in the bottom of the drawer . . . stretch out your arm, Madame de la Follette."

"His eyes are wide open," said Mademoiselle de Clergerie. "I think he's saying something. Oh, monsieur, surely he can't die without giving us his blessing at least?"

"He's got the constitution of an ox, he really has," Cénabre began, but the rest of his words faded into an indistinct murmur.

"Listen! Cénabre, where are you? Cénabre!" Chevance called, his voice trembling.

"I think this farce has gone on long enough, don't you?" Cénabre replied sharply. "I expected us to discuss things calmly and reasonably, and now, in this respectable house, you've begun to behave like a lunatic. You must be mad, stark raving mad, to doubt for a moment that we are alone here, when even the most superficial glance around the place will convince you that I'm being perfectly honest with you. I suppose, my friend, that you're delirious. You may be dying, Chevance, but listen carefully: I'm not going to let you die in my house."

"Oh, all I want is to die," said Chevance. "But please don't let me die like this, in the dark, like a blind man. Just let me *see* again, Cénabre, once, just once, only once more! Let me see your eyes at least! I've always been a useless man, and now I'm empty, completely empty, at your mercy. But you know as well as I do that this kind of darkness is like Hell."

"I'm afraid I must destroy your illusion," Cénabre answered. "I'm conducting an extremely interesting experiment, and so I absolutely refuse to countenance your stubbornness, which is threatening to ruin everything. Indeed, just listening to your moans is enough to convince me that you were never better. You're no more ill than I am."

While he was speaking, Chevance had begun to walk clumsily toward him, following the sound of his voice as best he could. It fell silent, so he put both his arms out into the darkness and drew back a soft, inert hand which he held to his chest, moaning.

"Leave my hand alone," growled Cénabre, half amused and half angry. "Leave it alone! You're mad!"

"I'm your friend, the only one you have left," the old priest said supplicatingly. "When you've pushed me into despair, you'll fall with me. God, I can't find anything to say to you, I'm getting totally confused. If you don't want me to be completely useless right until the end, let's get out of here. Let's go somewhere else, anywhere, so that you can at least see me die."

"I won't refuse you that," said Cénabre, "although I've got serious reasons for fearing a trap. And, my friend, supposing I did see you die, what good do you think it could possibly do me? It all seems very odd, very strange, to say the least."

He struck a light and blew on the touchwood, as Chevance had so often done as a little boy when lighting a fire of twigs at the edge of the Pâquis, roasting his chestnuts one by one . . . at first, the new candlelight showed up only the corner of the bare wall, but then immediately afterward Cénabre's wily features and finally his pink hand shielding the flame.

"Well?" he asked.

"You're a hard man!" Chevance cried, beside himself.

"No, I pity you," said Cénabre. "If it's true that you're dangerously ill, we need to settle our scores in full, with no delay. Your obedient servant, my friend."

"Who said anything about scores?" the old priest asked, trembling. "You're mocking me, as you always do. At the point we've reached, Cénabre, the only person you owe anything to is God."

"I threw you to the ground," the false priest said gloomily. "I'd give anything not to have laid a finger on you. Whatever I do, I'll never be able to escape you, I'm tied to your detestable little self for eternity, may you burn in Hell."

"Why are you cursing God, you fool!" Chevance stammered. "Why do you want me to be lost as well as you?"

He threw himself forward, but the ground seemed to fall away beneath his feet and all he could do was drag himself on his knees toward the tall, impassive shape.

"I've done what God requires of me," said Cénabre in the same dreary tone. "I've deprived myself of everything and I'm completely destitute. The man who has nothing owes nothing. Please note how correct my calculations have been. If I still had the slightest trifle left, I should destroy it at once, as it's my nature to destroy rather than to give. But no one could find anything to take back, since I've been the chief victim of my own unerring deductions. Like an insolvent debtor, I'm escaping justice because I'm so massively destitute. It seems to me that no one has ever been in a stronger position with regard to God. From that point of view, I'm safe. And in relation to my fellow creatures, dead or alive, I'm just as irreproachable, as I've got no obligation to anyone except you. *You alone* can call me to account for the *only* act of violence, or perhaps I should say the only unreasonable act, I've ever committed. However insignificant it might seem, it introduces an insuperable factor into a very delicate operation. Your forgiveness, if I were naive enough to accept it without giving anything in return, would destroy the whole undertaking, since it would be impossible to make an entry for 'forgiveness' in any proper accounting system. If not for you, you little snake, I would be free."

He raised the candlestick to the level of his chin, and Chevance saw a flickering, dazzling white point emerge from between the sad and staring eyes. The thin flame, no broader than the edge of a knife blade, suddenly reached his forehead, then his hair, and almost at once the whole head began to burn silently.

Before the old priest could make a movement or utter a cry it had lost all resemblance to anything human, even though it still seemed to be properly set on Cénabre's shoulders. To his great astonishment, what now looked like a blazing sphere turned toward him and seemed to bow down twice as if bidding him farewell. He felt no fear, only extreme fatigue, the kind of langor that precedes waking.

One of his outstretched arms was limp, and on the other he could feel the pressure of a shuddering hand near his elbow. Lowering his head, he realized that he had lain down on his back.

"Cénabre," he said softly, "Cénabre!"

All he could now see of the black shape was an indistinct shadow, shrinking and barely distinguishable from the pale light spreading over the wall. Then the shadow itself split in two, and he closed his eyes for a moment to avoid following its bizarre movement across the room, in which the faint sounds of life were beginning to stir.

"I've done all I can. Don't ask me to try anything else," said a distant voice, seemingly hanging in space. "I think he'll stay lucid till the end now."

The echo of the last words lingered, seemed to fade away, and then returned, finally merging into a more generalized rumble of sound that soon consisted of no more than an inexpressibly pure, steady monotone or vibration that quickly faded in the real morning light . . . the whole room had just emerged from a blue mist, like cool, limpid, ethereal water so welcome to the dying man's eyes. Reluctantly, his gaze then fell on the familiar objects and very soon afterward he turned, with a heartrending groan, toward the limpid gulf of the wide open window. Only then, taking his last deep breath, did he open his eyes wide and stare long and hard at the pale wall of the alcove, without, however, any sign of recognition. Finally he noticed the disordered bed, the bowl on the sheets, a crimson stain, and, suddenly, his bony and already corpselike hand with its nails ringed with purple. The wretched dawn was floating across the ceiling, and acrid whiffs of the morning rain reached his nostrils.

He saw the whole scene, but in a confused way. His eyes wandered from object to object as if he could no longer control their delicate muscles and then slipped insensibly toward the daylight filled opening of the window in which the pale disk of the sun was rising in a fleecy mist. While he was making an enormous effort to turn his head away a little, however, his eyes met the attentive, patient, purposeful gaze that, in the depths of his dream, he had felt resting on him perhaps for hours, and he clung to it as if it were the only fixed point in a universal flux. Even before he had made any real sense of it, he submitted to its gentle command and felt its mute appeal. The circle of his life was gradually narrowing, and no doubt at the center of the last spiral there was nothing but this pensive light, suspended between day and night, keeping a vigilant watch at the surface of the darkness . . . for a moment, the silence seemed to become even deeper but then was suddenly broken. No longer a vague noise, but a voice, certain and sure, with a tone and inflection he recognized in a flash, had just sounded in his ears. The old priest's surprise was so great, and his return to consciousness so brutally sudden, that he tried to jump out of bed, even though he could not even lift the blanket with his weak and icy arm.

"Try to keep still," Chantal de Clergerie said. "You'll be able to speak in a moment, I'm sure. Can you hear me?"

He indicated that he could. Already his eyes had seen too much of the squalid disorder of the little bedroom: an overcoat thrown across the table, a pair of bloodstained medical oversleeves, towels scattered here and there, a long woollen stocking hanging from the window sash lock and, on the corner of the mantelpiece, the leftovers from his last meal, an empty wine bottle and a hunk of bread. The humble collapse of his wretched life was there, visible everywhere.

"I'm going to die, my daughter," he said.

Hearing the words, she slipped gently to her knees and rested her chin on her clasped hands, still holding the old priest's wandering gaze with all the strength of her calm, proud eyes.

"I think so," she said. "At least, that what *they* said. I'm very happy. This morning you were so weak that we thought your heart had stopped beating. I've often said that I would like to die first, do you remember, and that you would be able to bless me for one last time. But you're doing your little daughter a great honor by keeping her with you right to the end."

"I'm going to die," he repeated, with something like harshness in his voice. Then he turned his head toward the wall and was silent.

Through the half-open door of the narrow room he called his parlor they heard a discreet laugh, which was soon lost in the sound of voices speaking softly. Every time there was a gust of wind, they could hear the whistle of the kettle and the hissing of water falling on the stove.

"Would you like me to close the window? Are you cold?" Chantal asked.

She could see him painfully moving his tongue, gradually spitting out thick phlegm, and almost at once the air rustled in his lungs. He made a gesture of surprise, however, and clenched his jaws, and the death rattle ceased.

"What's wrong with me? Is there nothing we can try?" he asked, after a further period of silence.

For some time, Chantal stared in utter amazement, without saying a word.

"I'll call the doctor," she said. "He's in the parlor with Papa."

The dying man, however, silenced her with an imperious look and relapsed into his strange rumination, eventually saying something of which she caught only the last few words:

". . . no one . . . just you . . . I want to know . . ."

She hesitated, frowning, her thin face drawn and almost aged by an inner revelation and the discovery of something so harrowing that every trace of innocence immediately seemed to disappear from her somber eyes.

"You've had an attack of uremia," she eventually said slowly, putting her mouth as close as possible to Father Chevance's ear. "You were delirious last night. You never stopped asking for me, and perhaps for Father Cénabre too? They told Papa about six o'clock. We brought his doctor, Dr. Glorieux, here with us."

She gathered her strength, and added just as clearly:

"He says there's not much that can be tried now, and that you will soon be with God."

He seemed not to hear, but his head sank a little further into the pillow and the air could be heard whistling in his lungs again. Then, as had happened earlier, the death rattle stopped suddenly. Chevance, who had just been looking toward the entrance to his parlor, turned to Chantal with an indescribable look of terror and determination in his eyes.

"I understand," she said very quietly. "I'm going."

She walked across the bedroom, put her head round the half-opened door, closed it, and came back and knelt noiselessly in the same place.

"I think they're asleep. Your concierge has lent them two big armchairs. They didn't hear us. Is there anything else you want?"

"Nothing," he replied.

His shoulders twitched a little, then he lay still with his eyes closed. Beneath the sheet, all his muscles were visibly and horribly slackening, and the death rattle now sounded more like the hollow sigh of an exhausted animal than any human cry of distress. Chantal hid her face in her hands.

"Have you really nothing to say to me?" she asked. "Nothing? Are you displeased with me? Won't you commend your daughter to God . . . presently . . . in a moment?"

She stopped talking and listened, pressing her eyes and face with her open hands like an anguished child. All she could hear was the same monotonous moaning, rising and falling. It was suddenly faster, and she could make out individual words and phrases above the bubbling in his lungs.

"I don't want . . . don't want . . . don't want . . ."

"Don't want what?" she asked.

"I don't want to die, my daughter," he answered clearly.

She lowered her hands and looked straight at him with a guileless curiosity more awesome than any scorn. His voice was no more than a breath, and she sensed rather than perceived how harsh it was. On his gray face, a touch of red etched in the contours of his cheeks for a moment and then disappeared.

"My God," she cried naively, "is it so hard? I didn't think it was. They assured me that you wouldn't suffer anymore, that the delirious stage was over, and that kind of thing. They said you'd die lucidly and peacefully. So all we need is to be patient for a short while. Talk to me, it will help you. Do you remember? I've got good hearing. Even if you only move your lips, I'll be able to understand. Just remember that they might come in at any moment, and that in any case I shall have to call them in the end. All we have left in this world is these few short moments. Am I wrong to ask you for them? Are you angry?"

She held the old priest's eyes with her own, trying to look into their very depths. All she could see in them, however, was an unyielding obstinacy verging on stupor, so she delicately took his hand, which was already stiff, and placed it on her forehead.

"Bless me, at least," she said. "It will help you. Bless me once again, as you have so often done, one last time."

She felt his rigid fingers slip from her head to the nape of her neck like five little wooden spatulas.

"Be quiet," the dying man said. "You can't help me, you or anyone else. What's the point. It's hard to die, my daughter. No one wants to die," he added after a silence.

She bravely tried to smile again, her eyes full of tears.

"You haven't blessed me," she said. "Will you deny me that too?"

"What does it matter to you?," he replied curtly, his voice

suddenly stronger. "What could a blessing from a man who'll be dust tomorrow be worth? Why not let me die in peace? What do you have to give me, my daughter?"

"I'd like to give you what I have," she said softly, "what you like so much and I no longer need — I shall never need it again, ever — my joy, my poor joy that you loved. I've always obeyed you easily and happily, as you wanted me to. And after all, it's quite possible that the happiness was pointless . . . but what does it matter? Wasn't it you who were lost in wonder one day at the great things God can draw from the laughter of a little child just for Himself? . . . perhaps it's right that I should learn to be more careful with the marvelous hope that I thought would never dry up and was so unthinkingly lavish with, as if it were a worthless present. After all, hope is the divine word, and the word of God is gentle as well as frightening. I've smiled too much at death and everything else, and it's only fair that today I should see its true face. I *have* seen it. I accept it as it is, as you've shown it to me. I'm truly receiving it from *you*. And now . . . now . . . how can I put it? I'm asking you just to be happy now . . . happy as I was, this morning, when I saw you sleeping so peacefully, so calm, already out of our presence, half in the dark and half in the light. Don't turn away from me like that, forever, with a last sad word. After God, you've been the source of my joy. Take it back. Use it all, I beg you, all at once, just to go these last few steps. If you want to leave me in doubt, don't spare me. But if it's true that by some miracle you need me, I think I could perhaps find a way of helping you . . . if you wanted me to, that is . . . *do* you want me to?"

He made a sign that he was unable to speak and little by little lifted her hand to his mouth. The same compelling look in his eyes told her that she was his daughter. Then she wiped away the sticky scum from his lips with a corner of the sheet and gently pressed his clenched jaws with her fingers.

"It's not good for you to watch me dying," he finally said. "It does no good at all. Go away!"

"I will, then," she replied. "Don't talk anymore. Keep a little of your strength back. We asked for the parish priest of Saint Paul's at five this morning. His curate on call came to give you extreme unction, but he promised to come back himself as soon as you were conscious again. I can tell him. Our car's at the door."

"No!" said Father Chevance.

"I'll go for anyone you like," she said without daring to raise her voice, "anywhere. The doctor will take my place here. I should have called him already."

As he watched her, there was a momentary flicker of the old simplicity and humility on his stiff face. She understood that he was giving her this last look and that there was nothing else in this world that she could ask him for.

"You were a child," he said. "It's my fault. I was one too. I have to go to my death as a man, truly naked. I'm not even a sinner, I'm nothing but a man, as naked as when I came into the world. Don't try to find any meaning in all this. It's not wise to come too close to a dying man like me. Tear me out of your heart, my child. Throw me away as He himself has thrown me away, without bothering to turn around once toward his humiliated servant."

She saw him hesitate for a moment, as if, under duress and regretfully, he had said something incomprehensible to anyone else and impossible to communicate to the living.

"Mary, servant of the dying," he said.

He closed his eyes, slowly and patiently breathed in again and, with his eyes still closed, continued speaking in an embarrassed way that brought a touch of color to his face.

"I wanted you to ask you to bring . . . Father Cénabre here, because I would have liked a final absolution from him. That's no longer possible. It hardly seems suitable to disturb him to no purpose. Please give the curé of Saint Paul's my apologies. My time has come now."

The blanket he was holding with both hands rose imperceptibly and then fell back. Chantal thought he had died, but suddenly his voice was audible again, extraordinarily sharp and clear:

"My little daughter," he said, "I've taken what you've given me."

Only then did she realize that she was trembling convulsively and unbearably. As soon as she tried to control the trembling, it became much worse. It was not exclusively fear, or pity, but those and something else, something like a supernatural satiety, a disgust in the soul itself. Since dawn, she had kept loving watch at Chevance's bedside, expecting something vaguely more uplifting, a sign from God, for which she had kept her pure soul open, and now an unexpected, unforeseeable disappointment was secreting a hopeless bitterness into the secret source of her joy. She could not go on and stood up, still trembling, her shining head bent, solemnly silent. Not a single word escaped from her lips, for she had just traveled falteringly to the place beyond words: any word would now have been a lie. The dying man had been her hope, her honor, her pride, the sweet anchor of her life, and she had lost everything at one and the same time. But what did it matter? A treacherous doubt had passed over her, but if it had killed her it would have done so without sullying her. She was standing before God, as denuded as any creature, but unshakeable in her willed, unreserved, and uncomplaining acceptance. At that crucial moment, all she could try to do was place herself so as to allow the divine blow to penetrate the depths of her being as easily as possible. Timidly her fair little hand tried to find her old friend's slow, almost imperceptible heartbeat, and suddenly and silently she innocently saw, absorbed into her being and espoused forever, the mysterious humiliation of such a death.

The same evening, Monsieur de Clergerie spoke to his daughter.

"Chantal, after this trial, which was the hardest you've ever had to go through and which will have an effect on the rest of your life, I think we really have no choice but to pick a firm and wise adviser, a real clinician of souls. I must say that what Father Chevance wanted is clear to me now. There was a good reason why he kept repeating the same name while he was delirious. In my view, he was entrusting you to Father Cénabre. He is a dear friend, and I shall speak to him tomorrow. I hope that you'll fill the empty space left in his noble heart, which is so discreet and misunderstood, by the absurd and senseless death of poor, mad Pernichon."